Breakaway House

by

Arthur W.Upfield

ETT Imprint
Exile Bay

This edition published by ETT Imprint, Exile Bay 2020.

ETT IMPRINT & www.arthurupfield.com
PO Box R1906,
Royal Exchange NSW 1225
Australia

First published by Angus & Robertson 1987
Published by ETT Imprint 2015
with the help of Upfield scholar Kees De Hoog

Copyright William Upfield 2015, 2020

ISBN 9780994309655 (ebk)
ISBN 9781925416657 (pbk)

Table of Contents

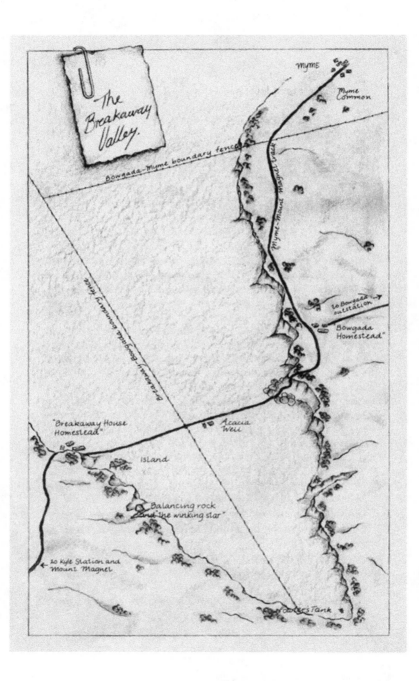

The Breakaway Valley.

Myme
Myme Common

Bowgada-Myme boundary fence

Myme—Mount Magnet track

to Bowgada outstation
"Bowgada Homestead"

Breakaway-Bowgada boundary fence

"Breakaway House Homestead"
Acacia Well

Island

"Balancing rock and the winking star"

to Kyle Station and Mount Magnet

Cooler's Tank

CHAPTER I

BREAKAWAY MEETING

THE brilliant yet balmy sunshine of early September fell on a hatless man lounging on a wide seat made of gum saplings, a man whose strong face would have aroused speculation in the observant–had he been anywhere else but just where he was. Here, on the lip of a Murchison breakaway, colourful space with far-flung boundaries so overwhelmed one with a panorama of scintillating tints–an intoxicant to the imagination and a vision of freedom known only to swift birds–that a solitary man was lost in the grandeur of his surroundings.

This was the rock-bound coast of a sea that never was. Never had the ocean roared against the rock-strewn foot of this curving, hundred-foot cliff which swept away to the north-west to end in a mighty headland of black and brown stabbing into a sea of dove-grey saltbush, and, to the south, curved out to westward to end in an escarpment of ironstone and granite rubble amongst which specks of mica reflected the sun as though an escaping thief had thrown away all the jewels of India. Perhaps it was familiarity, or perhaps some secret sorrow or flaming hope, but Brett Filson seemed blind to this imposing picture.

To reach the cliff, you left his homestead by the front door, walked through the small vegetable plot lovingly cared for by Soddy Jackson, the cook, passed through the garden gate, crossed the Myme-Magnet track, passed through another gate in a six-wire fence, pushed the hundred yards through thick mulga and, abruptly, burst out upon the granite edge of a precipitous cliff one never dreamed was there.

Such was the surprise Western Australia gave to Harry Tremayne when he, having left his saddle-horse in the Bowgada yards and inquired for Brett Filson, followed Jackson's careful directions.

With the wall of dark green bush at his back, Harry Tremayne barely noticed the figure on the bush seat, the man whose hair was almost white, whose left shoulder was slightly lower than the other, and in whose right hand was the comfortable handle of a serviceable stick. Against his will his gaze was drawn instantly to the electrically attractive vision of colour and space.

"Wanting to see me?" the seated man asked with quiet yet distinct articulation.

Tremayne started, as though from a reverie, and walked with the mincing stride of a horseman the few yards to confront the Bowgada squatter. "Mr Filson?"

He looked down on the face of a man who knew suffering, encountered the hazel eyes of one who was courageous, a man hardly forty years of age, and yet...and yet...

"Yes, I'm Filson. What can I do for you?"

Brett Filson examined the tall young man standing squarely before him, instantly approved of the powerful shoulders, slim hips, and feet encased in riding boots. He liked, too, the wide-spaced grey-blue eyes, the features chiselled as though from the dark wood of the omnipresent mulga itself.

Tremayne seated himself beside the squatter of Bowgada, tobacco and papers magically appearing in his hands. "I'm Harry Tremayne," he stated in the soft slurred accents of central Australia. "I've been up for a look-see at Myme which, I'm told, is a very rich mine. Thought I'd come along to have a yarn."

"Good! For that I shall be owing you something," Brett said, smiling at the bushman's habit of never at once coming to business. A stockman, probably, this Harry Tremayne. In fact, a stockman, most certainly. Looked efficient and dependable.

Brett's eyes turned away, to peer into the haze partially obscuring the turrets and domes of an opposing breakaway on the western horizon. When again he glanced at Tremayne it was to find himself being thoroughly examined. "Satisfied with me?" he asked.

Tremayne nodded, before lighting his newly made cigarette. "I was told that you're a man to be trusted, but I'm apt to rely a lot on my own judgment," Brett was informed. "Until this minute I was undecided whether to tell you I was a stockman wanting a job, which I'm not, or a policeman with a special commission, which is the truth. Interested?"

"Of course," replied Brett, noting how the slurred speech of the bushman became submerged in the clipped tones of official authority.

Imagination transformed Tremayne into a bird which slipped off the edge of the cliff a few yards from them, glided downward steeply and then more levelly to speed over the rock-strewn slope falling away to the dove-grey plain, onward into the light beams which seemed not of the sun, ever onward to mount at last over the mysterious summits ten miles distant.

"Not a bad view," were the four words which dispelled the fantasy.

"Er–no," Tremayne agreed, suddenly grinning at the older man. "It's a great view, one in miniature equal to anything America can show us per medium of her moving pictures. Now–oh yes! I was telling you that I'm a

6

policeman on a special job. Do you remember the case of six months ago when a man was found shot at the bottom of an old mine shaft away out from Myme?"

"Yes."

"He was a C.I.B. man sent up to investigate the suspicion of the mine directors that a lot of gold was being stolen. He'd not been on the job three weeks before he was murdered. His reports contained nothing definite save his belief, unfounded on fact, that a keen, well-organised gang was operating.

"The chief dispatched half the police force to rope in Hamilton's slayers. They achieved nothing, drew a blank, fell down on it. There was a young uniformed policeman stationed at Pinjarra who, having a month's leave due to him, asked permission to take a run up here and try his luck. Robbins was a likeable chap, keen on his job, and well coached in detective work by the chief himself, who was his father. When I refer to the 'chief' I mean the Chief Inspector, not the Commissioner.

"Robbins got his chance, Mr Filson. He arrived at Myme with a swag lashed to a bike, looking for work. For a month he knocked about among the old prospectors and dry-blowers on the outskirts of Myme, and when he did get a job at the mine, on the surface, his leave was extended. Being a strong young fellow, and intelligent, he worked his way into the crushing plant and laboured among the cyanide vats. Finally, he reported his opinion that the gold was stolen in the ore, and not after its treatment, which meant that it had to be treated elsewhere.

"As you can see, the problem then facing him was to discover the locality of the snide plant. Find that and the murderers of Hamilton would be found, because only the men who feared Hamilton would have killed him, and the only men who feared him were those whom he was there to get–the gold-stealers.

"Robbins–that wasn't his real name, but the name he was known by at Myme–first examined the country north, east, and south of the town, and, knowing of the breakaways, at last decided to look them over.

"Which was how it came about that he arrived here one evening–to be exact, August tenth–and stayed that night and the following day and night at the pressing invitation of your generous cook, Soddy Jackson."

"I remember him. He asked for work," Brett said quietly. "But the busy time was just over."

"So he said," Tremayne continued. "The day he was here he wrote the chief a long letter, which wasn't unusual, describing your cook and other hands and you most fully. Apparently Soddy Jackson is familiar with your entire history."

"The devil!"

"Don't worry," Tremayne responded, chuckling. "Your dossier is entirely in your favour."

"That's fortunate."

"Yes–for me as well as for you," Tremayne agreed, again serious. "The letters Robbins wrote to the chief and to his mother he left with Jackson to post, which was done. Do you remember which way Robbins headed when he left Bowgada homestead?"

"Yes. Towards Breakaway House. If you use these glasses you'll see Breakaway House homestead at the foot of that round hill over there on the horizon."

The policeman accepted the proffered binoculars. His gaze leapt the ten-mile gulf and was presented with a low, turreted, battlemented ridge, blued faintly by distance, yet with the dark tints of the mulga growing at its summit and the blue-grey of the saltbush at its foot still clear to the eye. Like a small town nestling in a cove on a rocky coast, the buildings comprising the homestead of Breakaway House station dully reflected the sun with their iron roofs.

"Draw in a little. Do you see the hut and windmill halfway across?" Brett directed.

"Yes. I've got it."

"That's Acacia Well. It's one of my huts. Just beyond it is the north-south boundary fence separating Breakaway House from Bowgada. Near the hut is the track from station to station, crossing that valley."

"I see, and the valley being ten miles across, how long is it?"

"Almost forty miles. At the south end this and that west breakaway join, whilst to the north they grow further and further apart, their extremities eventually merging into the general level of the country.

"As you can see, in the long ago, a wedge of land approximately four hundred square miles sank hundreds of feet below the general level, leaving about eighty miles of precipitous cliffs. Wind and rain have together fashioned the breakaways, eroding great boulders from the cliff face, carving out caves and caverns which once provided shelter for the Aborigines, and now shelter cattle and sheep, kangaroos and dingoes."

"Plenty of scope for a gold-stealer's treatment plant?"

"Hereabouts nature is most kind to gold-stealers."

"I should say! You didn't see Robbins again after he left you that morning?"

"No," replied Brett Filson. "Offhand I couldn't tell you if he got as far west as Acacia Well, but we can find that out from Ellis who's stationed there. But–am I to understand that Robbins vanished?"

Tremayne gazed steadily at his companion on the gum-sucker seat, saying: "The letter he posted here was the last the chief or his mother received. Up until that time he'd written to his mother by every mail–once a week."

The policeman paused, maintaining a short silence, and then went on, "Something has happened to that lad. Something as bad as happened to Hamilton. For seven years I've been up in the Kimberleys; never asked for a transfer because I liked it. Would sooner be a trooper in the Kimberleys than an inspector in Perth. The damn bush has got me fast. It's my...it's my home. And when I heard that Robbins had vanished I demanded six months leave of absence, and got it per telegram. You see, Mr Filson, Robbins is my brother, and Chief Inspector Tremayne is our father. My father wrote to say that my mother's frantic about young John. All of which is why I'm sitting on this seat with you. I'm going to get those birds who killed Hamilton, a city man, and now appear to have killed John, also a city man. As I've already explained, I'm a bushman and I have a reputation for quick and accurate shooting and good tracking to keep up. If that snide treatment plant is anywhere along those eighty miles of the breakaway, I'll find it."

Observing the passionate face and the gleaming eyes of this lean, virile man, Brett Filson said earnestly: "Let me help. I can't do much. You see, I was smashed up in the war, but I'll do all I can. I remember Robbins–John Tremayne–a nice boy. Yes, let me help."

"You're being very decent, Mr Filson. Shake?" Tremayne was now smiling, if a little grimly. "You can begin helping me by giving me a job as your overseer. I understand you're short of one."

"Right! You can start tomorrow. We'll go back to the house now and clean-up for dinner. But, as you'll be living with me, don't for heaven's sake call me Mr Filson. My Christian name is Brett."

"I'll remember it, if you don't forget mine Harry."

CHAPTER II

BREAKAWAY GIRL

HARRY TREMAYNE settled into his place on Bowgada station as a keystone settles into a well-built arch.

His first impressions of Brett Filson remained unchanged; liking and admiration for the man intermingling. Badly wounded in the war and still suffering the effects of the wound, Filson was quietly triumphant over disabilities which in a lesser man would have produced a human wreck.

The few hands he had met were all up to Tremayne's standards of direct simplicity, generosity and bonhomie. Perhaps Soddy Jackson, who expressed political views strangely out of line with his behaviour, was an extraordinary character in a land of characters, but Old Humpy and Charlie English with his wife, Millie, and Alf Dodder were normal lovable bush people.

To them it quickly became apparent that Tremayne was woefully ignorant of sheep management, although an expert hand with cattle and horses. The new overseer made no bones about his lack of sheep knowledge, frankly admitting that his experience had been won on cattle stations where sheep were as rare as women. But as for bushcraft, there was nothing they could teach him.

The day he met Frances Tonger was overcast and cold. From the southern end of the breakaways blew a soft yet penetrating wind. He was riding southward along the Bowgada-Breakaway House boundary fence when he noticed in the distance a horseman riding towards him on the other side of the fence.

Here, in the middle of this north-south valley, the eastern breakaway, six miles away, resembled a rugged coast of headlands and bays, almost within stone-throw; whilst that to the west, at the foot of which nestled the buildings comprising the homestead of Breakaway House, and but four miles distant, had alongside it a chain of mounds which looked precisely like a chain of islands.

The brown filly he rode was vicious, a would-be man-killer. Unlike an honest, spirited horse who determinedly bucks right at the start of a day's work, this horse behaved well–until she thought that her rider's attention was momentarily relaxed. She seized her first opportunity after she and Tremayne had been out an hour, when, with astonishing quickness, she entered into a series of bucks. This failing to dislodge her rider, she determinedly tried to crush his offside leg against a solitary cork tree.

Naturally Tremayne's temper became ruffled and he administered a sound thrashing which only served to make the horse angry as well as vicious. He vowed that never again would he ride this horse when working, for a horse that bucks after an hour's good behaviour is a dishonest horse, a useless horse to any stockman, and one giving financial loss to its owner who employs men to ride out to examine sheep and their tracks and watering places, not merely to ride a horse.

Engaged in administering this chastisement, Tremayne failed to see the girl who cantered towards him and only when she spoke did he realise that the rider he had observed far along the fence was a woman.

In clear ringing tones she cried: "You beast! How dare you beat a horse like that?"

Astonished by this feminine voice, Tremayne ceased his belabouring and fell to staring at as pretty a face as he had seen for a very long time. Her presence so unsettled him that he forgot the filly; and the horse, knowing it, reared on her hind legs, pawed the air with her forefeet, sat down and rolled backwards like a playful pup. Within the cloud of grey dust which the filly stirred up, the girl saw Tremayne standing beside the undignified animal, and then, as the brute began to scramble to its feet, watched him leap back into the saddle. The Breakaway House girl saved the horse a thrashing commensurate with its vicious behaviour.

Tremayne dismounted. With the reins looped through his crooked arm, he led the horse close to the fence, where he leaned casually against a post and proceeded to roll a cigarette. "Good day-ee, miss," he said in a drawling voice, his eyes twinkling, yet his mouth compressed into a rule-straight line.

"You beast!" reiterated the girl.

"Dear, dear! I seem to be engaged in general warfare with the female sex this morning," he said lightly, looking up from his task to regard with unfeigned admiration the flushed face and supple figure of this young woman sitting on her motionless horse. Doubtless it was the effect of too much cigarette smoking which caused his heart to beat erratically, but that could not have accounted for the sudden trembling of his fingers. She was like one of those squatters' women of the old days, coldly surveying a ticket-of-leaver who had neither legal nor moral right to breathe the same air as she did.

Slowly his gaze moved downward, to note the open-necked dark blue poplin blouse, the well-tailored white cord breeches, and the polished, military-style, high-topped laced riding boots. On them his eyes lingered critically before beginning the slow upward movement, finally to rest again on her face.

"How's Perth?" he inquired irrelevantly, or what to a duller intellect would have sounded irrelevant.

She was mentally keen enough to know that his question contained a sneer at her city riding togs.

He realised that with satisfaction, as he watched her breast rise and fall and her lips part in anger. He calmly lit his cigarette.

"I would like you to know that I'm Miss Tonger," she said icily. "I shall ask my uncle, Mr Morris Tonger, to report your disgraceful treatment of that poor horse to Mr Filson. Why, you are a low cad! Indeed, you are!"

"I'm all that, and more," he agreed gravely. "I become, when the chance offers, terribly drunk and I smoke four ounces of tobacco every week. Sorry I can't offer you a tailor-made cigarette. My name's Tremayne—Harry Tremayne. Better mention it in the report. There's half-a-dozen fellows working for Brett Filson, you know."

Now furiously angry with this man who cared nothing for haughty eyes and icy tones, Frances Tonger determined to end this chance encounter. She jabbed her spurred heels into her horse's flanks, cut it smartly with her light switch, and the next instant she was sitting on a saltbush and her horse was galloping for home.

"What did you go and do that for?" Tremayne inquired mildly. "Your horse wasn't doing anything."

Seeing that the girl was unhurt when she sprang to her feet to stare after the fleeing horse, Tremayne strapped the fence wires together, persuaded his horse to step over them, and then, unstrapping the wires, approached her rigid back. With very genuine concern, he asked: "Not in pain, I hope?"

Mortified to the verge of tears, she refused to face him. Her voice trembled when she spoke after a silence, which eloquently proclaimed her fight to regain self-control. "Your melodramatic sarcasm certainly has not affected me, if that is what you mean."

"Good! You sound all right, anyway," he told her, suddenly chuckling, which angered her still further. Now in the saddle, he kneed his mount round her slim figure, so coming to look down into her face. "Just you stay right there," he advised cheerfully. "I'll bring Dobbin back quicker than he departed. By the way, what's the difference between melodrama and just plain drama? It's a question which has often puzzled me."

"Oh! You are insufferable!" she cried, her small hands clenched.

"That's what my bank manager told me last month when I asked him for the loan of ten bob. Well, as they say: 'I'll be seeing you.'"

Watching him depart in a cloud of dust, Frances Tonger fervently prayed that his horse would throw him and break his neck. Of all the uncouth louts, this man was the worst. Never had she been dealt with in such a fashion by a man; certainly not by those belonging to the circle of youths with whom she was friendly in Perth; gentlemen whose hair was always well oiled, whose hands were always lily white, and whose high collars were invariably speckless to match their speckless sports cars.

Having tidied her short chestnut-coloured hair, dusted her shining military officer's boots and hand-brushed her white cord breeches, she rearranged the set of her blouse and fell to watching the horseman streaking across the plain in pursuit of the runaway. It was then that she saw a second horseman converging on the runaway from the north-west, and presently she witnessed all three horses hunched together, and then the two horsemen came riding towards her with her horse between them.

Thus it was that Harry Tremayne met Frances Tonger and her uncle in the same morning.

Tonger was a larger man than he. His colouring was dark, and the weather had darkened his face, whilst too much drink had blotched it. The dark eyes were slightly protruding, and the lids above them seldom winked. He was dressed in a similar fashion to the younger man. "What happened to my niece?" he demanded in the manner of one accustomed to total obedience.

"She was thrown," Tremayne replied lightly. "Horse not used to spurs."

"She was thrown!" Tonger echoed. "Why, that horse couldn't throw a bag of vegetables." His black eyes examined the policeman with insolent minuteness. "Who are you?" he asked sharply.

"I'm a person of no social importance whatsoever," Tremayne replied, inwardly rattled by the other's tone. His voice became suggestive of the barking of a dog. "Who the hell are you?"

Tonger's eyes opened wider and blazed with sudden temper. A dull flush mounted into his mottled face, and he gazed at the younger man as though judging his ability to resist violence.

Tremayne rode on, leading the girl's docile horse and expecting at any moment his own mount to start another tantrum at the first unguarded moment. He gave Tonger another knock before he could recover from the first. "Well, who the hell are you?" he insisted.

Now Tonger's eyelids drooped, but his expression did not adequately hide the anger within him. Still, more civilly he replied: "I'm Tonger. I own Breakaway House station. You're on it now."

"Oh! Well if I trod on your feet you must blame your tone. I'm a stranger on the Murchison. My name is Tremayne, Harry Tremayne, and I'm working for Brett Filson."

"That so? Being a stranger to the Murchison, where have you come from?"

"From the Kimberleys. Been up there for years. I'm not going to tell you why I came out of the Kimberleys, or how much money I've got, because I don't see that it's any damn business of yours."

For a while they rode in silence, Tremayne watching his horse's ears, and beyond them the figure of Frances Tonger near the boundary fence.

Tonger, covertly glancing at Tremayne, noted the set of him, and his easy, assured seat. It was not lost on him that this young man's slow action concealed tiger-like agility, and that behind the soft drawl was knife-edged mental quickness. Yet the smart remained, stoking the fires of temper which flared up when they reached the waiting girl. His ensuing exhibition of uncontrolled anger astonished Tremayne.

The large flabby face became crimson and the big body trembled. "What are you doing out here in those togs?" shouted Tonger, leaning forward over his horse's neck. "Didn't I tell you I'd have no do-dahs on my place? I won't have you dressed in that Pommy togging. A habit was good enough for your mother, was good enough for your aunt, and is good enough for all the Tonger women. Breeches, even top-boots if you must be flash, but you won't wear high heels to 'em and spurs to mark my horses. You with heels..."

"Cut it out, Tonger," Tremayne said quietly.

Frances Tonger faced her uncle with scarlet cheeks, her eyes expressing hurt amazement. Tears began to slide down her cheeks.

"You keep out of this, you," Tonger snarled at Tremayne.

"Your horse, Miss Tonger," Tremayne said politely, holding her horse in position for her to mount. To relieve the tension, he went on: "Mr Tonger is right, you know. High heels on any kind of boots are dangerous. You see, a high heel might fasten you in a stirrup-iron trap."

With a little rush she was beside the horse and in a second she was in the saddle. For just one instant her tear-blinded eyes met his, and he saw in them her thanks for his courtesy. Then, in defiance of her relative, she dug her spurred heels into the animal's flanks and with one mighty plunge the horse was off to the homestead, the girl crouched along its neck.

"Say, you want to be a bit diplomatic with young women," Tremayne drawled coolly, which halted Tonger in his intent to race after his niece.

"I'm not taking advice from you on how to treat women," Tonger roared, viciously reining back his mount which was eager to follow the other.

"Perhaps my advice is worthless. To tell the truth, I haven't had much experience with women."

"Well, I have," snapped Tonger. "And any man with sense treats women like he treats horses. Good day to you."

"Hi! Wait a second. Miss Tonger left her switch."

Tremayne, picking up the elegant riding switch, proffered it to Tonger, and Tonger, snatching it from him, wheeled his horse away towards the homestead and the girl now far in the distance.

"So long!" Tremayne called out, casually rolling a cigarette as he watched Tonger lash his horse into a gallop and ride away directly westward, not straight to Breakaway House.

Having lit his cigarette, he spoke to the filly: "That's the kind of master you need, you hussy. One who treats horses like he treats women. One of the understanding sort is Mr Morris Tonger. And the thrashing you're going to get if you play the fool any more today will make you think that Mr Morris Tonger is on your back."

CHAPTER III

MISS "IT"

TWO miles southward of the point at which he had encountered Frances Tonger and her uncle, Harry Tremayne reached Acacia Well, beside which passed the Bowgada-Breakaway House track, and situated some two hundred yards distant from the boundary fence. Here he hoped to see Fred Ellis, who lived in the single-room iron hut built close to the windmill which raised the water supplying two long lines of troughing.

Unable to trust the filly by merely dropping the end of the reins, he secured her to the hitching post by her neck rope, and then prospected the hut. The door was shut, and after a glance into the interior and finding the tenant not at home, he began again to roll the inevitable cigarette whilst deciding whether he would wait or return to the homestead.

And then, round the angle of the hut wall there stepped a fine specimen of Aboriginal beauty. He first encountered her sloe-black eyes, round and soft, set squarely in a round face with fine and delicate features. About her short wavy hair was entwined a length of broad, Cambridge-blue ribbon. Her blouse was white, spotlessly white, and her skirt was of brown material. Her brown stockings were of silk, and her black shoes were fitted with Cuban heels.

"Good afternoon!" exclaimed the astonished policeman.

"Good day!" reciprocated the vision, in clear yet high-pitched tones.

The minx turned a little from the man, affecting shyness. Over the flame of the match which lit his cigarette, Tremayne again appraised this Murchison girl, less astonished now by her clothes–he had become seasoned to her Kimberley sisters who wore none–than by her taste in clothes. Here were no clashing colours but an ensemble the equal of that seen in the city.

"You must be Nora," he said speculatively. Brett Filson had told him something of the history of Nora and Ned.

"Yes," he was told shyly.

"Then where's your man–Ned?"

"Oh, he's out with Fred. They'll be home bime-by. You work on Bowgada? You got a job?"

Tremayne nodded, and sat down on the doorstep.

Nora squatted on the heels of her shoes and made of the hut wall a back rest. From somewhere she produced tobacco and papers in a tin and became engaged. Now and then he saw her sidelong glance at him.

"How long you been here?" he asked presently.

"Long time. You goin' to camp here with Fred?"

"No. I'm the new overseer. Where's your camp?"

"Back there in some acacia. You not come there. Ned would go crook."

"I don't want to go to your camp. You married to Ned?"

Abruptly she turned to look directly at him. Her eyes were veiled, and from between her lips a thin stream of smoke was spurted into his face.

"No," she said softly. "You married?"

Tremayne grinned. "I've seen cinema stars with less IT in them than you've got, my girl," he told her, "and less idea of what to do with it. You run away with Ned? Where's your right man?"

"He's in gaol. He kill a blackfella. N'gobi no good. He beat me. When he kill that man I told police. Police lock him up and I went with Ned."

"And Ned–he doesn't beat you?"

"Sometimes."

"I don't wonder at that, Miss Hazit. Your sort, black, yellow or white, can cause divorce and murder and suicide. Where did you learn to talk English and to dress so nicely?"

"Old Mrs Filson showed me. I used to run away sometimes from N'gobi and work for her. Then she died. Mrs Filson good woman. She says: 'Don't chew tobacco, Nora, and don't swear.' So I don't swear and don't chew tobacco," and again the cigarette smoke was impishly directed at Tremayne's face.

"You ever work at Breakaway House?" he asked, after a contemplative silence.

Miss Hazit nodded.

"When last?" he continued.

"Before Miss Frances come," Nora replied with a sudden hardness in her eyes Tremayne did not fail to notice.

"Oh. And is Mrs Tonger alive?"

"She died long time ago."

"Oh," the policeman said again, and refrained from continuing the conversation along this line.

Half an hour later, Miss Hazit stood up to gaze steadily towards the east, and Tremayne, following her gaze, saw the tiny shapes of two horsemen leaving the foot of the breakaway.

"Ned and Fred coming now?" he asked.

Nora nodded and vanished round the angle of the hut. When Tremayne moved to the corner he could see her crossing the clean river sand surrounding the place to an old grimy tent pitched in a clump of acacia. He turned back, smiling, to busy himself with lighting Fred's fire and placing a tea billy over the flames. That done, he stood in the open doorway watching the arrival of a very tall thin man riding an undersized hack, and a youthful Aborigine astride a mule.

"Good day, how are you? Where you come from? When you gotta go?" asked the white man without a pause.

"Good day!" exclaimed the black man, piercing eyes examining Tremayne before they were directed at the ground adjacent to the hut. In that one swift examination, Tremayne knew, Miss Hazit's man had accurately read quite recent history.

"I'm Tremayne, the new overseer. I might go in an hour or I might stop over till the morning. You Fred Ellis?"

"Yes, that's right. You stop overnight and have a pitch. I'll give you a bunk. Glad to meet you. Got the billy on. You'll do. Dry as hell," said Fred, of the untidy moustache, pale blue eyes and weak chin.

They unsaddled before the door and Ned led the three animals to the night paddock, in which he freed them. He brought back the bridles, and then disappeared towards his camp. He was dressed in tattered trousers, minus boots and hat, and his shirt was a rag.

"Glad you gonna camp. We'll have a cupper tea, then I bash up some wood. Gonna be fresh tonight," gabbled Fred, pouring water from a petrol-tin bucket into a basin. Even while he was spluttering in the soapy water, he went on: "See wool's gone up again. Squatters'll get cocky now—buy new cars, go for holidays. Won't raise wages, though."

"Make more work, Fred. Hullo, what's the matter over there?"

"That'll be Ned getting into his woman, trounces her now and then. It'll be the ribbon in 'er hair. I spotted it. He didn't give it 'er. Someone else did. Ned gets hotted up some when other blokes gives 'er things. Don't blame 'im. She's got wings, that tart, and Ned can't fly high enough."

Screams drifted across from the camp, intermingled with vocal evidence of Ned's rage. Fred Ellis turned watery eyes towards Tremayne and grinned. And Tremayne, grinning too, cut half a damper into slices.

"Leave 'em alone, says I," Fred stated wisely.

"Me, too," agreed Tremayne. "Got a tin-opener?"

"Yes. Kill a sheep tonight. Out of meat."

Miss Hazit's screams and Ned's yells continued while these seasoned bushmen stoically ate and sipped blue-black tea.

"Who gave her the ribbon?" Tremayne asked, looking directly at his host.

"Ain't sure. Expect it was Tonger. Tonger's a devil with the women. Used to get Nora over there afore Miss Tonger looked down 'er nose at him."

"Tonger's that sort?"

"You bet, and a bit more. Silly fool! He'll get a spear in his back or a waddy on his crust one day. Now what's to do?"

The sound of running feet heralded the arrival of Miss Hazit. For an instant her slim girlish figure was silhouetted in the door-frame. Then she was behind Tremayne who had risen from the table, sobs intermingling with her panting breath.

The outraged spouse soon followed, with the offending ribbon clutched in one hand and a doubled stockwhip in the other. Fred said, his voice a bellowing roar: "What's she done? You let 'er be. She's done nothink. 'Ave a heart, Ned."

The upper part of his shirt torn clean off his body, blood oozing from nail cuts across his magnificent chest, Ned held out his arms, the beautifully moulded arms of a god.

"Nora took ribbon from someone," he stated in fair English, due to long association with stockmen. "I make her tell me who it was. I give her the shoes and the dress from Ah Khan when he was here. What for she want to take things from other men, white fella, too?"

As the question was directed to Tremayne, he replied. "Search me!"

Ned's eyes clouded with unshed tears which no amount of will-power could keep in abeyance. The policeman was amazed by this sign of weakness but it enabled him to understand a few things.

Every penny Ned earned he spent on Nora, buying her the clothes she adored while he wore his own to tatters. He loved her as any man can love a woman, and was jealous of other men giving her things, as any man would be.

"Give me the ribbon," Tremayne said coolly, advancing towards Ned. "And don't use the whip in here because you'll raise too much dirt off the floor and the tucker is uncovered." He held out his hand, and, after a slight hesitation, Ned placed over it the blue band. Then standing aside, so that the two lovers came to face each other, he tossed the ribbon into the fire.

For a moment, while the flames destroyed the ribbon, there was utter silence.

Then Tremayne sprang at Nora: "Now didn't you promise Mrs Filson never to swear?" he asked quietly, his hands gripping her arms close to the shoulders.

His question produced an amazing change in the passion-distorted face. Magically it softened and became beautiful. Miss Hazit began to cry. Tremayne released her. Ned dropped the whip and took her in his arms.

"You won't do it again, eh?" he said, pressing his face against hers. "When Ah Khan comes again I buy plenty of ribbons, and a new dress, too."

Fred Ellis sniffed.

Tremayne smiled at this evidence of a romantic heart.

Slowly Ned escorted Miss Hazit out of the hut, his soothing, penitent voice dying away as he led his sweetheart back to their camp.

"They breaks out at different places at any old time," explained Fred, sniffing again. "Goes on like a couple of pigeons for days–then wallop, one of 'em cops it, hell let loose, and then they're canoodling for another spell."

"Why didn't Ned make an effort to track the ribbon-giver?" Tremayne asked.

"He knew the lover only come as far as the boundary fence, didn't get off his 'orse, sings out for Nora and Nora goes to the fence to get the ribbon. Likely enough promised to meet him some other time and place. Tonger took Nora to Breakaway House once just after Miss Frances come back to live there. Miss Frances flew off the handle when Ned complained to her. Only time she had 'er way with 'er uncle. He's gonna either get hanged or have a spear stuck in him. His sort always ends up that way."

CHAPTER IV

THE CATTLE DUFFER

THE night that Harry Tremayne stayed with Fred Ellis at Acacia Well was cold and starlit. The world slumbered in unbroken silence, undisturbed by the barking of a fox or the haunting, blood-chilling cry of a curlew. Set in an indigo sky, the stars gleamed unwinking; but low on the western horizon, some three miles south of Breakaway House, a solitary star danced, winked, danced, winked, vanished.

The time was a quarter to midnight when a mopoke nesting on the top limb of a dead wait-a-bit bush witnessed the passing of three huge shapes, and then, a little later, a fourth huge shape, humped like a water buffalo, followed by a fifth shape, low to the ground, and small and quick in action.

The mopoke on the dead bush was about midway between the Bowgada-Breakaway House boundary and the homestead of Breakaway House. To not one of Morris Tonger's hands would those five shapes have presented a mystery. The first three were prime steers, the fourth was an old cow with its hooves wrapped in bags, saddled and bridled, and in its saddle a man known over half of Western Australia as Mug Williams. The fifth shape was Williams' silently working heeler dog, Tiger.

"Go on up, Tiger! Gee 'em off a bit!" the night-rider said conversationally, whereupon the dog slid forward into the darkness and the three shadowy beasts ahead edged to the right and eastward. And when the duffer whistled the low musical notes of a bellbird, the dog obediently came back to take its station behind the cow doing duty as a riding hack.

Now and then Mug Williams looked over his left shoulder in the direction of that star which had danced and winked and finally vanished. The star was about six miles distant, placing Mug Williams three miles west of north of Acacia Well.

This was not the first time he had seen that star, but it was the first time he had seen it unaccompanied by at least two others. On a former occasion in this same paddock, in which sheep roamed with cattle, Mug had almost blundered into another night-rider whom he had shrewdly suspected was not of Tonger's stockmen.

The wonder of this nocturnal operation of stealing cattle was how Mug Williams was able thus to drive cattle from Breakaway House country with no visible landmarks to guide him. Here the earth was flat, the saltbush but a foot in height, with an entire absence of trees save here and there a wait-a-bit bush and a line of acacia trees bordering a shallow water-gutter. The world, blanketed by night, was as featureless as the ocean far from land where the mariner would be helpless without sextant and compass, or the heavenly bodies, to guide him.

But, this clear night, Mug Williams was able to follow a course dictated by three stars moving in the track of the sun and known to bushmen as the "Three Sisters". The Three Sisters, plus an intimate knowledge of every acre over which he operated, enabled Mug to move with sure confidence. When the duffer with his cattle reached the acacia-lined creek, in which water never ran except after very heavy rain, he figured his exact position from the lightning-smitten box-tree which they came to and passed by, and knew to cross the creek a hundred yards further up. And from this point it was comparatively easy for a man of Mug's experience to cross his cattle over the intervening two miles to the great area of granite rock lying almost flush with the surrounding land. Two hundred acres Mug estimated this rock surface to be and the Bowgada boundary fence of Breakaway House bisected it. An ordinary paddock fence would have deviated round it, but not so a boundary fence accurately running over a surveyed line. It was a five-wire fence, the posts being set wide apart, and each post kept upright by slabs of granite set against it.

Mug Williams was easily able to lay the fence flat by the removal of granite slabs from several of the posts, and thus pass from Bowgada to Breakaway House and back again, over the rock, without leaving a single track to betray his passage and the passage of stolen beasts. And should a curious stockman chance to observe three sets of cattle pads moving too far in what seemed to be an unnaturally straight line, how could his suspicions be further aroused when he saw no tracks of a following horse ridden by a man?

To use a colloquialism, Mug Williams was not born the week before. As every bushman fully understands, the bush may be likened to an open book, on the flat pages of which every living thing that creeps and crawls, walks and runs, must leave its mark indelibly to remain until washed away by the following rain, which might not arrive until a year afterwards.

Having reached the Bowgada paddock, in which only cattle ran, Mug re-erected the boundary fence, remounted his old cow, and, with the assistance of the dog, continued to drive the cattle on a north-easterly course, upwards over the lip of the breakaway, until they reached a wide, stony, empty creek crossed by the Bowgada-Myme Common boundary fence.

Across the creek, the fence did not dip down into its bed but was suspended at bank's height, its bottom wire at least eight feet above the bed. From bottom wire to creek bed hung strips of wire netting, the lower ends of which were fastened to lengths of timber. When water came down in flood, the timber lengths floated, lifting up the netting and permitting debris to pass without piling up against the wire barrier and eventually tearing it away.

This being Williams' return journey, the intelligent dog worked the cattle beneath the hitched-up netting with never a bark or a yelp, and halted them on the other side while Mug re-wired the netting bottoms to the timber lengths. He was now on common ground belonging to no squatter, and but four miles distant from the slaughter yard, on the outskirts of Myme, owned by Williams Brothers, butchers.

It was possibly twenty minutes after they had left the creek when the dog slipped up beside his master and growled persistently.

"Shut-up, you!" commanded the duffer, and with rein pressure brought the cow to a halt.

Dog and man tensed, listening. At first he heard nothing, but then Mug finally caught the sound of clinking harness. It came from the direction of the town and was heading almost directly towards them. Mug dismounted. "Go forward, sit 'em," he whispered.

The dog wagged his tail once and disappeared after the three steers, obediently circling them so that without fright they began to graze. And when they were all placidly feeding the dog lay down, becoming invisible.

Now on foot, Mug Williams leaned against the soft warm side of his "mount", his eyes trying to pierce the darkness whence came the ever-increasing sound of jangling harness, which is not to imply that the noise was loud. Presently, out of the darkness, loomed a gigantic shape travelling westward, on a course which would take it between the cow and the steers.

Doubtless the man riding the horse and leading four pack-animals did observe the grazing steers and the grazing cow, but that he did not observe Mug Williams pressed against the cow was certain. Four pack-animals led by one horseman here on the Myme Common at a quarter past two in the morning! Mug's lips were drawn into a thin straight line, and his eyes were but narrow slits.

Not until the last faint jingle had ceased to reach him did he again mount his cow and continue the drive towards the slaughter yard. And when at daylight the senior member of the firm of Williams Brothers reached the yard, he found six sides of three steers hanging, the tongues, hearts and offal in the brine tub, and three hides draped limply on a rail. Mug was asleep in a blanket on the ground.

The senior partner was a big and powerful man. With ease he lifted the heavy sides into a spring cart, covering them with a tarpaulin. He examined the three hides and saw that instead of bearing Tonger's brand, they bore the brand of one named Clark, which was quite correct, as they had formerly covered beasts owned by Clark and been legitimately sold by him to Williams Brothers. The hides Mug had taken from Tonger's cattle were now carefully buried half a mile from the yard.

Later, out of the blanket cocoon there emerged a little tubby man with grey eyes twinkling from a mahogany-tinted face that a painter could have used for a model of Buddha. The dog, which had made no sound on the arrival and departure of the senior member of the firm, now leaped against its master in affectionate play.

"Speak up! Speak up!" cried Mug. The dog at once vented deep-throated barks and raced in narrow circles round the man as he crossed to the bush stable to water and feed his horse. "That will do. I-s-s-s! I-s-s-s!"

Immediately the dog was silent. An obedient animal, carefully trained never to bark at night, Tiger was worth his weight in Myme gold to the junior partner and cattle buyer of Williams Brothers, butchers.

A little before seven o'clock in the evening of that day, Mug Williams turned up at Bowgada station, entering the kitchen to find the cook, Soddy Jackson, and Filson's half-caste housekeeper, Millie English, cleaning up. If Brett's inheritance of the station was due to his father who had created it out of the wilderness, it was wholly due to his mother that he now retained the services of this golden-hearted cook and the housekeeper, whom she had enslaved with her personality, even as she had enslaved the girl so aptly named Miss Hazit by Harry Tremayne.

"Good night, Mug! Now why the devil couldn't you get here when the tucker was on the table?" demanded Soddy Jackson, half turning from the large basin in which he was washing crocks. How the sobriquet became affixed to Jackson's surname was a mystery, but his fame as a cook was great, and although he professed passionately to be a Communist, Brett Filson, and his mother before him, knew that his expressed views were not a genuine reflection of his mind.

When Mug Williams answered the cook's sharply put question he was sitting comfortably at the table and Millie English was placing eating utensils before him. "Because, Mr Lenin, I was detained. But don't get narked, I don't mind eating by meself."

"Well you want to be earlier next time."

"Being in time smacks too much of capitalism, Soddy, and you being a good Boshivict shouldn't expect a comrade to be punctual."

"We're not having no cattle duffers in our Sovet," the cook pointed out loftily.

"You ain't!" Mug's expression was indicative of amazement. "Why, I thought cattle duffers and fire-stick wielders would be welcomed. Now, here am I, duffing the capitalists' cattle for all I'm worth, and you refuse to admit me into the fold. Why?"

"Cos the cattle you steals you sells to the down-trodden miners at Myme for money. That's why. If you duffed cattle to give to them poor slaves, it would prove that you was one of us."

That the cook's views on political economy were sincere would, to a stranger, be certain. It would also be evident that Mug Williams' views were not sincere. Mug's round ugly face was softened in appearance by his twinkling grey eyes which conveyed not the slightest perturbation at being called a cattle duffer.

"Now how can I give the meat away when every time I comes here you robs me at poker?" he inquired with assumed gravity. "You knows you robs me with them marked cards you and the others have been using all the winter. Going to have a game later, when I've 'ad a word or two with Mr Filson?"

Shrewdly he noted the gleam leap into the cook's eyes, the unmistakable expression of the gambler at the prospect of play; an expression which would instantly fade when the gambler's fingers touched the cards.

"I suppose so," Soddy Jackson said, as though bored. "I delight in taking your ill-gotten wealth. I ain't had no luck since the time that bikeman was here who the boss refused a job."

CHAPTER V

A DEAL IN CATTLE

SODDY JACKSON'S political views provided Harry Tremayne with ceaseless entertainment but, probably because he had known the Bowgada cook for a much longer period of time, Brett Filson no longer found him humorous. Jackson's views were entirely divorced from his actions. At the slightest provocation he would enlarge formidably on his dream of world revolution in which he was to take a prominent part, and yet he would not allow anyone else to set Filson's table, wait upon him, or clear the table afterwards, although Millie English, the wife of the half-caste boss stockman, might dust and scrub and wash.

When he entered the dining room that evening in which the squatter and Tremayne were smoking their after-dinner cigarettes, he said: "Mug Williams 'as come. Wants to see you. We're gonna play cards afterwards, although he's bit me more than once. Luck! Why, if I have 'is luck, I'll be the Chief Justice in the coming Soviet Republic of Orstralia."

"You would, I know, fill the office with credit," Brett remarked shortly. "But I thought your ambition was to be the public executioner?"

"I aim to be both, Mr Filson. I dreams of 'anging all the capitalists. Up they'll go. No droppin' 'em. No 'anging on their legs will be allowed. For centuries they have ground…"

"Get out, and send in Williams," Brett directed.

"…the workers into the dirt. The time is coming…"

"Get out!" repeated Brett with raised voice.

"…when the oppressors of the people…"

"Get out, for the last time, Jackson!"

"…sink beneath the heel of freedom. I'm getting out now." The door was closed softly.

Brett smiled dryly at Tremayne who lay back in his comfortable chair chuckling delightedly.

"He was with me during 1918 on the Somme," explained Filson. "And then he was cracked on 'universal brotherhood' and 'love your enemies' stuff and nonsense. Ran down our own king and royal family and praised everything German, even while he worked a machine-gun. He's the kind of Britisher whom no foreigner can understand."

"Good soldier?"

"The very worst, but he could manage a machine-gun. He brought me out of hell when I got smashed up, and when they told him he was to be recommended for a decoration, they gave him seven days extra fatigues for abuse and his views on decorations in general. Turned up here one day in twenty-two asking for a job, and got it. He shocked my old-fashioned, loyal old mother with his politics, and drew every pound he had on the books to buy a wreath when she died in twenty-six."

Tremayne was studying his host through the blue tobacco smoke, coming to understand a little the nature of the hell which had caused this man's mutilation. Old Humpy had described Filson to Tremayne as he was before he left Bowgada to go to war; abnormally powerful, a rodeo rider and a dancer of exceptional merit. And now here sat a man prematurely white-haired, one shoulder higher than the other, and incapable of walking without a stout stick.

"There's another person, too, who still thinks a great deal of your mother," he said steadily.

"Everyone did, but to whom do you refer?"

"Miss Hazit—I mean, Nora, Ned's woman."

"Ah! You've met her. But why Miss Hazit?"

"Because she has IT in full measure. A more adept coquette than the average white woman!"

"You've named Nora well, Harry. However, go slow."

"Don't worry. I'm less interested in her than I am in Tonger's character. Trouble over there once?"

"I believe so, although I'm not familiar with the facts," Filson replied slowly. "Ever since Tonger's wife eloped on the arm of a shearer shortly after I came back from hospital, Morris Tonger has been gradually going downhill. All men are animals, but he's more so. Before he offered his niece a home at Breakaway House, he was always in trouble with one or other of the Aborigines. But after Frances came back to live there I believe there was some sort of scene concerning his moral habits and he did at least have the decency to discontinue his romantic affairs at the homestead itself."

"How did Miss Frances come to stay at Breakaway House with such a man as he obviously is?" Tremayne inquired.

"For you to understand that I'll have to go back in history. Old man Tonger had two sons, Morris and John. He made his sons equal beneficiaries under his will. A stern puritan of a man, his sons trod the broad and winding road. Old Mrs Tonger having died long before her husband, the two sons experienced no benefit of restraint. They both married good women, and all sympathy is to be extended to Amy Markham who married Morris.

"John married a Perth girl who died when Frances was only three years old, and he himself arranged it so that he died in delirium tremens when he had but one shilling of his fortune left.

"Amy Tonger rescued the baby, Frances, and the child was brought to Breakaway House, where she lived and was taught by a governess. On Mrs Tonger's elopement, Morris sent Frances to schools in Perth, and, after her education was complete, continued to support her in Perth with an allowance which did not compel her to earn a living. But then, some two years ago, he abruptly announced that he no longer afford to make her the allowance, and asked her to come and keep house for him. And she thought that better than starving in Perth. Met her?"

Tremayne nodded, and described in detail his encounter with Frances and her uncle. "My! She's a peach, Brett," he exclaimed fervently. "Engaged?"

"I think not."

"Then I'm going to hang my hat up on her."

"It doesn't appear that you've made a very good first impression," was Brett's dry opinion.

"Never thought of making an impression, good or bad," Tremayne said with obvious regret at the lost opportunity. "I own I was a little rattled by her manner, but I didn't mean to be offensive."

"You'll have an opportunity to apologise at the Breakaway House Ball. It's…"

The door opened to admit Mug Williams who inquired: "Have you them beasts ready for me to take away in the morning, Mr Filson?"

"Sit down, Williams, and let's talk. This is my overseer, Mr Tremayne. This, Harry, is Mr Williams. He's a butcher in Myme, and rumour has it that he duffs cattle, although I find that hard to believe." Filson was now smiling grimly.

The little fat man's eyes had lost their twinkle of good humour. "Glad to meet you," he said, nodding to Tremayne. "This is a 'ard world and a man gets accused of things he never dreams of doing. Why, it's because I'm so soft that they calls me Mug. Any wideawake fellow can do me down. Even Mr Filson, 'ere, always beats me in a deal. What about them cattle, Mr Filson?"

"There's seven in the yard."

"Seven! Phew! That's more than I really wanted," the cattle buyer said, regret in his voice. "Trade ain't as good as it was. What them miners is doing with their money beats me. Their wives don't get it, that's certain. And the pubs don't get it either. Must be the 'orses. None of the favourites have won lately."

"How many beasts do you want now?" asked Brett patiently. "Will you take two?"

"Well, I was thinking of taking more than two. What were you thinking of asking for them beasts?" Mug Williams spoke with vocal tones indicating that the subject of cattle bored him almost to prostration.

"Fourteen pounds, five shillings a head."

"You must be thinking of our last deal when the market was high."

"No. I'm thinking of this one."

"But I want to take more than two of 'em."

"There are seven in the yard. My lads will help drove them off the place in the morning."

"But I can manage them meself, Mr Filson."

"You'd better have my boys' help," Filson insisted, a shadow of an amused smile about his lips. "You see they may break back on you, become boxed with other cattle, and then you might forget the number you really bought."

"Well, if I buys only two, and them two I can't manage–I'm not admitting it–it ain't likely I'd forget how many I bought, and go on with only one."

"I agree, Williams. You most certainly would not go on with only one. Will you have a snifter?"

"When we've finished the argument, Mr Filson. I'll not be too proud then."

"What argument?" Brett asked blandly.

"What? Why, about the cattle. I'll tell you what I'll do, quick, 'cos I'm thirsty. I'll take the seven off your hands at a tenner a piece."

"Better have the drink. You're likely to get a sore throat arguing."

"But I ain't got the money. Trade's bad, I tell you. It must be the 'orses."

Brett shook his head. Tremayne was grinning behind a weekly journal.

"What you really want is poor stuff, Williams. Try longer," advised the squatter.

Mug Williams' good humour vanished and into his grey eyes leapt a cold, hard light. His voice was metallic when he said: "That swine! I ain't dealing with him since he chased me off into the breakaways for nothing. You 'eard about it?"

"I did hear that he accused you of taking four extra beasts," Brett admitted, chuckling. "He's a tough nut."

"He's worse than a tough nut, Mr Filson. He's at the back of a pretty queer...He's gonna end up sudden like." Tremayne's eyes were peering over the top of his paper, veiled by drooping lids. "Perhaps a spear will run through his tummy one of these days. A man who messes about with black women always ends up that way. There was Alwin and Messingham who looked for and found black trouble. Well, I'll give you eleven pounds each for them beasts."

"Better have a drink. You must be getting dry."

"Hard! You're as hard as those breakaway rocks. I'll give you me limit—me limit, mind—twelve pounds each for the seven."

"Have you ever known me budge, Williams?"

Mug Williams sighed in despair. "Give us that drink, Mr Filson. A double nobbler, please. I'd as soon talk to a black about 'is corroboree rites than to you about cattle."

"Help yourself, Williams. You'll find those beasts well over the seven-hundred pound weight I set."

"I ain't arguing no more," Williams stated sadly. "Your bringing up Tonger 'as spoilt the argument. The lousy dog! A nice crowd over there for a young innocent tart to mix with."

"What kind of a crowd?"

Keen, shrewd eyes regarded Tremayne, who had spoken. They examined him very carefully. Then: "Oh...a bit loose like. Well," Mr Williams rose, "I'll be getting across to the men's 'ut for a game of poker. Here, Mr Filson, take the money till the morning please."

From a hip pocket the cattle buyer extracted a roll of ten-pound notes and a small wad of one-pound notes. From the latter he "lifted" one pound.

"You'll find a hundred and forty-three pounds there," he said solemnly. "Lock it away safe, and if I should come back for a pound or two, don't you let me have it at any price. Poker's my cross. And don't trouble about assistance in the morning. I can manage 'em."

"You'll be escorted off the place," Brett said decisively.

"All right! Have it your own way. Good night!"

Once more cheerfully grinning, the little rotund man gaily waved a pudgy hand and vanished.

"There goes a modern Robin Hood," Brett said, with low laughter as he locked up the money in the safe in the corner. "Ten years ago he and his brother started the butchery in Myme. Everyone thought him a bit simple, but suspicions of cattle duffing are becoming strong against him. And yet he's that honest that it's not necessary to count his money or to give him a receipt for it. He's got just that one mental kink for duffing cattle."

CHAPTER VI

A FOX HUNT

THE Myme mail was dispatched from Mount Magnet every Tuesday and Friday, and this particular day in late September Harry Tremayne, in Brett's absence, took the Bowgada bag from old Hool-'em-up Dick.

Among his own letters was a report submitted by the police at Mount Magnet in which was the statement that no one recollected seeing a young swagman with a bicycle on or subsequent to August tenth. Further inquiries at Kyle station, situated midway between Breakaway House and Mount Magnet, produced information to the effect that such a swagman was not remembered to have visited that place either.

There had also arrived by the mail a parcel addressed to him by a Mount Magnet storekeeper, and with this parcel, as well as his lunch and quart pot, strapped to the saddle, Harry Tremayne rode away from the Bowgada homestead astride Major, his own intelligent horse.

At a leisurely walk the horse carried him down the south track from the house for about half a mile, where they abruptly skirted the precipitous face of a breakaway "bay" similar to that above which Tremayne had first met Filson, and on the far side of this sea-less bay the road turned westward and fell in steep gradients down the side of a headland to the flats below.

Near to the bottom, at the extremity of the headland, the road wound in and out among huge granite boulders sundered from a stratum of rock near the summit, whilst in several places a conglomeration of such boulders made small hillocks of rock. Here was a position which the war veteran Filson knew could be defended against a battalion by a single machine-gun.

But on this clear, warm and brilliant late morning Harry Tremayne was singularly unappreciative of scenic beauties and unconcerned with military strategy. Even at the foot of the headland the higher ground level permitted him, when once clear of the rock debris, to observe the sun-reflecting roof of the hut at Acacia Well and those roofs grouped into Breakaway House homestead farther westward.

More than likely, at that very moment, Brett Filson was at that distant homestead, lunching there, on his way to Mount Magnet where he would catch a train to Perth to undergo his periodical medical examination–still a necessity after all those years.

From Breakaway House he would ring Tremayne, and if then he should order that English be sent out to overlook certain beasts in an east paddock, it was to be understood that the swagman had not been seen to arrive at Breakaway House; whilst if he directed Fred Ellis to be set special work it indicated the opposite.

To concur with Tremayne's ostensible presence at Bowgada, it would not have done for him to make inquiries concerning a man who had disappeared some time before his arrival. Brett, however, would say that he had been asked to make inquiries by the man's aunt who had received his last letter from Bowgada.

From the first, Harry Tremayne regarded the occupants of Breakaway House with suspicion. He had not told Filson, but in his brother's last letter, his brother had said that he had obtained information, the implications of which demanded an examination of the breakaways west of Myme.

At Acacia Well, both Ellis and Ned remembered the swagman with the bicycle. They were crutching sheep in the adjacent yards that day and the swagman had taken his lunch with them. There was no doubt then, that Tremayne's brother had left Acacia Well for Breakaway House, but it appeared likely that at some point between these two places he had vanished.

The information that Tremayne gathered concerning Breakaway House indicated that as a small pastoral community it was not normal. Its owner was a loose liver. He was so partial to black and half-caste workers that there were but two white men on his books, the men's cook and the boss stockman. Of the cook, Tremayne had learned little, but the boss stockman was legally married to an Aboriginal woman, he having been given and accepted that way out by the police.

All this was not extraordinary to a man with Tremayne's experience of the Kimberleys, but it was not a set of normal conditions on the Murchison where squattocracy is older. Here at Breakaway House the number of Aborigines and half-castes was much higher than a view of its area would require to work it. Yet despite this fact, the condition of Tonger's fences, his cattle and his sheep emphatically indicated neglect. Both as a stockman and a policeman, Harry Tremayne's interest was captured by Breakaway House.

He was boiling the quart pot at the foot of an outcrop of ironstone some two miles from Acacia Well when he observed near the east breakaway, and about three miles to the north-east of his then position, two columns of smoke rising into the still air.

This signal indicated that one Aborigine desired another to come to him without delay. Likely enough, it was either Ned or Miss Hazit signalling to his or her conjugal partner then at Acacia Well. Whichever one it was, there at the base of those smoke columns presently would be Ned, whom Tremayne wanted to see that day.

And between two islands of rubble, beside a watercourse bordered by flats covered with small chips of snow-white quartz, reminding one of a well-kept graveyard, he found Ned and Miss Hazit crouched over a small fire on which they were cooking short lengths of goanna.

"Good day, Mr Tremayne!" Ned shouted, springing to his feet to welcome the second boss.

"Day, Ned!" Tremayne replied cheerfully. "I was boiling my quart when I saw your smoke, so I emptied it and came on to boil it here." Having refilled the utensil from the canvas bag slung from his horse's neck, he added: "Which one of you signalled?"

"Ned did. I was at Acacia Well," replied Miss Hazit, demurely refraining to look up from her task of cooking. "You must have ridden fast."

"Yes–I came along. I brought Fred's shotgun. Ned wanted it."

"You bet. Over in that burrow is two or three foxes," Tremayne was informed with a frank smile. "I seen them tracks. Then I gathers wood and leaves for the fires way over there in that acacia and..." Ned paused to yell his mirth, "up one of those trees went this bungarra. Cripes! I had him cooking when Nora got here."

"Oh! And what about the foxes?"

"They're orl right. They keep shut-eye. Bime-by me and Nora get 'em out. You wait!"

Miss Hazit was dressed precisely as she had been when she shamelessly flirted with the overseer at Acacia Well. To be sure, there was a hole in her right stocking, and a bad ladder on the calf of the other, but she was as clean and as fresh as on their first meeting.

Later, Tremayne watched these two at work fox hunting. In other parts of the world foxes are hunted with expensive hounds by people mounted on more expensive hacks. In other parts of Australia men go to enormous labour in laying poisoned baits and setting traps. These two Aborigines, ignorant of foxes and their habits until quite recent years, revealed a cunning cleverness truly surprising.

Miss Hazit softly circled the burrow, marked amid the white quartz chips by the brown earth of the excavations below, and expertly examined the "run-outs" for tracks, finally silently indicating a particular hole.

Twenty odd yards from this hole Ned squatted down, made sure the double-barrelled gun was full cocked, and waited immobile after waving to Tremayne, still near the fire, to sit down.

Miss Hazit then brought her head close to the mouth of the hole and coughed loudly several times. Continuing to cough louder at short intervals, she walked back to Tremayne, shuffling her feet as she went.

Nothing happened. Ned, seated like a carved Buddha, rested his cheek against the gun-stock. Miss Hazit then proceeded to throw quartz chips much like a boy skimming a stone over water, each piece of quartz bounding from the burrow to fall some distance beyond.

A fox leisurely appeared out of the hole selected by Miss Hazit, the strange sounds having mastered its curiosity. Blinded by the sunlight, it sat down blinking its eyes, waiting for them to become accustomed to the light in order to ascertain just what caused these most curious noises. And then a second fox appeared. The standing Miss Hazit presently was seen by the first fox which rose on all feet ready to dash below, but Ned fired twice rapidly and the two foxes fell dead.

A third fox appeared, to run blindly across the quartz chips, and because Ned was fumbling to reload the gun, Miss Hazit with screams of delight snatched up a stick and gave chase. Ned began yelling orders and curses, and Tremayne found himself joining in the hunt. He and Miss Hazit tore after the fox, which now could see and dodged this way and that with deceptive casualness. Miss Hazit's high-pitched excited laughter and Ned's roared orders to get out of the way, so confused the animal that it never had a real sporting chance.

"Take that—and that and that," shouted Miss Hazit, gleefully battering the fox, which was wholly unnecessary as her first blow had killed it. Her black eyes were little flames, her white teeth revealed by the widely parted lips. She was a living picture of the huntress when the world was young: straight, finely moulded, and with a figure to be envied by any woman.

"Good, eh?" Ned cried on reaching her and Tremayne. "Plenty tobacco now. Plenty new clothes for you, Nora. Mr Filson give order on Magnet storekeeper when he come back from Perth. Now you scalp 'em, Nora, and get back to camp. I gotta go see to White's Mill. Fred says so."

He set the gun down on the body of the fox and proceeded to cut tobacco for a cigarette before giving the knife to his woman. She could do the skinning and take the skins and the heavy gun back to Acacia Well. He had work—real work—to do.

"I'll be going with you," Tremayne told him. "So long, Nora!"

"Goo' bye!" she replied and, because Ned was not looking in her direction, the minx pursed her lips at the overseer, with her eyes almost hidden by the lowered lashes.

At White's Mill he worked on the loose nuts of the mill-head and the giant fan, while Ned let out the water in the long line of troughing and scraped away the green weed growing on it. And the job done, Tremayne brought out the parcel he had received that morning from Mount Magnet and opened it in front of Ned's fascinated eyes.

"Remember the other day that ribbon you took from Nora and I burned," he said, looking up at his tattered companion.

Ned nodded assent, his enraptured gaze still centred on the mysterious parcel.

"Do you know why I burned it?"

This time Ned did look at his questioner, to shake his head.

"Nora being your woman, she had no right to that ribbon. And the man who gave it to her had no right to give it to her either," Tremayne patiently explained, in his voice a hardness which diminished Ned's curiosity in the still unopened parcel. "Nora fine woman, eh? You love Nora, eh? You going to keep Nora, eh?"

"Cripes! You've said it, boss," Ned assented vigorously, using a common Americanism.

Tremayne pressed on in his task of imparting wise philosophy, tugging at Ned's ripped and soiled trouser-leg: "You find fella for Nora to love, eh? She clean in white woman's clothes, you like wild black. You wear ragged trousers, no shirt, no hat. You look like mangy camel."

"Yes, boss," agreed the crestfallen Ned. "You said a mouthful."

Tremayne could not restrain a smile. Quickly he laid open the contents of the parcel. "You put these on now," he ordered sternly, presenting the astonished Aborigine with a pair of white moleskin trousers and a sky-blue shirt. "And you give these to Nora and tell her you bought them off me." A pair of grey silk stockings and a yard of wide pink ribbon were also presented.

Without looking up, Ned finally said after a pregnant silence: "You good fella, boss. I bin a damn fool."

CHAPTER VII

SUSPICIONS AND FACTS

JUST a week later, when Tremayne reached the Bowgada homestead late in the day, he found Brett Filson returned from Perth. "Well, how did the quacks treat you?" he asked cheerfully while waiting for Jackson to bring in his dinner.

"They're as sympathetic as they know how to be, but they and I know perfectly well that I'll never again be a whole man," replied Filson, whose weather-tanned face displayed lines of fatigue.

"Better half a man than a dead one."

"That's the philosophy of a whole man."

Tremayne gave his attention to the plate put before him by the cook, who did not veil his displeasure at the lateness of the dining hour. Filson's mood was obviously influenced by his having been to Perth buoyed with hopes, destined to be destroyed yet again, and the tragedy or this once athletic bushman, so courageous and likeable, saddened Tremayne.

"Do you think Tonger was speaking the truth when he said he didn't remember my brother passing through Breakaway House?" he asked, deftly changing the subject.

"It's always difficult to decide whether Tonger was speaking the truth or not. Have you made any discoveries?"

"Nothing of great importance. I've thoroughly examined the whole length of this east breakaway on your country, poked my nose into every hole and cave, and read all the tracks to be seen. There are caverns enough in which to imprison a thousand abducted persons, run all the coining and gold treatment plants in the world, and one series of caverns which would make a fine resting place for a bunch of Mug Williams' duffed cattle. But as for tangible results–nothing."

"I saw your father as you asked me to," Filson said as Tremayne, having eaten, rolled the inevitable cigarette. "He sent a message."

"Which is…?"

"He's hoping you'll be quickly successful in establishing the fact of your brother's life or death, for your mother's sake."

Tremayne was grave when he responded: "He has a reputation for wanting results in ten minutes. He's never had outback experience, and doubtless imagines that the Murchison is but a little longer and wider than Hay Street. This is a job on which one has to go slow to make haste. I'm always thinking of my mother, which is why I'm travelling slowly but surely. You know, I could be wrong, but I feel there could be more to this than just gold-stealing."

"Really! Why do you say that?" asked Filson, surprised.

"It's just a feeling, but it seems to me too many people have been killed or made to disappear just to protect a gold-stealing racket."

"What do you think it could be then?"

"I really don't know. Perhaps drugs. But there's not enough to go on and as I said, it's just a feeling."

Tremayne changed the subject. "Ever noticed mysterious lights on the Breakaway House breakaway about two and a half to three miles south of the homestead?"

"Mysterious lights! No."

"There were two at the same spot two nights ago. Looked to me as though someone was signalling with a flash lamp. Do you know how Mug Williams gets Tonger's cattle to his killing yards outside Myme?"

"No. I'm surprised and yet not surprised. Have you proof?"

"Of course. He picks them up in the paddock west of Acacia Well, drives them to a big area of surface rock over which runs your boundary fence, lays the fence down and passes the beasts through into Bowgada, then cuts 'em to a wide shallow creek running into Bowgada from the Myme Common, lifts up the netted flood fence crossing the creek, drives them out of Bowgada, and is then about four miles from his slaughter yards."

"You tracked him?" Filson asked grimly, in his eyes a hard glint.

"Naturally. He rides an old cow and doubtless uses a silent-working heeler dog. I've seen the cow he rides, faintly saddle-marked."

"Oh! Then he'll have to be arrested. I once told him if he was duffing cattle he'd get caught in the long run."

"He's not going to be arrested for cattle duffing by longer, anyway."

"Why not?"

"'Cos Tonger does a bit of duffing, too."

"Tonger!" Filson looked astonished.

Tremayne nodded. "Yes. Not cattle–women."

"Oh."

"Besides, I want Mug's cattle-duffing activities to use as a lever to blackmail him."

Two keen hazel eyes examined the lounging man idly drawing at a badly made cigarette. "You are a policeman, aren't you?" Brett said slowly.

"Was," Tremayne corrected. "I wrote my resignation a few days ago. As a policeman I would have had to use lily-white kid gloves. As a private bloke I can use any weapon with freedom, from a gun to blackmail. I'm going to blackmail Mug Williams into telling me what he's seen, heard and done while engaged in his illegal night work."

"Your father didn't tell me of your resignation."

"I only sent it down by the last mail. I post-dated it."

"And you think Williams knows something?"

"Sure! The night he was here, you remember, he got rattled at the mention of Tonger's name. Pulled himself up in time to avoid making any accusations. Ned knows something, too. Yet, despite the fact that Williams hates Tonger, and that Ned hates Tonger for duffing his woman, both are afraid to talk. Why are they afraid? That's what I'm most interested in, and why I'm going to use any and every weapon Dame Fortune presents to me."

"What do you suspect? You can trust me, you know."

"I can, and I'm going to, Brett," Tremayne said in the direct fashion he could use when he wished. "I suspect a lot, but can prove nothing. Why those flash-lamp signals on the Breakaway House breakaway? Why is Tonger able to run a racehorse, buy himself a new car every year and give the annual ball started by his father in the good old days of prosperity? Why, when his run is in such a bad state, and his sheep and cattle are going to seed? And why does he tell you that my brother never reached Breakaway House when he did?"

"He did reach Breakaway House! How do you know?"

"That day, in the afternoon, Ned sent Nora to the Acacia mill-head to oil it. Although the distance is four miles she could see my brother opening and closing a gate half a mile from the homestead, the gate being on a rise and her native eyesight being up to standard. Tonger made a bad mistake when he said they hadn't seen my brother. He should have said that my brother stayed the night there and went on to Kyle station the next morning."

"Strange…it's very strange."

"It is, Brett. It is, too, very interesting. I'm going to the Breakaway House Ball tomorrow night, firstly to have a look round, and secondly, to remove any wrong impressions Miss Tonger may have of me. I'll bet my last zac that if there's any funny business going on over there then she is ignorant of it."

"Well, you'll be able to go all right. Every station owner or manager or overseer in the district is automatically invited. But," and Brett smiled wryly, "every man must take a female partner."

"Is that so?"

"It is. Without a partner you would not be received."

"Then I'll take Miss Hazit."

"Blacks are barred."

"I'll take Millie English."

"Half-castes are barred. It's a swell social function. More, it's an old institutional custom established fifty-four years ago. Like old man Tonger before him, Morris Tonger receives as his guests to the ball even those whom he normally dislikes. Tonger is a well-bred man who has gone down after he reached years of discretion. You could punch him on the nose tomorrow morning and he'd welcome you politely tomorrow evening. But without a lady friend you cannot go."

"Who are you taking?"

The faint light of amusement in Brett Filson's eyes faded at this question.

"I've decided not to go this year," he replied quietly.

"Why not?"

"Because it's hardly fair to the lady. You see, I cannot dance and she thinks it's not fair of her to be dancing when I'm sitting out all the time. I believe, however, she'd be pleased to go with you if you agreed."

"Do me! Who is she?"

"A Miss Sayers. She's the daughter of the Myme Hotel licensee. Shall I ring her up and tell her, if she wishes, that you'll fetch her tomorrow afternoon? You could be back in time to dine here before going on to Breakaway House, and, of course, you would have to take her back to Myme after the ball."

Tremayne made no decision while he rolled yet another cigarette. He was wondering why that note of sadness had crept back into Filson's voice.

"Good-looking?" he asked without glancing up, knowing that a man's voice will betray him when his face remains a mask.

"Very," Brett said readily.

"Old?"

"Not much over thirty."

"Good dancer?"

"Just wonderful."

"What's her Christian name?"

"Ann."

Abruptly Tremayne's gaze rose to Brett's face, to see Brett staring into space, his face vacant of expression. It was only for an instant, and then his own gaze became again centred on the cigarette. "I'll go tomorrow afternoon," he drawled in sharp contrast to his preceding, almost barked questions. "But don't telephone. Give me a short letter of introduction. I can then use it or not at my discretion."

"But I'd like her to go, Harry. Indeed, she's a very fine woman."

"In which case I'll present the letter."

Then Tremayne abruptly diverted the conversation. "How does it come about that an Australian Aborigine who cannot read glibly reels off Americanisms as Ned does?" he inquired. With secret satisfaction he noted how Filson's face regained expression. So Miss Sayers as a subject of conversation was dangerous to this semi-wreck of a man.

"That can be easily explained," Brett said. "Nora was tribally married to an Aborigine called N'gobi; promised to him when she was born, taken by him when she was about thirteen years old. She sometimes ran away from N'gobi and my mother would become her protectress. She also educated her in domestic science and taught her to read. After a bit, N'gobi would become tired of living alone and take Nora away again, my mother having no power to keep her, even though Nora feared and hated N'gobi, and wanted to stay.

"Then, in a fight, N'gobi killed a rival for your Miss Hazit's hand, and they put him in gaol at Kalgoorlie where he will be for a long time. After that Nora came and stayed here with my mother for two years. My mother thought a lot of her and she of my mother, and, as I said, she learned to read.

"Just before my mother died she decided to go with Ned who was born on Bowgada and has always lived here. He had the same chances as Nora, but was never her mental equal. Plays poker till the cows come home, and was the best draught player of all the hands. And now he borrows American novels from Fred Ellis and gets Nora to read them to him. Fred's a great fan of American literature."

"Both Ned and Nora are exceptional," Tremayne said.

"Yes and yet it's odd you know. It's not necessary for her and Ned to live as they do. They could have a hut of their own here at the homestead, but refuse it in preference for an old tent or a bough humpy."

Tremayne described his last meeting with this couple and the method he adopted to arm Ned against all rivals.

"The stuff I gave them didn't amount to thirty shillings," he said. "But two days later Ned sent, per Hool-'em-up Dick, the three fox scalps worth six pounds in bonus."

CHAPTER VIII

AT THE MYME HOTEL

"HO! You going to Myme today?" Soddy Jackson asked when Tremayne appeared dressed for the trip.

"You bet," Tremayne replied carelessly. "But you're stopping here."

"I ain't arguing. You can bring me back a couple of bottles of brandy. I'll get the money."

"Oh no, I can't cook."

"I didn't say you could. I ain't talkin' about cooking. I'm talkin' about brandy," Jackson explained patiently, an expression of strain on his chalk-white face.

"And I'm talking about my inability to cook," Tremayne countered seriously. "If you drink two bottles of brandy, how can you cook? And if you can't cook and I can't cook, how do we get on for tucker tomorrow?"

"The drunker I gets the better I cooks," Jackson stated warmly.

"Good! Then I'll bring you back six bottles of brandy so that you can become properly drunk and can properly cook–if you obtain a permit in writing from the boss."

"That's fair," cried the white-haired, bow-legged stockman called Old Humpy.

"Course you've got to bring the blasted boss into it," complained the cook, aggrieved when reminded of Brett Filson's iron rule concerning liquor on his station. "The capitalists can swill their booze; but no, no, no, to the down-trodden slaves wot produces their wealth. Thank Gawd, the day of our freedom ain't far orf! When that does come I'm gonna get drunk proper so's I can 'ang the blighters more slowly. I got a letter from the executive of the movement in Sydney the other day appointing me chief executioner-to-be."

"What's the screw, Soddy?" inquired Charlie English, Millie's husband, a big, powerful man whose disposition made him popular with everyone.

"Five pounds a 'ead," the cook promptly informed them. "I reckon to make a 'undred quid a day."

"You won't be making it for long, Soddy, old top," drawled Tremayne. "For why? Because when you and your hunch have done all the rough work cleaning up the capitalists, the F.S.S. will start operations. We members of the F.S.S. are only waiting for you Bolshies to do all the spade-work."

"What's the F.S.S.?" demanded Jackson.

His features immobile, his eyes almost invisible beneath the lowered lids, the ex-policeman replied in soft sinister tones: "The F.S.S.," he began in explanation, "stands for the Fire-Stick Society. There are nearly forty million members scattered throughout the world. Very little is known about us because we're a real secret society. We aim to wait calmly until the Bolsheviks have overthrown the capitalists. Then we're going to start on the Bolsheviks. We're going to put a fire-stick into every person's house, and into every public building. We don't believe in law and order, in houses and buildings. We don't believe in anything but the universal application of the fire-stick to the world."

"But the people gotta live," gasped Soddy Jackson, a dull flush indicating rising indignation. "The people…"

"We're not going to hang Bolsheviks or shoot them," Tremayne continued. "No. None of those la-di-da women's ways for us. When we get busy, millions of saw-edged knives are going to slide back and across Bolshie throats. For why? Because we're not going to have Bolsheviks ordering us about like the capitalists are doing."

"Well, of all the bloodthirsty…"

Old Humpy roared with laughter; English's white teeth were flashing in a smile. Soddy Jackson glared at Tremayne, both hands gripping the edge of the pastry table. Tremayne, with grave seriousness, departed whistling Rule Britannia.

The "overseer" drove to Myme in Filson's powerful-engined car, following a track which now and then skirted the apex of breakaway bays, where one momentarily glimpsed purple-shaded views. Presently the road gradually turned to the north-east and for several miles passed through dense mulga.

Ten miles from the homestead the mulga began to thin. Here and there were little clearings carpeted with white and yellow everlasting flowers, among which the buttercups formed sheets of gold, and the daisies nodded modestly. Another two miles, and from the scrub-top ahead slowly rose a knob of gold which magically grew as the car drew closer. Eventually Tremayne was facing a three-hundred foot hill smothered in buttercups, appearing like a nugget of pure gold undreamed of by the most optimistic of prospectors or company promoters.

"Ye gods!" he breathed, stopping the car to examine something which, even he, with his wide experience, had never before seen the like.

It was more wonderful than a dying gold-seeker's hallucination. Not a mark, not a blemish, not a square foot of vacancy marred this huge mound of gold that sent, even against the zephyr wind, a perfume which haunts a man for years. It stood to the east of the track. The sun shone full down on it. It dazzled–nature's effort to dwarf the seven wonders of the world.

"Some nugget!" commented Tremayne, and drove on with reckless speed, as a man might who had once looked deeply into dewy violet eyes and smelled violets.

While yet three miles distant, thousands of ugly mulga stumps thrust upward from natural flowerbeds, mute evidence of the mine's ravenous hunger for furnace wood. Further on, even the stumps had been dragged out to feed the fires, and here the beauty of the flower carpets was unmarred.

The track led him to one end of the main street of the town, beyond which reared ugly poppet heads. First appeared single houses, all built of the same corrugated iron–the curse and also the blessing of Australia–and then adjoined shops without architectural symmetry, as though the inmates of a madhouse had laboured with feverish activity for just one day. The only brick-built structure was the hotel.

A little rotund man ran out to meet him. "Good day, Mr Tremayne! Come in and have a snifter," invited Mug Williams.

"Have a snifter!" echoed Tremayne. "Why, of course. That's what I'm here for."

Mug Williams' mouth widened and his small grey eyes narrowed in evidence of his bonhomie. "Come on in," he entreated. "Don't waste time."

"Waste time!" Tremayne said, again in echo. "Lead me to the blessed fountain. I want to be waited on by beauty."

The lines of Mug Williams' face stretched further in a smile. He winked by lowering the lid of his right eye the remaining fraction of an inch.

The saloon bar was empty of customers but behind the counter waited Miss Ann Sayers. As Tremayne walked the short distance from doorway to counter he made up his mind what he would do.

She was fair, was Ann Sayers. Her dark blue eyes were set wide apart in a face which could not possibly conceal guile or conceit. She was Helen to Frances Tonger's Cleopatra, and Tremayne was to come to know that she could intelligently discuss racing and horses with the keenest of sportsmen, and with equal facility talk of all the famous murders and all the famous gold strikes. Her position behind a saloon bar demanded versatility even in a mining centre. In her private life her interests were centred on music and books.

So it *is* that, thought Tremayne, as Williams and he breasted the counter. "Morning, Miss! I've been a teetotaller for fifty years, but Mr Williams tempted me and I have fallen."

"Meet Mr Tremayne from Bowgada, Miss Sayers," said Mug. "Mine's a pot."

"Two pots, please. I'm happy to meet you, Miss Sayers, and oh, so glad that I was tempted and fell," Tremayne drawled without smiling.

"Are you staying at Bowgada?" she asked, just a trifle eagerly.

"I'm overseer out there, Miss Sayers. Well, Mug, here's the skin off your chest. I'm going to the Breakaway House Ball, so I came in to see if I could hire a dress suit."

"You won't hire no dress suit in Myme," Williams pointed out with a chuckle.

"Well, I can't go to a ball in a lounge suit."

"Why not, Mr Tremayne? More than half the men will not be in evening clothes. And anyway, to be able to dance well is much more important than evening clothes," interposed Miss Sayers.

"Good!" Tremayne said, still unsmilingly. "I can throw a leg. Well, I've to do some shopping before lunch. See you later, Miss Sayers. *Au revoir!*"

He and Williams had reached the doorway when Ann Sayers said softly: "Mr Tremayne!"

Tremayne strolled back to the counter, now smiling affably.

"I forgot," lied Ann Sayers, revealing the lie in her eyes and by the faint flush in her face, "I forgot to ask how Mr Filson was keeping."

"Oh! He's all right," Tremayne replied indifferently. "Of course, he'll never be much good again. Pretty useless, poor devil."

"I...you've no right to say that," she told him sharply. "Mr Filson was badly wounded in the war. He's deserving of all sympathy. He's..."

She paused, Tremayne's broad smile making her stop. Purposely he allowed her to see in his eyes what was in his mind. A crimson stain mounted into her creamy face.

"I forgot something, too," he said calmly. "I have a message from Mr Filson. He said that if you cared to accompany him to the Breakaway House Ball he would be delighted to escort you. I'm to tell you, in addition, that he's remembered every moment of the last ball at Breakaway House."

"He said that?" she whispered.

Tremayne nodded. "Of course. Think I made it up? Will you be ready to leave at five o'clock?"

"Yes, Mr Tremayne. I shall be very glad to go."

"All right, then. How many maids in the hotel?"

"Two."

"Engaged to be married."

"Both of them."

"Oh. What about the cook?"

She was now looking curiously at her questioner. "Violet Winters is not engaged to be married, nor is she married."

"Well, I'll see you after," and, smiling again, Tremayne raked his hat and walked out of the bar to join Mug Williams on the footpath.

"What kind of a woman is the cook, Mug?" he asked the little man.

"Hefty, forty, nifty," was the succinct answer.

"Take a drink?"

"Too right, I will."

"I'm referring to the cook, Mug."

"Oh...'er. Yes, too right!"

"See you later then."

Tremayne again entered the hotel and in the main bar purchased a bottle of beer. With the bottle concealed inside him coat, he found his way to the kitchen.

"Morning, cook. Nice day," he said charmingly to the tall and broad woman mixing a salad at a side table. She swung round, to glare at him from his boots upwards.

"Good day!" she responded sharply, indicating that she had not the slightest desire to talk with a stranger. Her face was red and damp, made so by the stove heat. Wisps of greying hair straggled down her forehead. Her eyes were brown, and not at the moment soft like a doe's eyes.

"I've just thought up a good idea," Tremayne said with undaunted cheerfulness. "If I were to produce a nice cold bottle of beer, would you produce a nice hot cup of tea?"

The woman's irritation was smoothed away as though by the hands of Cupid. From a savage virago she became pleasantly maternal.

"You fetch that bottle and see," she said.

Tremayne winked brazenly and produced his bottle. While the cook made a pot of tea he took a cup and saucer from the dresser, and a bottle-opener. Then he filled the glass and she filled the cup.

"My name's Harry Tremayne," he said lightly. "Yours is Violet Winters. We're introduced. You know anything about the squatter's ball?"

"Too right! I cooked for the squatter's ball two years ago."

"Did you? Well, what about coming with me tonight? I'm working for Filson. I'm leaving with Miss Sayers at five sharp. Will you come?"

"Oh, boy!" she chortled. "Do you mean it?"

Smiling and nodding, Tremayne walked to the range, and there slipped into its maw the letter of introduction Brett had written to Ann Sayers.

CHAPTER IX

TREMAYNE BEHAVES QUEERLY

AFTER lunch at the hotel, which he took at the licensee's table in the company of the host, Mr Sayers, his wife and Ann Sayers, who had only come to Myme to "look after" her parents, Tremayne went shopping for Brett and himself, during which time he telephoned the squatter.

Filson's immediate requirements concerned the Bowgada homestead, but Tremayne needed clothes, and he took this opportunity to expend the balance he felt owing on the fox-scalps on clothes for Miss Hazit and her worshipping man. At five o'clock he was ready to leave with the Bowgada—and Breakaway House—guests.

"How do I look?" asked Violet Winters, as she entered Miss Sayers' room. "I want to look nice 'cos it's years since a boy took me to a dance."

Ann Sayers checked the laughter which hovered on her lips when she saw the pleading light in the small brown eyes of the great ungainly woman. The cook wore a low-cut, short-skirted, one-piece gown of vivid blue voile trimmed with lace. The shortness of her dress emphasised the size of her silk-stockinged legs, and the low-cut neck-line, the vastness of her bust.

"Let me do your hair and a few other things, and you won't know yourself," Ann Sayers urged, melted by the appeal in the other woman's eyes and voice. "If you feel right, you'll be happy; if you feel wrong you'll be miserable."

"Do you mean it?" asked the wondering cook, for socially, even in Myme, they were far apart. She wondered more when the barmaid rearranged her plentiful greying hair, touched her brows with pencil and her lips with rouge, and dusted her face with powder. "Why it ain't me!" she exclaimed, on looking into a mirror. "What a lot of difference a little powder does make! And I'll always be doing me hair this way." Outside a klaxon blared impatiently. "Oh, drat him! Hark at him!"

"Let him wait. Never be in a hurry to meet a boy," Ann Sayers advised from her wider experience of men.

"But...but he might go without us," Violet protested.

"Not he. Anyway, I'm almost ready. Now, now, wait for me! Don't hurry so!"

The cook's triumph was complete when, sallying forth ahead of her companion, she found the presence of some dozen people forming an avenue similar to those which greet a bride emerging from a church. The two women were both respected and admired in Myme and there was quite a little crowd to greet them, among which were Mr Sayers, his wife and the entire staff, Mug Williams, two current drunks and the bank manager, while gathered about Filson's car were several curious cows and small children.

"Are you waiting for us?" Miss Winters asked Tremayne, who stood flanking the open door of the tonneau.

"Are you Miss Winters?" he inquired, displaying astonishment and admiration on his face.

Nodding happily, she squeezed his arm before he handed her into the car.

Tremayne then helped Ann Sayers in and fussed with cushions for their comfort. When he was finally seated behind the wheel, he called to the children: "Take those cows away and drown 'em, please. I want to move off." And with a cheer from the crowd he began the homeward journey, at first having carefully to avoid the many mobs of goats.

He did not speak again until they had passed through the gate that indicated the Bowgada boundary. Having shut it behind them, he leaned with Australian casualness against the car. With that beaming grin which was so very attractive, he drawled: "I've got strict instructions not to bounce you up to the roof, and to get you to Bowgada at six o'clock punctually. It's now a quarter to six and we have yet twenty miles to go. Consequently, we'll have to travel at the speed of eighty miles an hour. So if you should get bounced up to the roof occasionally, don't say anything."

"If you shakes me face to pieces you'll hear more about it," Miss Winters said with mock sternness, resolutely repressing a giggle.

"It might be as well to get on with the journey, Mr Tremayne," suggested Ann Sayers sweetly.

"We'll be there on time, don't worry. This car can do a hundred and ten to the hour if coaxed a bit," Tremayne told them, unhurriedly rolling himself a cigarette. He was beginning to like this open-faced woman more and more.

He proved to be not the reckless speed demon he had threatened. However both women implored him not to be so careless in his manner of driving; he only had one hand on the wheel and spent most of the time half-turned towards them so that he could converse in his cheerful way.

The urgency for speed was overstressed apparently, because he stopped the car for a minute so that his passengers could gaze enraptured at Round Hill, now a flaming gold reflecting the light of the westering sun; and again he pulled up when not far from the homestead so that they could enjoy the superb view of the breakaway valley from one of the many deeply indented "bays".

The sun was setting when they arrived at Bowgada, stopping outside the front gate which gave entry to what should have been a flower garden but was in fact devoted to vegetables. Filson came out to welcome them, his limp and his stick much in evidence. He was warm in his greetings yet controlled. Talking gaily, they entered the house where Millie English met them to escort the women to the guest room.

"I thought I made it quite plain that I wasn't intending to go to the ball?" Filson said to Tremayne when they were alone.

"You did that," Tremayne agreed nonchalantly.

"I thought, further, it was understood that you were to ask Miss Sayers to accompany you to the ball, as you seemed keen on going?"

"You bet!"

"Why don't you look at me?"

"Look at you!" Tremayne exclaimed, transferring his gaze from the cigarette in the making to Brett Filson's eyes. "You ain't that handsome that a man's got to look at you all the time."

For a space each tried hard with no success to bore into the other's mind.

"Surely you've no objection to explaining why you brought the cook?" Filson pressed, trying not to be impatient.

"Objection! Of course not. I'm taking her to the ball."

"But what about Miss Sayers? You cannot take both to the ball, you know."

"Then in that case, Miss Sayers will have to remain here until my lovely Violet and I get back from the ball–unless you change your mind and take her yourself."

"I don't quite get you," Filson said thoughtfully.

"Well–it seems simple enough to me. You'd better do a bunk now and get dressed. Miss Sayers is quite looking forward to going."

"I still don't quite get you," Filson persisted.

Tremayne sighed. "I want to go to the ball and regulations state that I must take a female partner. Isn't that right?"

Filson nodded, by no means as dense as he made himself appear, which did not deceive the ex-policeman.

"Good! I'm glad you follow me. Now, I go to Myme ostensibly to fetch Miss Sayers because you wanted her to go–not me. On the way I lose your letter of introduction, and while wondering what to do about it, I fell into the hotel kitchen–and there I saw my own sweet girlie. Get me?

I'm for her and she's for me, understand? But I've got orders to bring Miss Sayers, so's there's nothing else for it but to bring 'em both. Quite simple."

"You're not by any chance an adept at making two plus two equal four, are you?" Brett asked quietly.

"I couldn't say, Brett, but I'm no damned good at answering riddles. You hurry up and get dressed now. I'll have to get busy, too. See you after," and Tremayne walked determinedly through to the kitchen.

"Good night, my noble hangman! How're things up your street?" he asked the busy Soddy Jackson.

"You keep away, I'm engaged in my slavery," the apostle of Bolshevism returned surlily.

Tremayne drew close to Jackson's rigid back. "Have a smoke-stack?" he asked, thrusting a cheap but fat cigar into Jackson's line of vision,

"Thanks! Put it on the dresser," Jackson said ungraciously.

"And when you've done your work, have a drink on me," and Tremayne slipped a half-bottle of whisky into Jackson's disengaged hand.

The metamorphosis in the cook was an interesting phenomenon. Turning, he beamed upon Tremayne and the tip of his tongue slid backwards and forwards between his lips.

"You're a good 'un, Mr Tremayne. You're one of us," he said enthusiastically.

"Not a bit, you're a Bolshie, I'm a fire-stick wielder. There's a lot of difference."

"Well, I'm gonna join your Fire-Stick Society. I always did think Bolshevism was a bit lukewarm for real men."

"Goodo! I'll arrange your invitation," Tremayne told him, and bolted to his room.

THERE was nothing indicative either of flamboyant wealth or genteel poverty in any of the four people who sat down to dinner at Bowgada homestead that early evening. Four people who, elsewhere, would live on different planes of human society, here came into jolly association. Many a peeress has appeared less tastefully, if more fashionably dressed, than was Violet Winters; whilst in a city one would travel far before hearing a better modulated voice than that possessed by Ann Sayers. The fact that Brett Filson wore evening dress was to Tremayne no cause for either regret or jealousy. That man of the far north, where fine feathers do not make fine gentlemen, was dressed in a navy blue lounge suit and a soft-collared sports shirt. He was the kind of man who would not wear a starched shirt to attend a king's levee.

At the close of a well-cooked, but simple dinner, Millie English–despite Jackson's protestations–removed the cloth and brought them coffee. Tremayne drifted over to the wireless on which he found a station relaying music, and Violet Winters took her coffee with him. For Brett, the evening was crowned by a *tête-à-tête* with Ann Sayers during which they discussed music and novels, and never once permitted their eyes to hold in meeting longer than a split second.

At eight o'clock they left for Breakaway House, Ann and Brett occupying the tonneau and Violet sitting beside Tremayne who drove the car.

Sliding southward, the mulga scrub, revealed by the headlights, appeared to be a world occupied by gnomes and fairies, and when they arrived at the sharp turn above the steep descent into the valley, it was to see a young moon hanging above the western breakaway slipping into a gulf between two dark spires outlined against the blush of the sky. And there a little to the north of west, a column of fire leaped upward from an invisible base.

"It doesn't seem worth going on," Tremayne cried. "Breakaway House will be a cinder by the time we get there."

"The house will be all right," Brett assured him. "That fire is the beacon lit every ball night to call us to the dance. Tonger, as his father before him, spends a lot of money to have that beacon constructed."

"Good idea, isn't it, Mr Tremayne?" said Ann with a low, gay laugh.

"It is, Miss Sayers."

"Tonger's hands invite their friends to their own party round the beacon. Tonger permits them to kill a beast and gives them a case or two of jam and a bag of flour," Brett further explained.

"He must be generous," Tremayne opined.

"No one can justly accuse Tonger of being mean."

Beyond, ever beyond, flamed the great beacon welcoming them and others to Breakaway House. Twice they were stopped by wire gates. The flat land of the valley offered but an occasional shrub or cork tree to maintain touch with reality; for the road was good, and only its ceaseless unwinding before the headlights and the purring engine prevented the illusion of a magic carpet.

"Comfortable?" inquired Tremayne of his companion.

"Lovely," replied Violet, sighing happily. "Why can't life always be like this?"

Presently, looming out of the darkness came the spidery outline of the mill and the low, box-shaped hut of Acacia Well. Beside the track, Fred Ellis awaited them.

"I opened the gate for you," he called. "You needn't stop to shut it. When me and Ned come home after sundown we found Nora cleared out. Ned raising hell, gonna start a war, thinks she's gone to the dance."

CHAPTER X

BREAKAWAY HOUSE BALL

WITH Acacia Well behind them, the beacon appeared to rise and then, a little later, on its left and below it, winked many lights which rapidly grew in brilliance. Higher still rose the beacon. They could see its leaping flames, and could discern the black shapeless mass of the breakaway on which it burned.

All the homestead gates were wide open. Beyond it the lights of three cars blazed as they descended the long slope from the high ground. Tremayne put their car much nearer to the shearing shed than the mass of parked cars, and turned it to face the homeward run. From the shed issued the music made by an improvised orchestra. Between it and the homestead, the men's kitchen was a hive of industry. From the homestead, which had every window lit up, came the sound of happy laughter and raised excited voices. Then Morris Tonger was beside the car, opening its doors.

"That you, Filson?" he said, ignoring Tremayne.

"Good evening, Tonger! I've brought my overseer and two ladies," Brett said, assisting Ann Sayers out. Having introduced the ladies, he formally introduced Tremayne, and Tonger said with studied politeness:

"Oh, ah! That you, Tremayne! Glad you came. Well, go along all of you. You'll find my niece serving coffee in the drawing room of the house. Excuse me now. Here are other guests arrived."

The lights of the approaching cars showed them up as though it were day. They revealed Morris Tonger's big and mottled face and his magnificently proportioned figure within well-cut evening clothes. The Bowgada party walked to the rambling bungalow house, Brett leaning heavily on his stick, Ann walking by his side–following them Violet Winters and Tremayne, who restrained her impulse to hurry forward to give her arm to Filson. Tremayne liked Ann Sayers for also leaving his friend a little independence.

Guests were walking from house to shed. Uniformed maids were busy between house and men's kitchen. Obviously Tonger was doing the thing in style, keeping up his father's reputation for hospitality.

At the homestead door a quiet, efficient-looking girl relieved them of their coats and wraps, and, on direction, they found Frances Tonger serving coffee in the drawing room.

"Hello, Brett! Awfully glad you came," exclaimed a tall girl in a sea-green dress. "Let me introduce you all to Miss Tonger. Why, Miss Sayers and Miss Winters! Well, well! Wonders will never cease."

The malice in her voice jarred. She was the daughter of a man who owned a run near Youanmi and lived mostly with her married sister in Perth. In that city the father was never mentioned because he had remarried an Aboriginal woman when his first wife died.

"It's the rule that one must not come without one's friends," Brett said calmly. "Have you met Mr Tremayne? Tremayne, Miss Tinley-Bucklow."

"So pleased to meet you, Mr Tremayne."

"Charmed," drawled the overseer, whereupon Miss Winters stepped in. With her mouth close to her cavalier's ear she said in what was supposed to be a whisper: "Don't you be. She's not half as nice as she appears."

Whereupon Miss Tinley-Bucklow fled, permitting Brett to introduce his friends to Frances. Dressed strikingly in a creation of unrelieved black, she was a superb representative of that type of woman diametrically opposed to the blond type represented by Ann Sayers. Frances was genuine in her welcome–until Tremayne's turn came to be presented.

"How do you do, Miss Tonger?" he said, standing squarely before her. She held out her hand, although there was cold fire in her eyes, and he bowed over it with the suaveness of Brett Filson. "I'm a stranger on the Murchison, and because of it I am the more indebted to you for your kind invitation."

There was now none of the slurred bush drawl. His expression plainly indicated deference to her beauty, and respect for her as his hostess. Try as she did she could detect no mockery in his voice or see mockery in his twinkling eyes. With a sense of annoyance she found herself judging him in his favour.

"The Breakaway House Ball is famed as far north as Wyndham," he was saying. "I do really consider myself fortunate in being present this year. If you will honour me with one dance I shall always thank my gods that I left the Kimberleys."

She was no less surprised than several of her friends when she found herself giving him her dance card. Afterwards she excused herself on the plea that he proved himself sufficiently a gentleman not to publicly remind her of their first meeting. When he returned her card there was a faint expression of wonder allied to the hardness in her eyes. Tremayne smiled gaily, and stepped back to permit the presentation of another party of guests. Even whilst welcoming these fresh arrivals she visually sought him out, and found him waiting upon the enormous woman in the blue gown.

She thought what an extraordinary person was this Miss Winters to be brought by a man like Tremayne, who was even more extraordinary. And, months later, she declared that the most extraordinary thing of all was the tiny thrill which touched her heart when, glancing at her dance card, she discovered that Tremayne had impudently written his name carefully against two waltzes.

Within the great shed all was movement and colour and merriment. Bunting and paper streamers hung beneath the roof. The interior fittings had been removed and the fake floor, which old Tonger had had constructed in his day, laid over the floor proper.

Violet Winters danced with her eyes shut in the safety of Tremayne's arm. He was giving her the treat of her life, and he happily guessed as much. This third dance was the second they had partnered. In the middle of it Violet felt her escort trip and opened her eyes to see a man she knew as Buck Ross cease dancing, and snarlingly demand why Tremayne was so clumsy.

"You appear to be deliberately looking for trouble," Tremayne answered, white with anger. "You attempted to trip me a minute ago."

It became proved that Violet Winter was a superb liar, although in fact she was right. It became proved, too, that she had not lived in mining towns, and in mining camps before living in mining towns, without having gained an extensive knowledge of men.

"Buck Ross, you did that on purpose," she said, and, disengaging herself from her partner's hands, she stepped swiftly to the scowling man beside who stood his embarrassed partner. Violet's hands became pressed against her hips. Her head was thrown back and her eyes were pin points of gleaming light. "If you do that again, Buck Ross, I'll slap your face so hard that your head'll be turned back to front. Mr Tremayne can't make a scene here, but I'm never slow in taking up an argument."

"Excuse me, Miss Winters," urged Morris Tonger, inserting himself between her and Ross, whose dark face had become crimson. "Mr Ross, there's a gentleman outside who wants to see you. I'll take your partner if, Miss Pink, you will so honour me."

Perhaps none but Violet and Tremayne and Buck Ross witnessed the fury in Tonger's dark eyes.

Tremayne was astonished to see Ross's demeanour replaced by one of sullenness, and he watched the fellow's broad back as he made his way through the dancers to the main door. Tonger's voice recalled his attention.

"Sorry, Miss Winters, you were quite right in your action. I happened to see Ross trying to trip Mr Tremayne."

"But why, Mr Tonger?" exclaimed the overseer. "I don't even know the man. I've never met him before."

The squatter shrugged before swinging away with the interested Miss Pink.

"I know why he did it, Mr Tremayne," Violet said, anger still remaining in her eyes and voice. "He's been wanting to marry me for a long time. Now you keep your eyes open. He's a bad customer, is Mr Buck Ross."

Tremayne was now smiling, and when she saw how amused he was, she said impatiently: "I mean it. He wouldn't fight any man fair. He'd get his gang at Myme to smash you up."

Tremayne continued to smile broadly. Violet shook him with the hand laid on his shoulder. "Stop it!" she commanded in the manner of a lord of the kitchen. "Do you hear what I say? Be sensible, do. You keep your eyes open for Buck Ross."

"What does he do for a living?"

"Anything bar honest work. He's got a small mining show four miles out of Myme, but that's only an excuse for humming beer."

"Ever been in gaol?"

"Not yet, but there's still time."

"That's comforting," Tremayne told her. "What about a drink?"

"I'm dying for one," she replied honestly.

"Have you known Miss Winters long?" Frances asked Brett Filson abruptly after Tremayne and Violet had moved off to the bunting-hidden cocktail bar in a far corner of the shed.

"For several years. She's a forthright woman."

"They appear to be fast friends already."

"Bush people make friends–and enemies–quickly, Miss Tonger. For instance, it didn't take me long to accept Tremayne as a friend after accepting him as my overseer."

"No?" she responded sceptically.

"No. I like Harry Tremayne," Brett went on in his quiet manner. "I like a man who has retained his boyishness, as Tremayne has. He often says the most outrageous things, such as one would expect of inexperienced youth; yet there are occasions when I feel sure that he has much experience, both of life and of men."

"Men–not of women?"

Brett smiled at her. "Don't ask me to leave firm ground for quicksand," he pleaded.

"Did he tell you of our encounter near the boundary fence, Mr Filson?" Frances asked with slight colour.

"Something of it," Brett replied guardedly.

"Did he tell you how rude he was?"

"He didn't appear to realise it until I pointed it out to him."

"Did he tell you how I fell off my horse and sat on a saltbush?"

"No, he didn't tell me that," Brett cheerfully lied, and became both amused and a little astonished when she broke into a ripple of slow laughter.

"I felt so foolish, I could have killed him. I wonder if he would lose his *sang-froid* if an earthquake happened?"

"This is my dance, Miss Tonger, I'm positively sure," said the object of their conversation. "Why I'm so positively sure is because I made a note of the dances you so kindly granted me, and I've been counting and checking the dances already passed."

To Filson's delighted amusement, she said coolly: "I'd forgotten. Is this really your dance?"

Gravely unsmiling, he said: "Yes. The moment of your execution has arrived."

Frances stood up. "Very well. Let's get it over quickly, please," she told him coldly.

Brett had hard work not to laugh out loud.

Then just as they were moving off, Tremayne, who was facing an open side door of the shed, said: "Just excuse me for a moment, please, Miss Tonger. There's a little matter which requires my attention. I'll not be long."

In silence Frances and the seated Filson watched Tremayne walk rapidly to the door and vanish beyond it.

"Well...what..."

"Sit down again, please," Brett urged. "Tremayne apparently has found a long-lost friend."

"Then he might have waited until after our dance to greet his long-lost friend. He's the most provoking man I've ever met."

CHAPTER XI

TREMAYNE'S TRICKERY

IT had been an almost instantaneous picture, that which was presented to Tremayne from beyond the side door of the shed, and it compelled him to leave Frances Tonger at the moment he was to hold her in the dance. Such a picture would not have called many men from the prospect of dancing with Frances, for it showed an Aborigine being knocked down.

Without attracting attention, Tremayne reached the side door and left the building. When his sight became accustomed to the outside darkness, he was in time to observe Ned rushing on the man who had hit him, and, an inborn sense of fair play controlling him, he stopped short to watch the result of that purposeful rush. He saw the powerful figure of the white man draw upward to its full height; saw, too, what looked like a short stick brought down quickly on Ned's head. Without a sound Ned collapsed and lay still.

"What's wrong," Tremayne asked softly, approaching the white man.

"Black hanging around when all Aborigines have been ordered up to the beacon," calmly replied the smiter.

"You are, I perceive, Mr Buck Ross. I also perceive in your hand a length of shoeing iron," Tremayne said in tones suggestive of snapping steel.

"That's me. And you...why, if it isn't Mr Blooming Tremayne. Now, this is a lucky meeting."

"Your peevishness seems to have started from about an hour ago. Why?"

"Who wouldn't be peeved at a bloke barging into him on a dance floor?"

"Ah! Who, indeed?"

"And now that you're here, I'm going to show you who's the cock of the farmyard."

At their feet Ned groaned and moved.

"So you hit him with a bar of shoeing iron?"

"I did. He got what was coming to him. And now you're going to get all that's coming to you."

"You don't say, my poor innocent, ignorant, Buck. Let's start, then."

Tremayne's right feinted to Buck's stomach, and, as the man's body bent forward to avoid the blow, Tremayne's left fist uppercut him on the jaw.

Considering that the light reflected through the shed door was poor, the blow was beautifully timed. Ross lay on his back, and Tremayne secured the bar of iron and tossed it far into the night. "Get up, my dear friend," he requested.

"You...you...!"

Ross arose to stand swaying on his feet. The overseer waited. For Ross the world at length became steady, whereupon he rushed Tremayne. And Tremayne hit him a second time at the same point on his chin. Ross crashed earthwards to lie as inert as poor Ned had lain.

Had lain is correct, for now Ned was on his hands and knees, fighting nausea and dizziness so that he could get to his feet and continue the battle. The top of his head was gashed, and blood streamed down his face. The language he used was excusable, perhaps.

"Steady, Ned! Steady, old boy. Take things calmly," urged Tremayne, assisting Ned to his feet. "Come over to the car and sit down."

"Bime-by, boss. I finishing Buck Ross first."

"He's finished," Tremayne pointed out with candid simplicity. "Like the sluggard, he slumbereth. Go easy, now. You had a terrific wallop."

Without doubt the bar of iron was less soft than a band leader's baton, and, although at the time Ned's spirit was willing, the mangled flesh was weak. Tremayne got him to the Bowgada car and made him sit on the running board. "Don't you go from here," he ordered sternly. "I'll be back in a minute."

Crossing to the men's quarters he entered the kitchen, where he found a big fat man in chef's regalia working with the assistance of two women, both almost as fat as he. "Good night! I want a strip of clean calico. A lady has slipped and hurt her leg."

The untruth saved time. It produced a square yard of linen and a tin of Zambuk, with which he hurried back to the car. "How are you feeling now, Ned?"

"Pretty crook," Ned replied, to add with a brave chuckle: "Cripes, boss! He did swipe me. Put me right on the spot, he sure did."

"Yep, he sure did," agreed Tremayne, unable not to grin. "Come over here. There's a horse trough in which you can drown your head."

He tore the linen into strips while Ned bathed the gaping cut, and rendered first aid as best he could before taking Ned back to the car. He ordered him into the tonneau, and then got in himself to at once work at cigarette making. "What happened, Ned?"

"I bin come after Nora, Mr Tremayne," Ned began in explanation. "When me and Fred got back to Acacia Well Nora had gone walking– walking to here. I came on over her tracks. That Tonger, he got her over here, giving her ribbon. I saw her helping Miss Frances in the house, Nora all dressed up fine. New dress and stockings and white apron and cap like she uster wear for Mrs Filson.

"Then I seen her going from kitchen to the shed, and I run after her. She see me coming and ran past Buck Ross into the shed. And he saw me, and when I got to him he hit me. Then he hit me with something I don't remember. Tonger's got Nora and he'll keep her for days."

"How did you come here from Acacia Well?"

"I run," replied the black simply. "I reckon I'm a damn fool. I forgot to ride the mule."

"Of course," Tremayne agreed, understanding how easy it had been for Ned to forget when he knew Miss Hazit's destination. It was as well, perhaps, that the average Aborigine is a peace-loving man.

"Do you know what you must do?" he asked.

"What, boss?"

"You must stay right here. I'll fetch Nora at the first opportunity, and I'll drive you both back to Acacia Well. And when you get Nora back to Acacia Well, when you have given her the hiding you have made up your mind to give her, you open up the parcel here I brought from Myme. If she's not too dazed, she'll appreciate the pretties. Now, will you stop here quiet?"

"You'll fetch Nora?" Ned pleaded anxiously.

"I won't leave Breakaway House without her, but if you interfere there'll be nothing doing."

"All right, boss. I'll have a shut-eye. You good fella, Mr Tremayne."

"Right! You stay put and be ready to calm Miss Hazit when I bring her along."

"Miss Hazit! Who's she?"

"That's Australian name for Nora, Ned."

"Cripes! Miss Hazit! Good, eh?"

Leaving Ned chuckling despite his aching head, Tremayne strolled back to the shed. Matters were turning out just as he anticipated, which was why he had stopped the car away from the main mass of cars, and facing the homeward road for a quick getaway. Within the shed he found that the waltz dance was over, and Frances dancing in the Lancers. Ann Sayers was sitting it out beside Brett Filson, and Tremayne did not become a third person until the next dance was announced by a foppishly dressed man whom he had learned was a Mr Henry Wonkford.

"Miss Sayers, our dance, I think," he said cheerfully, when he stood before them.

"I...oh! Could you not find it in your heart to excuse me? I've been dancing all evening, Mr Tremayne," Ann said calmly.

"You haven't, Miss Sayers," Brett pointed out. "You did not dance the last number."

"Well…"

"I like to see you dancing. You dance beautifully," Brett said, smiling quizzically.

"Very well, Mr Tremayne. But I do feel tired."

"I don't doubt that," Tremayne told her seriously. "But when you've danced two seconds with me, you'll have forgotten it. Thank heaven the old boy in the mid-Victorian clothes puts on plenty of waltzes."

Smiling at Brett, they swung away, remaining silent until they had made a full circuit of the floor.

"What do you think of my friend and boss?" he asked her.

"I think he's a fine and gallant man, Mr Tremayne. He never complains. He's always cheerful, always courteous, and yet he must suffer."

"What he wants badly, Miss Sayers, is a wife to look after him."

Ann's brows lifted. Her eyes, blue-black in the electric light, regarded him steadily.

"I don't doubt that," she said.

"Just fancy a man like Brett living alone year after year with no woman to care for him after Mrs Filson died."

The blue-black eyes were masked. Her face became partly hidden from his searching gaze. For a space they did not speak again. Then: "I'm afraid you're not dancing very well," he told her serenely.

"Mr Tremayne!" The blue-black eyes were now wide, looking fully at him. "Your mind doesn't appear to be occupied with this dance, anyway. Are you in love? Well…Mr Tremayne!"

"Isn't that a question a very old friend can ask?" he blandly inquired.

"A friend of nine hours?"

"Is that all? It seems more like nine years. We are old friends, I hope."

"Oh, yes. Very old friends."

The ghost of a smile was playing about Tremayne's mouth. It fascinated her.

"Then I'll tell you something if you'll promise never to say a word to anyone. Will you?"

"I promise."

"I'm a bit worried, Miss Sayers," he said hesitatingly. "You may think Brett Filson is standing his racket in a good spirit, but as a matter of fact I've found him in tears of despair on three occasions. I have, without his knowledge, gathered all the strychnine and the arsenic about the place and buried it. I couldn't very well take the guns away, but I have removed the cordite from all the cartridges. He doesn't use an ordinary razor, so there's no danger from that direction. The cook keeps his butcher's knives safe, but..."

"What are you trying to imply," Ann cut in.

Tremayne was doing it well, and he knew it. He had no unsophisticated young lady to deal with here, and he was entitled to feel proud.

"To imply—nothing! Only if you could buck him up a little, I'd be glad. You see, I like old Brett. He's a square-rigger, and I just hate to see him down in the dumps. If I came in for you, say, every Saturday afternoon, would you come out to Bowgada for a game of bridge or something? You could bring Miss Winters or a friend to make a fourth."

"I...I couldn't do that, not unless Brett—Mr Filson suggested it." A gleam of understanding entered her eyes. "Stop! Take me to a quiet corner," she commanded.

He found a seat behind a stand of pot plants, and there he regarded her slightly strained face.

"Well?" he asked.

"What are you driving at, Mr Tremayne? I dislike mystery. What's in your mind?"

Holding his face sideways to her, he said: "Why don't you marry him? Go on, smack my face."

Ann remained motionless, staring at him.

"You little fool," he said softly. "Wasting precious hours. Go on, smack my face."

Out of the corner of his eye he watched her teeth bite her under lip, saw her eyes cloud.

He leaned back then against the wall, staring straight ahead of him.

"I like you, Ann. I liked you when Mug Williams presented me to you this morning. You're a good sport not to smack my face. Last night Brett said he wouldn't be coming to the ball, that last year he'd brought you and that he'd like you to come tonight. He suggested I bring you. He gave me a letter of introduction to you. I guessed, Ann. He'll never ask you to marry him. He thinks he's only a quarter of a man now. He's not weak like I am. He's bigger than ever I'll be. He's big enough, and damn fool enough, never to ask you to marry him. As you love him, what are you going to do about it?"

"I love him!"

"Of course. You're not going to be stupid enough to try to deceive me, are you?"

"No. No, I'll try not to be stupid. Look at me, Mr Tremayne, please. You guessed it. Now you see it. But what can I do? I...I can't make him propose to me. I can't tell him I love him until he proposes, can I? Tell me what I can do?"

"You can call me Harry, to begin with," he said. "I was sure he loves you, but I wasn't quite sure you loved him until you told me. Sorry if I had to trick you a bit. But now you can leave old Brett Filson to me. I'll make him see reason."

And then Ann Sayers' arm was resting on his shoulder, and her forehead was resting on her arm. Quite softly she was crying.

CHAPTER XII

WHAT THE PARSON SAID

TO Frances Tonger this was a night of nights, a time of gaiety and excitement which helped to alleviate the usual dullness of station life for a girl who had become accustomed to city life.

Her uncle was a model of courtesy, revealing to her and to his guests the best facet of his character, reminding her of what he was when she was a small child. Elderly Mr Wonkford, reputedly rich and owner of pastoral country south of Breakaway House, old-fashioned in his manners and dress, was a beau still, and one of her more obvious admirers. And then there was the slightly eccentric Major Gatley-Tomkins, arrayed in full regimentals and dancing with gooseneck spurs affixed to field boots. These two leavened the throng, added personality to the whole, and provided a salutary brake on the effervescent spirit of youth, especially as represented by the likes of Buck Ross.

"They say that heaven knows not time, Miss Frances, but having lived in heaven, I do not believe it," Mr Wonkford told her when the music stopped and ended their dance. "Were I a genie I would wipe out all these people, retaining only the orchestra that we might dance forever."

"That's very nice of you, Mr Wonkford," Frances said, smiling up into his long face, which so reminded her of pictures of the Duke of Wellington. "I've enjoyed it very much. Thank you!"

"From me is due all the thanks. And now, permit me to find you a seat. My duties as Master of Ceremonies compel me to leave your side." He guided Frances to a vacant chair between a vivacious widow who had buried three husbands, and Morris Tonger who was talking with a visitor to a neighbouring station, a jovial man who had stolen much gold during the palmy days of the fields and now lived in respected retirement in Perth. Bowing low, Mr Wonkford added: "*Au revoir*, Miss Frances! Never again will I act as Master of Ceremonies."

"Quaint old bird!" remarked the widow when Mr Wonkford had left.

"Very nice, though. I like old-fashioned people," Frances returned.

"I don't. They make me feel old."

"They make me feel young."

"They make me want to grow Dundreary whiskers," interrupted Harry Tremayne. "I believe that with them I would look extraordinarily handsome, but, alas! I'm a slave to fashion. I have the honour, Miss

Tonger, to present myself as your partner for this waltz. You see, old-fashioned gentlemen make me talk old-fashionedly."

"Where did you learn it?" inquired the widow.

"Not in a drawing room, madam."

"And not in the stockyards, eh Tremayne?" Tonger put in, a smile on his face but none in his eyes.

"You're right, Mr Tonger. I'm a good Roman in doing always that which the Romans do."

The widow examined Tremayne with increased interest, and Frances, although she badly wanted to refuse him, got up to dance in preference to talking to this woman whom she detested.

When they swung out on to the floor, Frances knew that here was a partner who could really dance. As Ann had done, she shyly studied his face, trying to guess his age, unable after two minutes' silence to determine if he were younger than twenty-five or older than forty. When he grinned at her she doubted that he was older than twenty.

"You dance well," he assured her unsmilingly–and then looked at least forty.

"I'm less interested by your compliments than by the reason you so rudely left me."

"Ah! Couldn't we defer explanations until after the dance? The confounded band will stop at any second."

"I would like an explanation–now."

"Very well," he said sadly. "Just when we were about to dance I saw someone knock down a friend of mine known on Bowgada as Ned. It appears that without his sanction, Miss Hazit had left home for Breakaway House, and he came to take her back."

"Miss Hazit? Who's she?"

"Her Christian name is Nora."

"Oh! But she's not a 'miss' and her surname isn't Hazit."

"No? My mistake. I thought it was."

For a few seconds there was silence between them. Then Frances burst out laughing. He knew the reason for her merriment, and shrewdly guessed the subject that had occupied her mind during the preceding period of pensive silence.

"You're a keen observer," she said more soberly.

"I am. And you do dance well."

"Better than your friend?" she asked, wanting to hurt him.

"Yes, but so you should. You're younger and lighter," he argued, as though to insist that his compliment was not flattery. "My lovely Violet is a bit thick in the fetlock. She is, too, a bit thick in the forearm. But, nevertheless, physical thickness and fitness is no criterion of a woman's goodness of heart or quickness of mind."

"Your lovely Violet!" she echoed softly. "Are you engaged?"

"Eh? Oh—I beg your pardon. I didn't quite catch what you said."

"I asked a quite plain question. It was not an impertinence; for you referred to Miss Winters in endearing terms."

Regarding her with knit brows, he said: "Do you think so? Is calling her 'my lovely Violet' a term of endearment?"

"Well, what am I to say to that?" she expostulated, for the first time laughing at him, her expression making him hold his breath. And seeing the flare of admiration in his eyes she laughed again.

After a little silence, he said: "Referring to Miss Winters as I did doesn't strike me as a lover-like figure of speech. You see, I call my mother 'Queen of my Heart'. My sister I call 'Puss Cat', and you, to myself, 'Breakaway Flower'." The sudden flush which swept into her face did not deter him from adding: "Now, now! Keep cool! Never get excited at what Harry Tremayne might say. I speak from my heart and think with my mind and never mix the two. Frankness is a guarantee of innocence."

"Of that I'm not too sure."

"Do I look like a villain?"

"No..."

"Or an angel?"

"Decidedly not."

He sighed deeply. "Why do you say that? I've been thinking what a jolly fine fellow I am."

"If you thought less and talked less you might be worth knowing," she told him bitingly. Then searching his face with her eyes, she struck him a shrewd blow. "Are you related to Chief Inspector Tremayne?"

"Who's he? A stock inspector or a rabbit inspector?" he asked, successfully masking the surprise her question gave him.

"Police," she replied simply.

At that he laughed and daringly squeezed her waist. "If my old dad heard anyone referring to him as a policeman, and a chief inspector at that, he would sue for libel the first day he got out. Why, he's a butcher, the head butcher in Fremantle gaol."

"I don't believe you. I know Mrs Tremayne and Mr Tremayne very well. You take very much after Mrs Tremayne."

He was growing desperate beneath this stroke of ill fortune. "Look here!" he said. "I'd like to swap stories with you. Do you know that big balancing rock three miles south of here along the breakaway?"

"Yes...But I don't swap stories with mere acquaintances."

"Being your very dear friend, I'm glad to hear you say that," he told her swiftly. "Wednesday at three o'clock I'll be riding by that balancing rock, so I'll turn in to it for an hour. When you leave here you ride out round the point of the headland, then along the foot of the breakaway till you come to a deep bay. In the centre of the bay is a short promontory on the lip of which is the balancing rock. Before you reach it, take one of the several cattle pads leading up through the great cracks in the breakaway lip, and there, at the base of the promontory on high land, you can secure your horse to a cork tree. When I arrive, we'll climb to the top of the balancing rock, and there admire the scenery and have a good old pitch."

"A pitch!"

"Conversation," he corrected himself.

"I shan't be there."

"You will be there."

"I tell you, I shall not be there, Mr Tremayne."

He sighed. "You're like the parson in the song giving out the church notices. When he announced the meeting of the Young Ladies' Guild, he said: 'I shall be there,' like I'm saying now. What did I say? The music is stopping. I knew you'd spoil this dance. Now, remember! Three o'clock on Wednesday afternoon to the tick."

"I shall not be there."

"You will be there."

"I shall…"

"Don't waste breath. Life's too short. You'll have to give me another dance to make up for this one." He looked at her card dangling from her dress. He was astonished to see that no man's initials were against the very last one. Hastily he inscribed his own. When he looked up Frances saw that his mood was no longer gay. The expression in the depths of his grey-blue eyes shocked every nerve in her body.

"Thank you very, very much," he said, in tones so low that his voice was barely above a whisper.

He guessed! He guessed why there were no initials against the last dance on her card. Frances became furious with him. "Oh, you are insufferable."

"So you said on another occasion," he bantered her, the old mood returned. "*Au revoir*, till the last dance. Here's Mr Filson just dying to talk to you, and there's my lovely Violet waiting for me to take her to supper. *Bon jour, Herr Filson!* I leave to your protection Breakaway–er–Miss Tonger."

"You've been having an exciting time, Miss Tonger?" remarked Filson, as Tremayne sauntered across to Violet Winters.

"So much so that I wouldn't be able to stand too much of it, Mr Filson. But you must be having a very quiet time. Don't you care for bridge?"

"Not while I can watch you dancing."

"That's very nice of you, and as a reward you may take me to supper, if you like."

"I should like. I should like ever so much."

Despite his limp, Brett Filson was a distinguished figure in his dress clothes, against which were splashed the colours of several decorations. He escorted Frances round the ballroom in preference to winding a precarious passage through the throng gathering for another dance. They found seats at one of the big tables in the decorated wool room.

"Feel calmer now?" Brett asked.

"Much," Frances replied. "Your Harry Tremayne is, what shall I say…"

"Delightfully boyish? Golden-hearted? A real man's man?" Brett suggested.

"No…none of those nice things."

"Dear me! You astonish me, Miss Tonger."

"Did you know him before he came to Bowgada?" she asked, looking directly at her escort.

"No."

"Do you know that his father is chief of the Criminal Investigation Branch, Perth?"

"Er…yes. Did he tell you?"

"No. Mr Tremayne hasn't done all the guessing tonight. I know his people well. He bears a striking resemblance to his mother."

"Does he?" For a little while Brett pondered. Here was a turn of the wheel which would have to be checked. "I wonder, would you mind keeping that a close secret?" he asked. "You see Tremayne is up here on a confidential mission."

"Oh! I'm not sufficiently interested in Mr Tremayne that I would gossip about him or about his secret mission. I may wonder what that secret mission is, because it must be a police mission. You see, Mrs Tremayne told me all about her son, Harry, who was doing some fine work up in the Kimberleys among the Aborigines."

"I would share a little secret with you were it not for my promise," Brett conceded. "I promised not to divulge the nature of his mission. Will you promise to keep his identity a secret?"

"Yes, of course. It's no business of mine."

Again there was a pregnant silence between them. Watching her unobtrusively Brett saw that she was looking in the direction of Miss

Winters and her escort leaving the supper room.

"Would you grant me a favour?" she presently asked him.

"Need you ask that? Command me."

"Take me outside where I can have a cigarette, will you?" she entreated. "I'm just dying for one and I haven't yet plucked up sufficient courage to defy my uncle's prohibition."

Brett laughed delightedly. The girl pleased him with her warm camaraderie after the cold aloofness bordering on snobbery which he had found in her on her return from that sojourn of years in Perth. "Let us conspire against your uncle without loss of time," he urged.

So it was that they two, leaving the supper room, came to that door beyond which Tremayne had seen Ned knocked down. Out in the darkness the air was balmy and soft.

Brett led his companion along the wall of the great iron building till they reached a stack of weather-seasoned fence posts which provided a seat.

"Ah! That's lovely!" the girl murmured ecstatically, inhaling deeply.

Across from them was the men's kitchen. Bustling figures were revealed through the open doorway. Girls journeyed from the kitchen to the supper room laden with trays. One emerged from the kitchen. They saw distinctly that it was Nora. She was coming towards the shed, when a man dashed out of the skirting darkness, snatched her up in his arms and raced with her to Filson's car. Then the car engine purred, the headlamps sent forward their beams, and the car speeded off towards Bowgada. They both saw that the man who had carried Nora away was Harry Tremayne.

CHAPTER XIII

THE AFFAIR AT ACACIA WELL

"MR TREMAYNE is behaving rather peculiarly, don't you think?" Frances said in those icy tones she knew so well how to exercise.

"Well, one might assume that he should have lived in the days of James I, Miss Tonger," Brett agreed, unable to decide whether to be angry or not. That Tremayne was merely abducting the girl seemed to him to be improbable.

From beyond the kitchen a dark figure appeared, ran towards them, and then passed by into the ballroom.

"Let's go in, too. I want to dance," Frances entreated, with just a hint of desperation replacing the chilling tones.

"Wait a few seconds," she was urged. "Come to the corner."

They gained the corner of the shed, passing the side door, and now had the big double doors on their left. Light poured from this entrance intensifying the darkness of the night.

Three men emerged from the ballroom, one of whom Frances recognised as Buck Ross. Ross spoke rapidly, and one of the other men ran to a small shed some distance away. Ross and the other man hurried to the parked cars and trucks.

"What shed is that—where that man has gone to?" Brett asked and was informed that it was the skin and hide shed. "Do you know what's kept in it besides skins and hides?"

His question was put quietly, but she sensed its possible importance and experienced the first hint of rising excitement. "Yes!" she replied. "Poisons and dips. Look! What's he carrying to the car?"

"It looks like a drum."

"A drum? An oil drum?"

"Yes. What does a drum contain that might be stored in that shed, Miss Tonger?"

"Sheep dip. Hide paint. Tar."

"Tar!"

"Yes, tar," she affirmed tensely. "What do you think they're taking it for, Mr Filson?"

Brett made no immediate reply. He watched the man with the drum reach the car in which the other two were waiting, its engine running and headlamps switched on. He saw the burdened man place the drum in the car's tonneau and step in beside it. Then the machine was rapidly driven away over the track Tremayne had taken.

"Mystery piled on mystery, Miss Tonger," Brett said, venting a grim chuckle. "If you'll excuse me escorting you back to the dance floor, I'll just amble along, too."

"I'm going with you," Frances said determinedly.

"Better not. The air will be cold driving. You've no wraps."

"I can soon get a coat. You'll wait? You'll not go without me?"

"Be advised. Go in and dance."

Frances caught at his arm and held it with pressure. "I don't understand what's going on, but I'm as anxious as you appear to be to find out," she said rapidly. "Take me, please, Mr Filson. I'm not a sook."

"Very well. Run for your coat. I'll take the first car I can start up easily."

Hobbling over to the parked cars, Brett selected a heavy six-seater standing in the outside line. The ignition key was in its lock and the engine turned over after the first few revolutions of the starting gear. Its low sound guided Frances to him, and, muffled in a raincoat, she took her place at his side. He was about to switch on the headlights when she said: "Couldn't you drive with the lights just dimmed?"

"Why, yes, but more slowly, although I know every yard of the track. Why dim the headlights?"

"Because they'd be less likely to see us following them. If they knew we were following they might do nothing."

Brett laughed delightedly at her cunning. With the lights dimmed, they slid away. "But isn't the reason of our little drive to prevent anything happening?" he asked.

"Yes—but only just before it begins to happen. I want to catch Mr Tremayne with that black woman, and to stop those men doing anything with that tar. It was tar in the drum."

"In that case we shall have to travel a little faster."

The dimmed lights barely revealed the wheel tracks of the bush road, and since the car taken by Ross and his companions would now be at least one mile ahead of them, even if one of them happened to glance back, he would be unlikely to discern them.

They soon reached and passed through the open gate half a mile from the homestead, the gate at which Nora had seen John Tremayne when she was oiling the Acacia Well mill, and, that passed, Brett knew that the track sank slightly lower than the general land surface and that his car lights would not be seen again by Ross until they were almost at his boundary gate.

He risked damaging the car and increased his speed to thirty miles an hour. Presently a pale light glowed in the distance which, when it became stronger, revealed the cut line of the ground rise near the boundary of the two properties. It became just bright enough to indicate its source as being motor lamps facing Bowgada. Lower still dipped the tracks until they met a narrow water-gutter less than fifty yards from the Acacia Well gate. Here Brett stopped the car.

"If you want to be a spectator in what might be a little drama, flavoured by comedy, I suggest we walk on from here," Brett said. "Tread carefully and remember your dancing shoes."

"I changed them for tennis shoes. Don't worry about me."

Together they reached the higher ground near the gate. Beams of light from two cars flooded the ground beyond the iron hut. In them a group of people danced like midgets. Yells and Nora's screams drifted across the intervening space.

"I can't wait with you. I must run on," Frances cried to Brett who was going as fast as he could.

"Wait! Keep by me, Miss Tonger," he ordered her sharply.

"Oh! I'll be all right. I must stop them."

Without further hesitation, Frances sped towards the group clearly revealed by the motor lights. A man lay stretched on the ground. Another man crouched before a man who covered him with a pistol. Two others were fighting a third man, and the third man seemed to be holding his own.

Nora was dancing about close to the combatants, shrieking at the top of her voice with excitement. "Go on, Mr Tremayne! Hit him! Kill him! Kill that Buck Ross!" she implored.

Frances halted just behind the motor lamps, concealed from any one of them who might look about casually, which, during these electric moments, would be most unlikely. From her toes to the top of her head her body thrilled and thrilled. The man crouching at the revolver point was Ned. She could see the whites of his eyes which glared fixedly at the man holding the weapon. His mouth was open; his bared teeth vying with the whiteness of the bandage around his head. She knew that the pistol had but to waver and Ned would spring. She felt like crying out at the courage of him.

One of Tremayne's assailants staggered back from a blow, sagged at the knees, and almost went to ground. He pawed his eyes like a man unable to see, staggered to his feet, looked dazedly about, and then lurched forward to something which gleamed whitely.

"Knock that black on the head, Jake, and come and give us a hand,"

Buck Ross shouted.

"Go on, go on," yelled Ned. "Shoot! Lift the gun to hit me—and I get you, you white fella devil."

"Kill him! Kill him!" screamed Nora, a strange caricature in her black maid's dress and crumpled maid's apron. Seeing the man pick up a big piece of white quartz, she looked round and pounced on a similar missile.

It was at this point that Brett Filson hobbled into the shaft of light and towards the combatants. Frances heard him say: "Jake Matthews, drop that stone!"

The man with the piece of rock swung round to face Filson, and without hesitation, hurled the jagged piece of quartz at the Bowgada squatter. It struck Brett full in the chest. For a second he seemed all whirling legs and stick before he crumpled and fell.

But the practical Nora who could kill a running rabbit with a stone was more deadly in action than Jake Matthews. Her piece of quartz struck Matthews at the back of his head, and he collapsed instantly, causing Nora to scream louder in triumph.

Frances ran to Brett Filson, who was supporting his body with his arms and coughing to regain his wind. The inert form of Fred Ellis began to move. So did Nora with her second missile. To make sure, she ran close to the man bailing up her Ned and, at short range, most unfairly placed him hors de combat. Even before he came to earth Ned and she were on him, clawing, smashing and yelling.

"Hey! Stop it, you two. You'll kill him. Take it easy," gabbled Fred Ellis, lurching to his feet and beginning to run towards the heap of humanity.

A sickening, smacking sound behind Frances, who was kneeling beside Brett Filson, made her turn her head just in time to see Buck Ross suspended in mid-air like an upturned land crab. Then the ground on which she knelt shook with the impact of his heavy body.

Next minute Tremayne was beside her, helping Filson to his feet. "Hurt much, Brett? That was a foul rotten blow, to be sure."

"I'm all right. Knocked the breath out of me, Harry. Look! Go and help Ellis rescue that man from Ned and Nora."

Tremayne rushed over and yelled at Ellis: "Grab Nora, Fred. I'll take Ned." He wound his arms around Ned's torso and pulled.

Ellis acted similarly with Nora. Both pulled at the same time, but neither Nora nor Ned would let go their hold on the senseless gunman and his inert body was lifted clear from the ground between them.

Tremayne laughed long and loudly, and his laughter penetrated the passion-inflamed brains. First Nora, and then Ned, let go their hold, they went limp in the arms encircling them, and broke into long peals of mirth, finally conquered by their inherent sense of humour.

"That's right. You calm down, We've 'ad enough excitement for one night. By cripes! How me 'ead aches," Ellis cried after releasing Nora.

"Get some Aspros, Fred," advised Tremayne, "and bring out a bucket of water. These birds will want reviving by the look of them. Ah! Here's Ross coming to. Now, Ross, get up and explain this business. Come clean or I'll have you locked up.

"You'd have me locked up!" Ross sneered, clumsily scrambling to his feet. "You got no right abducting black women and I'm going to have you charged with that, you flash upstart."

"What did you bring the tar for, Ross?" interrupted Brett slowly, unable yet to breathe without muscular constriction."

"What tar?"

"The tar you ordered one or your mates to fetch from the skin house. Don't deny it. I saw it brought. It seems to me that you're active in a little game of your own. As Mr Tremayne advises: 'Come clean'."

Being a man of substance and a Justice of the Peace, Brett desired strongly to take these three ruffians to Mount Magnet and hand them over to the police, but he wanted to ascertain what line Tremayne would take. Besides which, explanation was due from Tremayne too.

"Well, if you must know, we was going to tar this flash bloke for forcibly abducting a black woman."

"I can understand your righteous indignation, my gallant prince," Tremayne said banteringly. "However, as the other patients appear to be recovering, I'll leave the explanation to Ned. Ned, come here and tell Mr Filson and Miss Tonger all about it."

Ned told his story with relish, even laughed when he described how he'd been struck with a length of shoeing iron, while Tremayne mustered the other two and marched them to the group.

Ned continued: "So I was in the car when Mr Tremayne brought Nora and dumped 'er on top of me. An' Nora, she fight like an old ewe, an' Mr Tremayne telling me to go quiet and not bump 'er off. And then we get here with Buck Ross just behind us, an' we get out an' Buck Ross an' his friends start fighting. An ole Fred Ellis, he joins in..."

"So you see, Ross, your suspicions were entirely groundless," Brett said sternly. "As I don't wish to prolong this unpleasantness, and as no serious harm has been done, I'll take no further action–provided you three get into your car and go back to Myme at once."

Without a word they obeyed, and drove off to Myme via Bowgada.

"Nora, who told you to come to Breakaway House tonight?"

demanded Frances.

"Mr Tonger sent me word to go," Nora replied saucily.

"And I went after 'er," added Ned abruptly.

Frances turned towards the two cars without comment. "Come and get your parcel, Ned," Tremayne ordered.

CHAPTER XIV

A PROBLEM SOLVED

"NOW, Harry, if you'll take Miss Tonger back to Breakaway House, I'll come on after I've had a heart-to-heart talk with Ned and Nora," was Brett Filson's very welcome suggestion, at least to Tremayne.

"But are you all right?" Frances asked him anxiously.

"Quite, Miss Tonger," she was assured. "A little sore, perhaps, but nothing to worry about. Please don't delay on my behalf. Your guests will be wondering what has become of you."

"Very well. Are you ready, Mr Tremayne?"

"I'm always ready. May I drive?"

"Yes—if you wish, and aren't reckless."

"I'm the most careful driver in Australia, as you will concede when we reach Breakaway House."

His last boast Tremayne proceeded to justify by keeping the speedometer needle pointing to the figure five, and when the first half mile had been covered in silence, Frances asked: "Has this car rear bumpers?"

"Yes. Very strong bumpers, too. Why?"

"It seems likely that Mr Filson will crash into us no matter how slowly he drives."

"Life is full of risks, but they're so common that we seldom give thought to them," he said, and then abruptly turned sideways to face her in a casual, conversational attitude, steering with one hand. "I haven't yet apologised for being discovered by you engaged in fisticuffs. But, alas! I will never be a gentleman."

"Perhaps not. They say, once a policeman…"

"Now, now! Why harp on that?" he cut in, grinning. "Let's discontinue patting each other, metaphorically, I mean. Let's talk about you on Monday in the shadow of that balancing rock, a subject of unequalled interest, I assure you."

"Do you say those things for the sake of hearing your own voice?" Frances inquired with dangerous mildness.

The dash-light clearly revealed their faces to each other in semi-profile, and Frances noted the discoloration of the flesh about Tremayne's left temple, indicating the recent impact of a fist. Almost despite herself, she was quickly coming to see that beneath his flippancy was strength of mind and fine character.

"There are times," he told her with sudden gravity, "when a man is very like a woman in that he says things to prevent himself saying others, and does things to stop himself doing other things he badly wants to do."

"For instance?"

"The other day, when you fell off your horse because you were so angry with me, I teased you to prevent myself rushing after your horse and killing him. By the way, I trust that Mr Ross isn't a great friend of your uncle's?"

"Bosom friend, no. I believe, though, that they have mutual business interests. Why do you ask?"

"Because Ross is not the type of man I would have expected to find at a squatters' ball. And the same applies to his friends."

"They have money."

"Have they?" Tremayne looked into her eyes with disconcerting directness. "Tell me, does your uncle entertain much?"

"There seem to be always people coming to eat or sleep over night. But why these personal questions?"

"One more, and then I'll talk about moonlight and roses and melody. Are most of your uncle's visitors of the Buck Ross type?"

"Well..." she paused. "They're not very interesting. Do I rightly assume that you are interested in my uncle and his guests in an official capacity?"

"Unofficially, yes. I'm far more interested in some of your uncle's chance guests than in your uncle, and much more interested in you than in all your uncle's guests put together."

"I suppose that's to be my reward for information given?" she asked pointedly.

"If to hear truth is a reward..."

"If you don't drive more carefully, my reward will not be a compliment, but death. Tell me, how are your mother and father?"

"I haven't seen them for several years, but they are well, if worried very much about my younger brother, John." Watching her face relax from a hard, cynical mask, Tremayne made up his mind to take chances with this girl. He had sensed her disapproval in her replies regarding Tonger and his associates.

"Worried about John!" she asked with genuine concern. "Why, what's he done? I met him several times and liked him."

"He's gone and disappeared," Tremayne answered her with spurious levity.

"Disappeared! When?"

"He was last seen on August twelfth of this year."

"Where?"

"He was last seen alive at this gate just ahead of us by Nora who was then oiling the mill at Acacia Well."

Now she was staring at him, and no longer was he turned towards her. "I don't yet quite understand," she said quickly. "Please explain."

When he spoke his voice was hard and his face lyingly aged him. "John was up here on a holiday," he said, "a holiday spent in pushing a bicycle about. He arrived at Bowgada on August tenth. He left Bowgada on August twelfth for Breakaway House. As I have just told you, Nora saw him at this gate we're coming to. Your uncle doesn't remember seeing him at Breakaway House, nor do people at Kyle station, nor anyone at Mount Magnet. Swagmen aren't so numerous on the Murchison that no one would have noticed him. Up to the time he left Bowgada he wrote regularly to my mother. Since then she hasn't received a word."

"Well, he must be looked for. He must have gone off the track and become bushed. Why hasn't my uncle or the police organised a search party?"

"The police have. I'm the search party."

"That's not a satisfactory answer."

They passed between the stout posts of the now open gate before Tremayne spoke again. "You see, there are the Breakaway House lights," he pointed out. "From the gate, the homestead is plainly to be seen in daylight. There was no reason why my brother should get off the track and become lost. Can you remember where you were on August twelfth?"

After a pause she replied: "No. But I can find out."

"How?"

"I'm one of those possibly foolish people who keep a diary."

"Good! People who keep a diary are not foolish. If everyone kept a diary police work would often be much easier. You would, of course, remember seeing John about that time–if you had seen him?"

"Without any doubt. I haven't seen him since some time before I left Perth."

"I wonder how it is that my mother never mentioned you in her letter to me. I wonder, too, why my father didn't inform me that you were here at Breakaway House."

"Probably because I wasn't very intimate with them," she replied readily. "You see, really I was a friend of a friend."

"That would explain it. Well, I've driven as slowly as I could, but we're here. You're going to the house to change your shoes, aren't you? Just look up dates and tell me where you were on August twelfth."

"All right, Mr Policeman."

For a moment he saw her smiling face, and then she was hurrying off to the house in the gloom. Switching off the car lights, he pensively rolled a cigarette in the dark, fingers working automatically, mind occupied with this tangle of Breakaway House.

There was something queer about the place; that was certain. This Morris Tonger, an established squatter, a second-generation squatter, well educated, in every way able to associate with the squattocracy, and yet he included the Buck Roses of the Murchison in his visiting list and business activities. Everything was wrong with him and with his station. Nothing squared.

The noise of Brett Filson's borrowed car recalled Tremayne to his surroundings. He got out and crossed over to meet the Bowgada squatter.

"How does your chest feel?" he asked.

"A little sore, yet," Brett replied. "That swine might have killed me,"

"So might Nora have killed him."

"It was fortunate for us that she didn't. I told her and Ned that they must move camp to Fowler's Tank first thing tomorrow. They're too near to Tonger."

"They certainly are. Where's Fowler's Tank?"

"Twenty miles south of Acacia Well. Where the east and the west breakaways finally meet. Those two will be camped four miles from Tonger's land, not two hundred yards."

"Good hunting. Between 'em they'll commit a murder if they're not watched. Come on, let's go and have a snifter."

Just inside the main doors Ann Sayers and Violet lay in wait for them. Violet's wide mouth was drawn into a straight line. Her eyes were screwed into pinholes of suspicion. She noted the mark on Tremayne's temple and his disarranged hair. "Where have you been?" she demanded a little truculently. "Fighting?"

"Fighting! My dear Violet, this is a ball, not a war."

"Then how did you get that bruise on your temple?"

"That's the result of my temple coming into contact with the car hood. It's made me dizzy and very thirsty."

"It makes me thirsty to look at you. I'll go with you for a drink."

During Tremayne's absence something had happened. Both Violet and Ann were different towards him. Ann determinedly ignored him while Violet regarded him with cold disfavour.

"What's biting your little pink ear?" asked Tremayne, as they lifted filled glasses.

"Nothink. Only when a gent brings a lady to a ball, he doesn't go canoodling with a black woman."

"Forget it. It had to be done. I took her back to Acacia Well."

Violet sniffed.

"Come on, Violet, you promised me this dance," a man said from behind them, and as a further mark of her disapproval, she gushingly responded: "Of course, Tom. I'm just dying to dance. Let's go."

From a smiling contemplation of Violet's broad back, Tremayne turned to Ann Sayers. "What dance is this, Ann?"

"This is the last dance, Mr Tremayne," Ann replied, stressing the courtesy title.

"Then I must bolt. See you after, both of you."

"He has hurt Violet very much, and he has disappointed me," Ann said to Brett. "I was beginning to like him. So was Violet. She thought the world of him."

"What's he done?" asked Brett, quietly amused.

"We both saw him pick up a black woman in his arms and carry her off in your car."

"Did you, indeed? So did Miss Tonger and I. So did another man who informed Ross and another of his friends. They followed Tremayne, and Miss Tonger and I followed them. Not one of us followers of Tremayne's car knew that besides Nora, he had with him Nora's man, Ned. You see, when Ned could not induce Nora to go back with him to Acacia Well, Tremayne abducted the girl and took them both back."

From the wide parted lips and the bright eyes, Brett turned his gaze to his glass. If only he were a whole man, if only...What an ecstasy to look upon this wonderful woman and what a hell!

And on the floor, Tremayne, who was dancing with Frances, was also feeling ecstasy. The scent of her intoxicated him, swept him out of this mundane world as wind sweeps a dust-mote into a sunbeam.

"I looked up that date," she said.

"Not now! Wait until it's over," he implored. "Look up. I want to look at you."

"Look at me? Why?"

"Just because."

"On August eleventh, twelfth and thirteenth, I was staying with Major and Mrs Gatley-Tomkins," she persisted impishly, and, raising her face to his she laughed. Then quickly the laughter died and her expression became serious. "So you see I wasn't here to notice John's arrival. What..."

"No more. I'll tell you things and you can tell me things when we meet at the balancing rock at three o'clock on Wednesday."

"But I shan't be there."

"If you say that again I'll shake you. Dance, do you hear? How can you dance so divinely when you go on like a parson reading the church notices? That's right. Look up at me."

"All right, Mr He-Man."

CHAPTER XV

BLACKMAIL

IN accordance with Brett Filson's programme, his party returned to Bowgada at about two o'clock on the Sunday morning and, after coffee and biscuits, Tremayne drove the ladies back to Myme. When eventually he went to bed day was breaking. He slept throughout the day, and rose only in time to dine with Brett when the sun was setting.

"She was a great shivoo," he said, referring to the ball. "Good dancing, a little romance, good liquor, and an excellent fight. How's the chest?"

"Pain's gone. I aroused Jackson to rub it. Since then, I believe, Jackson has been selecting a weapon and seems to favour a sawn-off shotgun."

"The fact that the stone-thrower isn't a capitalist indicates that Jackson doesn't intend to waste hemp," Tremayne pointed out, chuckling. "Our cook is a real man's man. I wish I could be more sure of Mug Williams."

"He arrived this afternoon."

"Good! I wrote him a note asking him to call."

"Oh!"

"Yes. I'm going to blackmail him."

Filson glanced up from his plate to regard Tremayne with steady eyes. "I would rather like to know what you suspect," he said.

"I suspect a lot and know little. It's the little I know which leads me to suspect the lot."

"Tell me what you know," asked Filson, again engaged with his trifle.

"I know that I'm in love with my Breakaway Flower."

"Your who?"

"My Breakaway Flower—Frances."

"Indeed! Well, as a matter of fact, I knew that."

"The devil you did!"

"Yes. It was easy to guess. People who begin by irritating each other always end up by falling in love."

"Oh!"

Tremayne searched for tobacco and papers. Brett was smiling at him, but if the younger man felt discomfort his face did not show it.

When he spoke, it was quite casually. "Anyway, you're not the only good guesser on the Murchison. There's two people I've guessed are in love, although from outward appearances no one would think it."

"Oh! And who are they?" Brett inquired.

Tremayne made and lit his cigarette. Then pushing back his chair he rose to his feet to stand looking down at the man whose eyes refused to meet his.

"One of 'em is Brett Filson," he said, and added when he reached the door, "and the other is Ann Sayers. I would have married Ann if I hadn't fallen in love with Frances. I wouldn't have wasted no damn time—believe me."

When Filson turned it was to see the door shut and the handle being released by Tremayne, who was now beyond it. The calm which had reigned during the meal was suddenly dethroned by burning anger; anger with Tremayne, anger with himself and anger against his fate.

"Better let me rub that chest of yours," advised Jackson when he came in and saw his employer slumped moodily in a chair.

"Leave me alone. My chest's all right," Brett cried out. "It's my left leg and my left ribs that are all wrong. Crawling over the land like a maimed crab."

"Who said so?" demanded the now truculent cook.

"I said so. Didn't you hear me? Clear away the things and get out."

Slowly Jackson gathered the crocks on to his tray, covertly watching this man whom he had brought back from No Man's Land. Never before had he been spoken to in such terms, and rather than feeling hurt by them he was curious. "Young Harry" must have upset the boss. He would have something to say about that.

MUG WILLIAMS was lounging against one of the fence posts in front of the house, on this occasion no cheerful smile lighting his mahogany-tinted features. In the small grey eyes which encountered Tremayne's was a patent expression of anxiety.

"Pleased you came, Mug," announced Tremayne cheerfully. "Sorry if you've had to wait long but, as you know, I've been out on the tiles all night."

"Wot's all this about hinting at me duffin' cattle?" Williams demanded with the innocence of a little child, albeit an aggrieved one.

"Let's take a little walk," Tremayne urged pleasantly, to add with a chuckle: "That sounds like a policeman, doesn't it? What do you think of Soddy's efforts to grow vegetables? Cabbages and turnips looking fine. Let's go out on the breakaway and admire the scenery."

The little man's eyes shrewdly searched Tremayne's face, the invitation to take a walk seemingly prompted by something far more important than admiring a view.

Having crossed the track and passed through the gate beyond it, Tremayne said conversationally: "Good idea of Mr Filson's old father, and of Mr Filson, too, to preserve this strip of scrub from damage, don't you think? The idea, of course, was to maintain a natural windbreak without which the homestead would be exposed to the full force of the westerlies."

And then, when they stepped forth from the scrub to the narrow rock ledge: "Here it's very nice and quiet and private. We'll park ourselves on that seat and smoke and talk like old friends."

The sun had gone, draping the western sky with a crimson tapestry, the upper edge of which was orange, merging into yellow, and the yellow into bars of azure. Outlined against this fire was the western breakaway, its face masked by shadows, and purple-tinted mist floating at the base of each tower, pinnacle and hump raised above the general skyline.

The two arms of the bay above which they sat were softened and made lovely by the afterglow, like arms of grey and brown velvet reaching out over the peaceful valley which was already sinking into the bed of night. A flock of grazing sheep dotted the saltbush flats below them. The stillness was broken only by late crows lingering near the killing yard beyond the Bowgada homestead.

"Well?" Williams said at last. "The scenery's all right, but it ain't worrying me."

"No! Then what is?"

"Your note, Mr Tremayne. I don't understand the insinuations in it," Williams stated frankly.

"Indeed! And yet, Mug, it seems to me that you're up against it. Now just listen. I know that during last Monday night you duffed three steers off Breakaway House, took 'em into Bowgada through the fence which runs over an area of surface rock, and took 'em out of Bowgada on to the Myme Common by way of a wide, stony-bottomed creek.

"You rode an old cow. About a mile from the Bowgada boundary, you got off your steed and kept quiet while a man leading four pack-horses passed you. You then went on to your yard, killed and skinned the steers, and afterwards buried the hides in a gilgie hold close to a big kurrajong tree." Tremayne shook his head reproachfully, adding: "You should really have cut out Tonger's brand before you planted those hides."

The little man grunted, offering no comment.

"It does appear, Mug," Tremayne went on with painful cheerfulness, "that your day's work is done. You'll be put away for three years at the least, ten years at the most. They'll take you down to Fremantle where there are no views like that one, and lock you up every night in a cell with a hundred thousand bugs to torment you. The bugs are not so bad in the winter, but the winter has gone, and for seven months you'll be tortured with bugs. And a bushman like you, having lived in a land where there are no bugs, no fleas, no filthy vermin, will live ten years for every actual year you'll be in Fremantle gaol. I'm sorry for you, Mug. I was beginning to like you."

Looking sharply at the little man, Tremayne was not surprised by the expression of resignation on his face. At long last found out with ample proof, and with the certainty of imprisonment facing him, Mug Williams did not whine about a cruel fate, plead to be given another chance, nor offer to pay for the cattle he had stolen. He said, as his kind would say: "When are you going to give me in charge?"

Before replying, Tremayne gazed idly across the intervening space at the battlemented horizon behind which the orange and yellow edge of the scarlet tapestry was rapidly sinking.

"I haven't decided that, Mug," he presently said. "I've been contemplating compounding a felony. As a matter of fact, it's possible for you to purchase your immunity from gaol for your past thefts of cattle."

The little man's face showed his relief. Freedom! Well, if dearly bought, freedom was better than confinement. And he had heard about the vermin in Fremantle gaol. "Oh!" he breathed. "How much?"

Now that the moment had come to back his judgment of character with, perhaps, his life, Tremayne hesitated. It was his belief that Williams was not a member of any gold-stealing gang nor any group engaged in more nefarious crimes, but that during his cattle-duffing activities he had seen things of significance which would be of great value. But belief is not proof, and Williams might be a member of the association which had murdered Hamilton, and, probably, his younger brother, John Tremayne.

Brett knew about his mission; so did Frances Tonger. Could he, Tremayne, rely on Brett Filson's estimate of Williams' character? That was the point about which Tremayne hesitated now that the moment for decision had come.

"How much do you want? Play your hand," urged Mug Williams, happier now in thinking it to be a mere question of money.

"I will," Tremayne said with decision. "In return for my silence regarding your past duffing, I want all the information you can give me regarding the man with those packhorses, the contents of the pack-bags, and the destination of their contents. You can tell me, too, what you think those flash signals over there, south of Breakaway House, were made for."

Mug Williams whistled the first six bars of *He's My Daddy*. "I'd sooner do three years in the jug–even ten years–than get shot, or kicked to death, or found at the foot of one of those breakaways with a broken neck," he said with conviction. "I'm not going to mess about with that crowd, and I advise you not to either. It's a police job that. They're paid well to get killed; we're not."

"Are you serious that you would prefer gaol to parting with a little information?"

"Never more serious in my life," Williams assured the blackmailer. "I've bin on the fields since the year one. I've known many blokes who stole gold over a long time before getting nabbed; and I know others who were never nabbed, and who are living in Perth and Albany, 'ighly respected gents. They was tough nuts, most of 'em, but they wasn't criminals, if you get me, 'cos gold-stealing ain't a proper crime, and they was as suckling babes compared with the push running this show. You keep wide of 'em–well wide."

"Very well! You'll go to gaol then?"

"That's in your hands."

"It is," agreed Tremayne grimly. Into his weather-mined face crept an expression of savage determination. "Look! You thought I was going to blackmail you for money, didn't you," he said levelly. "I'm not that sort. As you know, a man named Hamilton was killed and flung down an old mine shaft. And my brother has disappeared. You might remember him–a young chap named John Robbins who worked at Myme for several weeks."

"Yes, I remember him."

"Well, I'm here to find out what happened to him. I'm not interested in gold-stealers as such. Like most of us on these goldfields, I don't regard gold-stealing as a serious crime. But I do regard murder as a serious crime, and, as I said, I'm here to find out what happened to my brother. You have got my word, promise, oath, never to mention you as my informant. Now, who's mixed up in this crowd? Tonger?"

"I'm relying on your word, mind! Yes, I think, he's one."

"And Buck Ross?"

Williams nodded.

"Who's at the top?" Tremayne persisted.

"I don't know."

"Think–for your freedom's sake."

"I tell you, I don't know," Williams said vehemently. "I've wondered often enough and tried to guess, but I've too much sense to go around asking questions."

"Is Jake Matthews another?"

"Yes. And so was Ted Winters, Violet Winters' brother. He was shot four years back by a policeman. I reckon Violet Winters can tell you more about things than I can."

"Oh, so she's in with them, too?"

"I don't think so. But she used to keep 'ouse for Ted in Myme."

"Well, what about those flash signals? What do they mean?"

"I can't tell you. I never took no notice of 'em," Williams replied earnestly. "I met pack trains before the other night, and seen riders when decent men are in bed. They leaves me alone and I leaves them alone. Our businesses don't clash, if you get me. Beside Hamilton who was discovered shot, there was Peterson found in a back street in Telfer Range up north, his ribs kicked in and him cold. A drunken brawl, they said. There was Sam Smythe, two years before him. He was run over by a truck driven by Tonger's boss stockman, Whitbread. Whitbread was fined for driving without lights. I know for a fact that Robbins never passed Breakaway House. You're going to be the next, and I'm gonna foller you. Can't you understand what you're up against?"

"I'm beginning to understand, Mug."

"No, you're not," Williams stated fiercely. "You think that this push is just a mere bale-'em-up Kelly gang, riding 'orses and shooting blokes to leave 'em alongside a track. Why, they uses motor-cars. They uses a plane; I've heard its engine. It lands some place near Breakaway House homestead. They ain't just pinching gold out of Myme. There's Teller Range and other mines. That's all I know, Mr Tremayne. Now we're quits."

CHAPTER XVI

THE ATTACK

HOW true the saying that "in the spring a young man's fancy lightly turns to thoughts of love"! Why, old Saint Anthony, ancient and withered, would this Wednesday have winked at a passing dryad, as he reclined on a bed of everlasting flowers beneath one of the vivid green kurrajongs. The sun, softly brilliant, made of the countless mica particles on the headland slopes cloths of diamonds, scarfs of rubies, and ropes of lapis lazuli. The air was as motionless and as clear as distilled water, perfumed like an Eastern harem, dwarfing distance and banishing from the eyes and the mind man's awareness of the chains binding him to earth.

When Harry Tremayne left Bowgada at one o'clock he rode southward along the road to Breakaway House, but coming to the turn west down the breakaway headland, he continued south riding in a line which skirted the apex of breakaway bays, and crossed the base lines of headlands and promontories, till he reached a wide fiord running east for many miles.

Here he dismounted and led his horse down the steep shingle-littered slopes which fell in the form of rock-lipped steps to a floor of white quartz chips so pure and so thick, that it looked like a glacier. Here the reflected sunlight had such a glare that it produced discomfort, and it was with relief that he presently gained the valley proper, and rode at a smart walk over the saltbush flats towards the western breakaway.

Six miles south of Bowgada, he was six miles south of Breakaway House, and three miles south of the balancing rock. No chance observer at Breakaway House would see him crossing the valley, as might have been the case had he crossed via Acacia Well.

To the south-west, far beyond the valley, rose an almost straight but oft-broken column of smoke, black against the blue sky. A similar column rose a little to the north of Breakaway House, broken into bars of brown, following one after the other to join in a cloud thousands of feet above the earth, a cloud capped with brilliant white like that of a water cloud.

"They don't look like corroboree calls, Major," Tremayne said to his horse, the bush habit of talking to dumb animals strong within him. "Those columns are too disjointed to be a simple signal. They convey a message more complicated than that. Oh! And there are Ned and Nora sending on that message or answering it."

Four thin straight columns rose from the low horizon at a point a little east of south where Tremayne knew was a watering station called Fowler's Tank, the place to which Filson had removed Ned and Nora.

"Something's got 'em going, Major. We'll pay Ned and Nora Hazit a visit in the sweet bye and bye."

With time to spare, the horse was permitted choice of its speed, and, now and then, choice, too, of a fancied titbit of saltbush. His master's mind was occupied with problems and theories raised by the conversation with Mug Williams.

The suggestion that the gold-stealers, if that's what they were, used an aeroplane held no water when Brett Filson tackled it, for the plane was owned and flown by the renowned Colonel Lawton, M.C., D.S.Q., a man of integrity, undoubted courage and wealth. He owned a huge cattle run in the Kimberleys and another somewhere near the Ninety Mile Beach on the north-west coast, and he never travelled from one to the other, or between them and Perth, or between Perth and Melbourne, save in his own plane. He and Morris Tonger were friends of long standing. Occasionally he visited Breakaway House where a landing ground had been prepared for him. The bait would have to be enormous to entice Colonel Lawton across the borderland of the law.

Four or five times during the year this flying ace paid a visit to Tonger, on his way either to or from his Kimberley station. Tremayne had once met him, finding him a keen quiet man, about forty-five years old, a man whose face was broken and scarred by many minor accidents, a man's man, a man to follow anywhere.

Frances would be able to tell him something about Lawton, although Lawton would have nothing to do with the job in hand. Hang it! This wasn't a time to think of gold and gold-stealing. It was a day especially created by the Almighty for a meeting between a man and a maid. There was the balancing rock in the dead centre of that knife-edged line of breakaway, and there presently he would be with Frances, gazing into her dark brown eyes and watching the smiles alternate with tiny frowns of displeasure at his levity.

So Violet Winters' brother had been one of the gang; met one night by two troopers as he was leaving Myme with a pack-horse loaded with fifteen ounces of ore, he had opened fire with a Winchester rifle and had wounded one of the mounted constables before he was shot dead. Silly fools, both those policemen! Why hadn't they allowed Winters to pass, and then tracked him to his destination? Such an affray was almost bound to have embittered Violet against all policemen, and she as a source of help appeared negligible.

"We're going along like the wounded knight in the picture, Major," he cried suddenly. "Hold up and keep moving."

Over saltbush flats, across quartz-studded water-gullies and wider sand-filled creek beds, as they neared it the balancing rock grew from a minute pebble into a stone. The dark headland to the north crept out to meet them, the headland beyond which lay Breakaway House; and, to the south, a low, sloping, rock-strewn bar of land crept out to cut them off from that quarter. It was as though the horse were a ship approaching a sheltered harbour within a rock-bound bay.

Immediately before them lay a wide belt of thick Bogota which they entered after crossing the north-south boundary fence along which, far to the north, could be seen the revolving fans of the Acacia mill. Tremayne found it easier to walk and lead the horse through the timber belt, the tough bogota being less like trees and more like giant bushes, and much tougher than mulga. In places they grew so thick that he was forced to make wide detours, using the water-gullies. This obstruction having been passed, he saw that there still remained thirty minutes to the trysting hour, but that the trysting place was only a mile distant.

From beyond the breakaway drifted rifle reports, reports containing a significant sharpness which denoted that the weapons used were military .303 service rifles. That there were two, Tremayne could distinguish; and he judged the riflemen to be then situated some distance beyond and directly behind the balancing rock.

Kangaroo shooters probably. They were using a type of weapon ideal for the purpose, provided the hunters were crack shots, for the cost of the ammunition was prohibitive to men making many misses.

Tremayne frowned. In general with bushmen he favoured the Winchester or the Savage for hunting purposes. The service weapon fired a bullet which travelled too far for safety, and cases had been recorded where such a bullet, ricochetting from tree or boulder, had travelled on for a mile or more becoming a grave danger to man and beast.

He was now crossing the imaginary line to be drawn from the horns of the bay. Before him the balancing rock, a huge hundred-ton boulder, was set on the extremity of a short precipitously-faced promontory which, had water lapped this dry shore, would have made a fine jetty.

Eagerly his eyes sought for a flash of white or colour at the foot of the balancing rock to indicate that Frances Tonger awaited him. For despite her steadfast statement that she would not keep the assignation, there had been something in her eyes during their last dance which made him confident that she would be there.

Still, he was a little early. It was yet ten minutes to three o'clock. And if he had to wait an hour, two hours, what would such a short period of time be when balanced against the reward of again being in her presence?

Horse and man reached the foot of the slope rising to the line of rock debris littering the base of all those miles of cliffs, a debris masking the weatherworn holes and caves and giant cracks in the cliff itself. This slope supported old man saltbush growing five and six feet in height, spaced widely over a carpet of foot-high annual saltbush. The mica particles sent upward their colourful flashes of reflected sunlight, and here and there lay quartz chips like isolated snowflakes.

Three hundred yards before him now rose the sheer blunt face of this short promontory, a hundred to a hundred and fifty feet in height. From this angle only the upper portion of the balancing rock was visible beyond the edge, betraying the fact that between it and the huge boulder was a ledge several feet in width.

Yes! There was Frances! She was there just back from the cliff edge. Tremayne could see a coloured handkerchief being waved in greeting, and he, all eagerness to be at her side, swept off his wide-brimmed hat and reined back his horse which, for three seconds, became motionless.

Tremayne just glimpsed the flash of the rifle before the light of the day went out...

TIME passed slowly, unnoticed by the man lying near an old man saltbush, and disregarded by the horse which nibbled at the saltbush and possibly wondered why his beloved master slept so long; time spent impatiently by three eagles circling above Tremayne, too suspicious to alight as long as the saddled horse lingered.

The westering sun had cast the shadow of the balancing rock far beyond the prone man and the grazing animal by the time Tremayne's eyes opened to stare up at the azure sky. His head ached atrociously, the Hammer of Thor pounding at it with ceaseless strokes. His throat was parched and his lips stiff with dryness. Effort demonstrated that to move his head was too painful, and, in any case, desire to get up was entirely absent.

What had happened? Oh! He remembered. He had been shot at, deliberately, coldly, mischievously shot at. Frances! No, no, no! It wasn't Frances—it couldn't be Frances! But who else? Who else knew, or was likely to know, he had arranged to come here? But it couldn't be Frances! What an absurdity!

There was Hamilton. They killed him and threw his body down a mine shaft. There was John. What had they done with him? There was

Peterson, kicked to death, and Smythe, beaten to death and allegedly run over by a truck.

It was about here he had seen those flash signals, signals which Williams had seen at other times. It appeared likely enough that near this balancing rock was something which had to be concealed even at the cost of a man's life. Why, having shot at him had not the gunman made sure of his work?

Go easy–tracks!

And an old man saltbush concealed him from the promontory and the balancing rock. It might well be that the person who had fired at him was still up there, waiting, watching, determined to fire again, in fact doubly determined to kill if he knew that his first shot had failed. For he would then also be aware that Tremayne knew it was a deliberate act.

Becoming satisfied that he was masked by the saltbush from any person on the westward heights, Tremayne eventually succeeded in the attempt to sit up. He could see his horse feeding further down the slope. The shadow line walled the passage of time, and his watch proved it to be twenty minutes after five o'clock.

So he had lain there two hours and a half, less a minute or so!

Oh, for about six bottles of aspirin! Oh, for the water-bag, strapped to Major's chest!

With his fingers he carefully felt the short gash along the scalp on the top rear part of his head. It had bled, but not much. On one side his hair was matted with blood. Well, "Lucky Tremayne" it had been up in the Kimberleys, and it now seemed to be "Lucky Tremayne" on the Murchison.

Looking about him, he saw the tracks of the horse, saw just where Major had been pulled up, saw where his own body had fallen and the one plunge the horse had taken in quick-passing fright. There were no other tracks. No one, man or woman, had come there to ascertain if he really were dead.

Two hours and a half now since he had been murderously attacked. Should he run on a zig-zag course to his horse and race away? During such movements they would be unlikely to hit him. Yet if he remained where he was, and waited, the person who fired that shot might come to investigate, in which case, he, Tremayne, would find out who the gunman was. Deciding to wait, he took from his pocket a small but efficient automatic pistol.

CHAPTER XVII

A PLEASANT HOST

SAVE for the eagles and Major's restless tail, nothing moved, and save for the occasional hum of a blowfly, attracted by the smell of blood, the early evening was soundless.

Tremayne wanted to smoke, but in the clear air of this perfect day, to do so would betray him to any watcher. His head ached less violently, and the pain of his wound was slight. It was now protected by his hat but he wondered if during his unconsciousness the busy flies had "blown" it. It would have to be scoured with carbolic.

No longer were the kangaroo hunters active. They had sussed on beyond gun-shot distance, or had called it a day. The attempt on his life worried him because he could not banish the suspicion that indirectly it was brought about by Frances Tonger. He had been so confident that she would be at the foot of the balancing rock, and if she had not actually fired the shot–perish the thought–had she found there the man who had fired it? What then had happened? She could not possibly have failed to see Major, and surely she would have regained her horse and investigated.

But, since she had not done so, either she had been prevented or she had not come. Had her absence been voluntary? If not, what had prevented her? And to whom had she said that he, Tremayne, would be at the balancing lock that afternoon? Or was there a watchful guard permanently stationed at some point within the arms of this wide "bay"?

Now what to do? Major's rump was towards him, and the pricked ears denoted that sharp eyes were watching something somewhere near the point of the southern arm. After a little while the horse showed signs of tenseness, and then he whinnied. He was calling to a horse, which might mean a man on the back of a horse.

Then into Tremayne's range came two horsemen, riding together towards Major, and after half a minute's speculation, he decided that one was an Aborigine and the second none other than Morris Tonger. Neither carried a rifle, nor were rifles fastened to their saddles in scabbards.

The Bowgada overseer pocketed his pistol and fell to making a cigarette. There was no further necessity to remain still and wait. Tonger would not attempt to kill him.

When they reached Tremayne's horse, Tonger's companion secured the reins which he handed to his employer, then dismounted and proceeded to back-track Major. For a minute Tremayne watched the tracking as the man walked faithfully over Major's meandering progress.

But then Tonger, suddenly sighting the seated Tremayne, uttered an ejaculation and hurried forward with the horses. "Good day!" he snapped. "What are you doing here?"

Tremayne rose to his feet to regard first Morris Tonger and then the other man who, on closer observation, turned out to be a powerful half-caste.

"I found that several of Bowgada's cattle had broken through the boundary fence from the paddock south of Acacia Well, and I took a look in this paddock to see if I could pick them up before they became boxed with yours. Then I got a crack on the head from a bullet which put me out for several hours, according to the sun."

"A crack on the head with a bullet!" Tonger echoed.

Tremayne bared his head and bent it forward for the squatter to inspect the wound.

"See any fly maggots in it?" he asked.

"No, but it's full of grit and dust." Tonger regarded the overseer intently. "I don't quite get you," he said. "Did you see anyone shoot at you?"

"No. I was facing that balancing rock when I got it," replied Tremayne, lifting the water-bag to his parched lips. "There were some fellows with service rifles hunting away back from the breakaway. That was just before three o'clock. I came to about ten minutes ago."

"Deuced strange, Tremayne! What the devil would anyone deliberately shoot at you for? Tell you what! It might have been, in fact it must have been, a ricochet bullet. I never did like those three-o-threes. They shoot too damn far. That'll be the Kenny brothers using them. They got permission to shoot on my place several days ago. You'd better come along to the house and get your wound fixed up."

"Thanks! I really have no business here, but I wanted to get those Bowgada cattle before they boxed and save trouble. Instead of which I got more trouble than I bargained for."

When Tremayne was mounted, Tonger asked: "Hurt much?"

"Like hell. A hammer keeps hitting the top of my head."

"I'll stop those fellows using service rifles. They'll be killing my cattle and horses next," Tonger remarked decisively. "You've had a very lucky escape. A fraction of an inch closer and we'd have found you dead."

"Service rifles are too expensive shooting anyway."

"Much. A man wants only to miss once in four and the profit on his skins is next to nothing."

Not a word from Tonger's hand. He rode a little ahead of them, a man whose daylight hours were clearly all in the saddle.

They presently rounded the northern point, on the other side of which was a half-mile range of cliffs ending in another point off which a low, scrub-capped island stood, its barren grey slopes in shade and its dark green cap of vegetation coloured by the westering sun.

Having passed between the island and the point, they now rode in sight of the homestead which was built in the centre of an estuary mouth rising in a long gradient to the higher level. It was the first time Tremayne had seen Breakaway House at close range in daylight.

The buildings were grouped in a line. To the left, the homestead proper; to the far right, the great shearing shed. Between these two buildings were the men's quarters, the combined office and store buildings, while to the front of the shed were cane-grass cart and motor sheds and the poison house. Beyond the men's quarters, on higher ground, were stockyards.

"Alec, take Mr Tremayne's horse and water and feed it. You'll stay the evening, Tremayne."

Although badly tempted, Tremayne decided to decline. "Sorry, but I must get back to Bowgada," he said regretfully. "I would be glad of a cup of tea and a wash though."

"You're welcome," Tonger told him pleasantly. "Come on in. I'll show you the bathroom. Then I'll get some stuff for the wound."

Tremayne followed the squatter into the house, through the hall, along the main passage, and then into a luxurious bathroom.

"Hold your head under the tap," Tonger advised. "I won't be long."

"Thanks. I will."

Having removed his coat and shirt, Tremayne permitted the cold rain water to gush into the open scalp wound. It "bit" at first, but when the adjacent hair had become saturated, he washed away the dust and caked blood.

Must have bled some, he thought grimly. Could have bled more. No sign of Frances. Where is she?

"Feel any easier?" Tonger inquired, returning. "Here, have a drink. Beer or whisky?"

"That's kind of you. Beer, please. Cold?"

"As cold as it can be got without ice. Yes, a near shave that. You'd better let me stitch it."

"Thanks. You a doctor?"

"Well, I've had practice with the blacks," Tonger replied chuckling, a very different man from the one who had raged at Frances.

Like old friends they drank each other's health, after which the squatter efficiently cleansed the wound with a strong carbolic solution and expertly stitched the lips together.

"Get Filson to have a look at it now and then," he advised. "At the slightest sign of trouble, see the Mount Magnet doctor. There's one at Myme but it's not often he can see straight. Besides, he'd want to cut off your head to prevent gangrene."

"Thank you very much. It feels good now. And the headache is going."

"Better be sure about the headache and finish the bottle. Then we'll go along to dinner."

Ever the courteous host, Tonger chatted while Tremayne completed a hasty toilet and then conducted him to a large plainly furnished room in which the table was set for two diners. Did that indicate that Frances would not be there? Through the open French windows drifted regular reports from the exhaust of the petrol engine running the electric light dynamo, and faint perfume from the standard rose trees in the narrow strip of garden fenced with white painted pickets.

"I understand that you had a slight argument with Mr Ross at the ball, some time after he tried to trip you on the dance floor," Tonger said coolly while they waited for dinner.

"Ah, yes! I was obliged to knock him out when he attempted to hit me with a bar of iron he'd used on a Bowgada black named Ned," Tremayne said, just as coolly. "Ned followed his woman over here. Objected to her staying. As it seemed likely that he would create a disturbance, and as the woman refused to leave with him, I picked her up and drove them both back to Acacia Well. Ross followed with two of his accomplices, intending to tar me for abducting the girl. One of the swine heaved a rock which floored poor Filson. I had the pleasure of knocking Ross out for the second time. The pleasure of knocking out the man who hit Filson is yet to he enjoyed."

"Go easy," Tonger advised smilingly. "Ross and his associates are a tough crowd."

"I like tough crowds."

"I suppose you meet hard cases up in the Kimberleys?"

"There may be an odd one or two, but they don't heave rocks or use their boots. In this case, it appears that Ross objected to me paying attention to Miss Winters. It seems that Ross and Miss Winters' brother were great pals. I wonder if he was mixed up in the business in which Miss Winters' brother was shot."

Tremayne turned and casually looked into his host's eyes. A trim maid entered with a loaded tray.

"It's quite likely. Ross is blackguard enough for anything," averred the squatter, motioning his guest to the table. "Yet I think the shooting of Winters ended what really was a criminal practice. After that there was no further trouble with gold-stealers. You know, I really believe that more gold has been stolen from our West Australian mines than has gone to pay shareholders' dividends."

"Quite likely."

"There was Tinker's Find—do you like your meat well or underdone?—away north of Myme. They knew gold was being stolen, so the directors sacked all the executive officers and employed an ex-policeman to search the miners when they left after each shift. The mine closed down in 1911. The manager retired to Perth. The policeman bought a nine-thousand-pound farm near Pinjarra."

The conversation was kept to the subject of gold-stealing, Tonger revealing an unexpected dry fund of humour. The meal proceeded pleasantly, but he made no reference to his niece, nor did Tremayne permit himself to inquire. This big, powerful man was a paradox, at times coarse and brutish, at others suave and cultured.

Tremayne could not fathom him, although he did reveal flashes of an iron will and a ruthless disposition. Did Tonger know of the tryst at the balancing rock? Did he know of the deliberate attempt on his life? Had he engineered it?

A telephone bell rang, and shortly after the maid entered to say that Brett Filson wanted to speak to Tonger.

Tonger nodded to her and pushed back his chair. "Excuse me, please," he requested rising. "I shall have to go over to the office. The instrument is over there, but an extension of the call alarm is in the hall."

"I'll be all right. I'll help myself to more meat in your absence."

"Yes, do."

He had been gone but a few seconds when the maid came in again and said softly: "Miss Frances asked me to get Hool-'em-up Dick to take this letter over to Bowgada, secret like."

Accepting the dainty pink envelope, Tremayne looked up into her face and encountered dark eyes which plainly forbade questioning.

Yet she answered the question hovering on his tongue. "She had to go to Perth," the girl whispered, and swiftly went out.

Badly though he wanted to open the envelope and read the letter, Tremayne dared not be found by his host with it in his hands. A feeling of elation fired him. Frances was not at the balancing rock that afternoon!

On his return Morris Tonger told him the reason for Filson's call. "Apparently N'gobi, Nora's husband, has escaped from the Kalgoorlie gaol."

CHAPTER XVIII

A NIGHT RIDE

BY the aid of matches and the pale light of the young moon, Tremayne read Frances's letter in the bed of a creek about a mile from Breakaway House. She wrote:

> Dear Mr Tremayne,
>
> Despite what the parson said, I did not go to the balancing rock. Did you? If you did, I hope you had an enjoyable time admiring the wonderful scenery.
>
> I am going to Perth to transact some business for Uncle and will be away for several days. Remember me to Miss Winters when next you see her. To Miss Sayers and to Mr Filson, too. Just between ourselves, do you think they are in love?
>
> Yours truly,
> Frances Tonger

There! No regret at being unable to meet him. Just a cool statement of fact to which was added a spice of impish sarcasm. She seemed to like the prospect of rushing off to Perth and leaving him to wait, possibly for hours, beneath a rotten balancing rock. And yet–she had written; had remembered him. And she had not written to say that she did not wish to see him ever again. She had stated that she would be away only a few days, and reading between the lines, that must mean she would not find boredom in a future meeting.

Well, it was a relief to know that she had not fired that shot; had not been anywhere near the devil who had fired it. But had she told Tonger about the tryst? Did she know of or suspect the attempt to be made on his life, and write the letter to cover her tracks?

Tremayne cursed himself for his horrible suspicions, and yet could not entirely rid himself of them. There are moments when a lover is not a reasoning man, when his mind is over-clouded by the passion of his heart, and then a wrong construction is placed upon every sentence, every act of the loved one.

Yet how did the determined killer know that he was to be at the balancing rock at three o'clock that afternoon?

There was no mistaking or forgetting the vision of the rifle flash, followed instantly by the stunning blow, before his fall into the gulf of unconsciousness. There was no mistaking the coloured handkerchief waved to him for the purpose it achieved, making him stop to become a motionless target. In the entire act, only the undue confidence of the marksman was at fault. Yes, he must have been very sure of success when he fired from the distance he did.

Tremayne mulled it over as he rode, and then, just as he was drawing near to Acacia Well, he hit upon a very likely hypothesis. Those kangaroo shooters operating back from the breakaway! That was it! His murder was to have been staged as an accident. That was why the killer had not been able to wait until he, Tremayne, was within a few yards of him. He was to be killed on the slope, several hundred yards from the face of the promontory. He was to be left just where he fell. In the course of time his body would be discovered by Ellis or Ned tracking his horse from Acacia Well, or by one of Tonger's riders attracted to it by the eagles. The police would be brought from Mount Magnet. Trackers would thoroughly examine the ground. That was why the killer had not come down from his perch to make sure he was dead. He could not leave tracks for the police party to read as easily as a summons.

It would have been remembered that the Kenny brothers were that day shooting above the breakaway. Tonger would mention it. They were using service rifles, and one of the ricochet bullets had unfortunately killed Tremayne. Was it not obvious? Naturally the killer's rifle would be in possession of one of the kangaroo hunters. A bullet fired from it would be microscopically compared with that found in Tremayne's body. Accident! A most unfortunate accident.

If this hypothesis were correct, then the Kenny brothers were members of the gold-stealing gang. That being so, the planned accident would have been the result of an arrangement evolved by some one man. Who was he? If not Tonger, who? How had he found out that his victim was to be in that place at that time? Perhaps Frances would remember confiding in someone; her uncle, one of the maids who betrayed her confidence.

They certainly had caught him napping, but they had erred through over-confidence, and had shown their ruthless blood-stained hands. To reason further–why did they want to kill him? Surely not for besting Buck Ross! Nor for taking Nora away from Breakaway House. They had found out through Frances–he felt sure it had been through her–that he was to visit the balancing rock, and through that same source they had learned that he was a policeman here on the Murchison to look into the matter of thefts of gold and the disappearance of one John Tremayne.

Only Brett Filson and Frances Tonger knew both his status and his mission. But only Frances knew he would be visiting the balancing rock. There he was again—back to Frances Tonger.

The hum of a car engine made him glance back to observe the lights of a machine a mile or so behind him. It was coming on fast, and when he and the horse were bathed in radiance, he urged Major off the track. Without lessening speed the big hooded machine roared by on its way to Acacia Well.

After a while he saw its headlight beams turn upwards as it mounted the steep rise beyond the water-gutter, his side of the boundary gate, but when he arrived at the gate twenty minutes later the car was but half a mile beyond the hut.

Reaching that, he discovered Fred Ellis entertaining company, for on dismounting he heard interspersed between Ellis's ramble another man's voice. Quite distinctly the voices issued through wall cracks and the open door.

"Too right, Alec. It's yours; only don't forget to bring it back."

"I'll send it over by Hool-'em-up Dick on Sat'day. That do?"

"Yairs, that'll do. Boil, blast you, boil!"

Within, Tremayne found the stockman trying to force a billy to come to the boil, and, seated on a case, the hand who had accompanied Morris Tonger that afternoon.

"Good night, Mr Tremayne—gonna camp?"

"No, Fred. On my way to the homestead."

"Goodo! Wait a tick, have a drink of tea. This is Alec, come across from Breakaway House with them travellers to borrer me accordion."

Nodding to Alec, Tremayne found a seat on Fred's bunk. "Going to stay the night or walk back?" he inquired, busy with his cigarette making and wondering why no mention was made of the accident.

"Reckon I'll walk back," replied Alec, expressionless. "Only four mile. Took a ride here when those travellers come through."

"Who were they?"

"Don't know."

"An' I never went to the car to look in. They'll be strangers to me if Alec don't know 'em," supplemented Fred.

Lifting the billy from chimney hoop to table with his felt hut, Ellis proceeded to stir the contents with a stained spoon before filling three tin pint pannikins, continuously gabbling away about nothing of importance, until he referred to the Aborigines' smoke signals.

"They bin at it orl day. There's bin hell let loose somewheres, they ain't corroboree fires, that I know. Ned and Nora bit at them, too. They won't 'ave done no work. They 'ad to ride the south paddock and overlook them weaners. They're that unreliable, sooner jabber over a two-stick fire than work, any day."

"Do you know what those signals were for?" Tremayne asked Alec.

The fellow was fingering Fred's accordion, and without looking up shook his head. Still no mention of an affair which surely should have been of the first conversational magnitude.

Liar, thought Tremayne. Here, evidently, was a very sly bird. Tremayne drank his tea, which he did not really want, and at the end of half an hour rose to leave.

"How's your stores, Fred?" he asked.

"Bit low on flour and sugar, anyone coming out send me a cuppler pounds of tobacco and a tin of mill oil."

"All right. Pity the boss doesn't have this place connected by telephone."

"Said he would long time ago. Means only a few posts and two 'undred yards of wire to connect with the main telephone line."

"I'll remind him about it. Well, so long!"

"Hooroo, Mr Tremayne. See you some time. Come and camp a night, want a pitch."

The lean scraggy figure arrayed in soiled clothes waved a hand and grinned a cheerful goodbye, watery eyes sparkling in the light of the suspended hurricane lamp. Fred Ellis was at home, content with his hut, and emphatically unwilling to exchange it for anything in the city.

Into the quiet world of low saltbush and treeless flats, illuminated by the ghostly light of the young moon drooping to the horizon, rode Tremayne, leaving Major to follow the track, his mind now occupied with this Alec. There was nothing significant in his ignorance, or pretended ignorance, concerning those smoke signals. That was natural to the race with which he was closest allied, but he might have asked how his wound was, or made some mention of the "accident", even though he was a taciturn fellow.

Until then he had forgotten Filson's message concerning the escape of N'gobi. Of course, N'gobi would make his way back to his own district, and knowing that, the police must have telephoned Filson to watch out for his arrival. The blacks knew as soon as did Filson; in fact, sooner than he. They set up a chain of signals from Kalgoorlie which finally informed Ned and Nora, who had acknowledged the message.

From all accounts, this N'gobi was a bad man. He would without doubt come back for his woman without vengeance in his heart, for it was unlikely that he would know who had informed the police against him, but he would bring his friends to Ned's camp to reclaim his woman and exact tribal justice. They would take Nora away from the man she liked and, if Nora was not in Ned's marriage class, then N'gobi and his friends would kill her, or, fearing the white man's vengeance, would point the bone at her; and if she was in Ned's marriage class, N'gobi would take her back, and Ned would have to fight N'gobi's friends and relatives, or be beaten into one whole bruise.

So intent was Tremayne on the likely outcome of N'gobi's escape that he permitted Major to walk off the track to nibble at a young bluebush. Suddenly he was recalled to his present surroundings by two distinct flashes of light in the far distance. He kept watching for a full minute for any repetition, but there was none. Imagination doubtless. Looking about to see where he was, he discovered that the east breakaway was behind him when he saw the flashes. The flashes then–if there really had been light flashes–were in the direction of Acacia Well.

When again on the track, he urged his horse into a canter, keeping his gaze fixed on the ground ahead to discern water-gutters before they were reached. Higher and higher loomed the line of the breakaway against the faintly moon-lit sky, now dark and featureless as the moon touched the horizon. Those flashes most likely were due to Fred Ellis carrying his hurricane lamp when he escorted Alec as far as the boundary gate.

He could now feel the long gentle rise reaching to the breakaway foot. A bluff-pointed shadow crept out to meet him on his right as he approached the mass of rock debris among which twisted the track before taking the final long and steep grade at a slant up the side of the right-hand shadow. And presently, like strange sleeping beasts, strange shadow shapes slid by him on either side–giant boulders. Major eased to a walk, ears pricked forward, head carried softly. There appeared to be something suspicious higher up along the track which excited his curiosity. A kangaroo? A loose horse? Or a mob of restless steers?

Tremayne could not forget those flashes. He could not discard the suspicion that they had been signals. The men in the overtaking car had dropped Alec at Acacia Well. They had all come from Breakaway House, or through Breakaway House, and if it had been Alec signalling what lay behind that?

Major was reined to a halt and his rider dismounted.

CHAPTER XIX

THE AMBUSCADE

FOR a full minute Tremayne stood still and listened. The silence became a sensation in his ears. The horse stood almost as quietly as he, his ears pricked, his nostrils slightly twitching.

Without haste, the overseer forced the animal to stand obliquely across the track, facing the edge of the steep slope falling to the water-gutter marking the gully bottom. And in this position Major again looked up along the darkened track, his attitude one of tense suspicion.

There was something between them and the topmost level of the track, unseen by the man, heard, if not actually seen, by the horse. That mysterious something might be wild things or domestic stock—or the travellers who had passed them in the car. Man and horse were but a bare mile from the Bowgada homestead; if the rider wished to reach the homestead by a different route he would have to return to the rock debris at the foot of the grade, strike north across the gully, skirt a headland, and so come to that bay commanded by the sapling seat where he and Filson had first met. It was an alternative route to take if he wished to avoid trouble; but, after all, avoiding trouble would not get him anywhere, and on this particular job trouble was to be sought, not avoided.

Leading the horse off the track, he lightly fastened the ends of the reins to a young kurrajong tree, and then, with his automatic in his hand, he once again intently listened from the centre of the roadway.

No sound came to his straining ears save the haunting wail of a curlew away out over the sunken valley. Supposing Tonger, or whoever had engineered the shooting attempt on his life, had sent those men after him to make a second attack? Alec had said he did not know them, but supposing the borrowing of Fred's accordion was a mere excuse to permit him to signal that Tremayne had left for the homestead, and somewhere up along this track the men who had been signalled lay waiting to shoot or in some way stage an accident? The locality would be quite far enough away from Breakaway House to permit its becoming the scene of an investigation without centring attention on Morris Tonger.

There was only one way to decide this question. He would have to scout forward, not along the track itself but parallel to it, and because, if he took the right side higher up the slope, he would be presented on a skyline, he stepped down the slope off the track and began to stalk with his head on the road level.

The further he proceeded the steeper became the slope of the headland. The ascending track began to follow a natural ledge widened with blasting powder, and the debris from the blasting had been pushed over the track's edge, requiring careful negotiation by a man whose life might depend on silent movement.

It was not lost on Tremayne that, although it was dark, he was placed at a disadvantage. He was forced to move while possible enemies could remain completely invisible by keeping still. Even in the darkest night a moving object is visible at short range.

Constantly halting to listen, Tremayne was gradually coming to believe that his suspicions were without foundation. His movements were executed soundlessly; not once did his feet snap a twig or dislodge a splinter of granite to rattle sharply down the now steep slope, a slope which became steeper still the further he progressed.

He saw the car and heard the horse at the same time. The horse was galloping up the track; the stationary car was further up the track, possibly two hundred yards. It emitted no lights, but its blurred outlines lay against the starry sky.

The horse's hoofs thudded against the granite track surface. With his eyes on the level of the track, Tremayne could see the sparks flashed outward by the iron-shod hoofs. An enemy come to view the result of the "accident" or a friend pounding after him to warn him of an attack? And then he saw the shape of the horse rushing out of the darkness, and saw, too, that the animal was saddled but riderless. It was his own horse, Major. It swept by him before he could make any guarded effort to stop it.

Major sped up the track, frightened by something down below, anxious to find his master or get to the familiar homestead. Two seconds after it passed him, Tremayne saw the body of the horse against the sky close to the rock wall which bounded the track's far side. The horse's shape blotted out the shape of the car. Then there came a muffled report. The rock wall moved. Featureless, he yet could see its outline, and the huge slab which split asunder. The slab was hurtling outward, toppling forward over the track, over the horse rushing to meet it. The horse screamed sharply–a scream drowned, cut off by the thumping crash as the rock slab smashed on to the rock roadway. Again the horse screamed. And from part way down the slope he heard the rumble of a miniature avalanche.

From the gully's bottom came another sound, the low roar of racing sheep. They fled to the open plain, and, as they went, Tremayne heard men's voices from the direction of the car. He gained the track, darted to the rock wall and into its deeper shadow, then moved cautiously along it, mounting ever upwards towards the place where that huge slab of rock had been blown out of its bed to send Major hurtling into the gully.

The beam of an electric torch sprang into being and began to play over a mass of rock lying on the track. It illuminated, beside the rock debris, the figure of a short tubby man who evidently was examining the result of this engineering feat. Another man joined him, a big man, and when he spoke Tremayne recognised him to be Buck Ross.

"Did we get him?" Ross said sharply.

"Yes, we got him all right. Didn't you hear the horse scream? The top edge of this slab of granite caught him nicely. Horse and man were knocked clean off the track. And look here, over the edge is a sheer drop of thirty feet."

The little man was a stranger to Tremayne. At first he thought him to be Mug Williams, but he was now sure that it was not Williams' voice.

"Good business," acclaimed Ross with a devilish chuckle. "That's a little score wiped out which was beginning to get my goat. I never like owing debts. Well, we might as well get on. We'll have to pass the homestead, but we needn't stop to tell everyone who we are."

"What about making sure that the bloke is out to it?"

"There ain't no need to mess around finding him to make sure," objected Ross. "Hit by that slab of rock wasn't like being patted on the back by a lovin' woman."

Again Ross chuckled with very genuine pleasure, and together he and his tubby companion walked up to the waiting car. The lights were switched on and the engine started before they reached it, proving that a third man was the driver. The engine rose into a high-pitched hum as the machine shot forward.

No tail-light gleamed on white registration numbers. Softer and softer grew its purring hum until the silence of the night reigned once more over the breakaways.

With matches to aid him, Tremayne examined the debris of rock on the track, estimating that, at the least, two tons of granite lay there, and some of the slab must have been sent forward off the track with the horse. From the gully rose no sounds indicating that Major lived; and, his match supply being low, he decided to go on to the homestead and return with Old Humpy and hurricane lamps to make sure that the horse was not lingering in agony.

HE discovered Brett Filson sitting in the living room with a novel in his hands, his feet on a second chair and a pipe between his teeth.

"Well, how have you been putting in the day?" Filson asked.

"Oh! So, so!" Tremayne replied casually, to add with more lucidity: "I'm going to help myself to a whisky neat."

"You'll find the bottle in the left-hand cupboard. Had a hard ride?"

"Very. I've been shot at, and Major has been killed by about three tons of rock blown out of the rock wall across the valley track. That car didn't stop, of course."

"No, it passed at high speed. But shot at? Your horse killed? Tell the tale."

Tremayne related his adventures, listened to without interruption by a man whose face became grimmer and grimmer as the tale unfolded.

"Those birds must have worked rapidly in laying the charge of gelignite," opined the overseer. "It beats me how they did it in the time. They got to work when that Alec signalled that I'd left Acacia Well. He was sent there for that, and who could send him, and that car-load of men under Buck Ross, if not Tonger?"

Filson rose to his feet and walked to the empty fireplace. He stood with his back to it, an angry frown drawing his brows together.

"We'll go over to Breakaway House in the morning and have it out with Tonger," he stated in tones likened to a whip cracking. "This sort of thing has got to stop. It's become a police matter."

"It's a police matter now, Brett," Tremayne said quietly. "Rushing things won't do any good. We'll lie low, and let 'em think as long as possible that they succeeded." The young man's expression was indicative of satisfaction, although his smile was without mirth and the drooping lids did not hide the hard, steely light in his eyes. "I want to go back now in the truck to make sure that Major is not living in agony. I'll take Old Humpy or English with me." Suddenly his face cleared and he laughed. "You know, Brett, these gentry are going to give me quite a lot of entertainment. John was right when he wrote the old dad that he suspected a criminal gang to be operating on these breakaways."

"That seems to be certain, Harry. Another thing which is certain is that a large force of police should be brought here to clean up the gang before they do any more damage."

"A large force of police would collect the small fry and let the big fish escape," Tremayne pointed out succinctly. "We can't act until we know the names of the big fish. Slow but sure is the policy to follow."

"All right," Filson assented reluctantly, and together they left the house, routed out English, and set off for the scene of the attempt on

Tremayne's life. They discovered the horse dead almost at the bottom of the slope.

"He was an intelligent beast, Brett," was all the younger man said about the horse he had broken and come to love.

They were back again in the living room in less than an hour. "I hope Dame Fortune will be kind enough to let me lay my hands on the swine who engineered that little stunt," he said savagely. "Here's the dad writing to tell me that he won't accept my resignation, and to remind me that I'm still a policeman and must always act within the letter of the law; but I pray the day will come when I can start shooting, and that day I'll not remember about being a policeman, you can bet."

To banish this mood, Brett said: "How's your head? Let me look at it." And then when he examined the wound and saw Tonger's expert stitching: "You weren't born to be shot. What are your next moves?"

"I'm going to examine Breakaway House inside and outside. And I'm going to examine every blessed foot of that breakaway bay which contains the balancing rock, Brett. Tomorrow I'll slip down and see Ned and Nora. I'm going to get Ned to come with me, and Nora can come here and stay with Millie English. She'll be safer here, for when N'gobi arrives there'll be some fun. Now tell me, old man, what do you really and truly think of Frances Tonger?"

"I like her."

"I more than like her. But only she knew I was going to the balancing rock this afternoon."

"Just what do you infer from that?" Brett asked levelly.

"I don't know. I love that girl, but I have horrible suspicions, cur that I am."

The squatter pursed his lips, looking steadily at Tremayne. He reloaded and lit his pipe before he said: "I think that your suspicions are rotten. What probably happened is that she innocently told her uncle that you wanted to meet her at that place and time. And then Morris Tonger found a business excuse to get her out of the way. You say she says she's going to Perth?"

"Yes, that's so. And I expect that's how Tonger learned about my appointment with her. Mind you, she never said she would be there, and when I think of it, I realise my cheek in putting it to her. By the way, when you rang up did he say anything about my being shot?"

"Not a word."

"Now I wonder," Tremayne said musingly. "He didn't mention that little matter to you. Alec said nothing of it to Fred Ellis. When Tonger planned this little stunt tonight–I'll bet it was him–he took a chance that no one bar the rifleman, Alec, and himself would ever know about it. He knew I saw the gun flash. He knows I know it wasn't a ricochet bullet which cracked me. He didn't arrange that 'accident' just because I was hoping to meet his niece, or might by chance discover something. No. He knows—I'll stake my life on it—that I'm a policeman up here to investigate the disappearance of John Tremayne. Phew! Things are getting interesting. Curse it! I wonder if Frances innocently mentioned that to him, too."

"You can depend on her innocence," Brett said quietly.

"One day I'll grovel on my chest to her to atone for my thoughts, Brett. I wish she were out of the way for good. I've a mind to wire the old dad to keep her in Perth for a week or two. He could lock her up if she refused to stay with my people. Say! On Saturday I want you to telephone Miss Sayers and invite her and my lovely Violet out for Sunday."

"Why?" demanded the astonished squatter.

"Because Bowgada is deuced dull on Sundays."

"That's not the reason. Tell me."

"Well then, because I want to learn a little history from Violet Winters. And I want to be reminded once more what a damn fool you are."

"I don't understand you," Brett said with abrupt stiffness.

Now Tremayne was grinning broadly. "Then don't try to," he said. "But invite those two for Sunday, if you love me. Send English in for them if you can't go."

CHAPTER XX

THE ISLAND

FRANCES drove away from Breakaway House after lunch on the Wednesday Tremayne had hoped to meet her at the balancing rock, accompanied by a hand who was to return with the car. She arrived at Mount Magnet, a distance of about one hundred and twenty miles, shortly before six o'clock, and there ate her dinner at the hotel, with plenty of time at her disposal to catch the 7.40 train to Perth.

While she was eating the hand approached her table to say that his employer had telephoned orders that he was to stay the night, and would Miss Frances be sure to ring Breakaway House as soon as convenient.

Evidently there was something her uncle had forgotten, so after dinner she telephoned him.

"Oh–that you, Frances?" Tonger said smoothly. "There isn't now any necessity for you to go to Perth after all as I've received a telegram clinching that business. Come back tomorrow. See Reeves, please, and ask for a case of whisky and a dozen syphons of soda. And don't forget to buy anything you may want for yourself."

"Very well, Uncle," she assented lightly.

"I hope you're not disappointed at not going to the city?"

"Not very. It's a long and hot journey just now."

"Good! I'm scheming to get away before Christmas. You and I will take a holiday trip to New Zealand for a month or so. We've both earned it, you know."

"That will be splendid," she cried joyfully at the prospect of a dream coming true. "If we don't go to New Zealand I shall be disappointed. All right, I'll get back some time tomorrow."

So it was about the time Nora drove a gig loaded with swags and hens and pups, and a family of cats, to Bowgada homestead, with Ned and Tremayne riding wide on the flanks in the hope of shooting eagles perched on solitary dead cork trees, that Frances sped back to Breakaway House.

The day having been windy, dusty, and unpleasantly hot, Frances was glad to be home to lounge away the rest of the day in the drawing room, writing up her diary and retiring early to bed, leaving her uncle at work on his books in the office.

The next day, Friday, was calm, brilliant, and cool, and at about two o'clock she ordered her horse to be brought in and saddled. Tonger being out, she had afternoon tea alone, and at four o'clock she left the homestead on one of those exploration trips which so delighted her.

For here at Breakaway House she was very lonely. Since leaving Perth she had missed the intimate society of youth. There were days together when she did not even see her uncle who never troubled to explain what he had done or where he had been. Since the scene, subsequent to her taking over the management of the house, a scene which had revealed her determination that the loose moral conditions she had found could not continue, the hands and servants showed little love for her, even if their respect was maintained. Of all the staff, only the girl who had conveyed the note to Tremayne was able to be admitted into her confidence. The rest treated her with an unfriendly reserve which conveyed their resentment of the altered conditions she had achieved.

Uncle Morris could manage his run and his men. His flirtations were no business of hers–provided they were not conducted under the same roof. His drinking bouts were horrid at first, but after she bravely bearded him concerning his behaviour to her, he conducted himself with greater circumspection, often confining himself to his office where he had had a stretcher bed fixed up.

Frances was no shrinking milk-and-water miss. She had inherited in full measure the stubbornness of the Tongers. It was this trait in her character to which Morris Tonger bowed with grace as his home comforts became vastly improved, more in accordance with that home governed so well many years ago by Amy, his much tried wife who had eventually eloped. Like the animal he was, he loved luxury; and never, even in his worst hours, did he fail to appreciate that his niece was a born housekeeper.

But affection, love! There was little on either side. Sober, Morris Tonger was bearable. There were even moments when he was the old Uncle Morris she had known as a child. And when sober he respected her for her self-assurance, her poise, and her stubbornness in the battles between them.

Yes, Frances was a lonely girl at Breakaway House, a girl starved of congenial company. Lonely evenings in the drawing room after lonely rides along the breakaways.

LEAVING the homestead, she set a course which would take her ship–a horse — to the point of the southern headland thrusting into the valley half a mile eastward of the house. The island off this point or headland appeared to be joined to it when viewed from the house, but on drawing close to the point a passage was revealed between it and the island, five hundred yards in width.

Less than half the height of the steeper rock-strewn headland and covering about ten acres, the island presented perpendicular rock walls supporting a crown of red earth covered in thick but stunted Bogota and mulga scrub. This crown now gleamed dully in the light of the westering sun.

The "strait" was carpeted with boulders set far apart over a mass of granite and quartz and ironstone splinters, a kaleidoscope of greys and whites and dull reds. Frances noted these colours with delight, and as usual was thrilled by the wildness of this sea-less coast. Her horse followed a stone-cleared cattle pad which brought her to within fifty yards of the island.

The sharp impact of one pebble against another distracted her attention from two magpies chasing a crow from the vicinity of their nest. It was not a natural sound, on this calm quiet afternoon, for it came from beyond her horse's head and not from the island's shore.

The second pebble she distinctly saw before it struck the ground. Strangely enough, it appeared to fall out of the sky, and on impact it smashed into tiny flakes. Interested by this peculiar phenomenon, she glanced upward to the island's summit to see curving outward and downward from it what appeared to be a piece of white quartz. When it fell beside the horse, interest gave place to astonishment, for the white quartz turned into a slip of paper weighted by a small stone. Mastered by curiosity, she dismounted, picked up the paper, and read in hurried scrawl:

On the seaward side of this island there is an easy path to the summit. Come up. I badly want to talk with you. H.T.

Harry Tremayne! What on earth was he doing up there? Why ever did he not come down instead of dropping this intriguing note at her horse's feet? Surely he was the most extraordinary man she had ever met! As though she did not know of the easy path to the top! Had she not often gone up there to see from its northern-most side the great sweep of country enclosing the homestead? Why the secrecy?

Again she read the note. With it crushed in her hand, she led the horse round to the south side of the island, gained its east side, and from there walked up the only slope, following a pad used more by kangaroos than cattle. When halfway up, dense scrub formed walls which almost met, but at the top she came out into a tiny clearing skirted by giant boulders among which the scrub trees grew. An Aborigine stepped quickly into sight and smiled at her. She recognised him as Ned, the Bowgada hand. He motioned her to follow him.

With increasing mystification, she obeyed, and presently saw through the thin tree trunks Harry Tremayne standing against the angle formed by two great rock slabs. Here, evidently, he and Ned were camped, for on the ground were two light swags, leaning against a rock were two rifles, beside a small smokeless fire was a billy-can, and hanging to tree branches were dilly bags and what appeared to be the skins of eagles.

"Welcome to my Cannibal Island, Miss Tonger," Tremayne cried, when he had ordered Ned to take charge of the horse. His eyes were alight and dancing. Her two hands were taken for an instant into his strong brown ones, and when he released them, the note remained in one of his. "I saw you about to pass by and I simply had to invite you to accept our poor hospitality."

Tossing the spill of paper into the fire, he addressed Ned: "When you've fixed Miss Tonger's horse, put on the billy. Miss Frances–I thought you were on your way to Perth."

"I would have been, only Uncle recalled me from Mount Magnet. But what are you doing here? What does all this mean?"

"It's quite a story. Might I make you a cigarette?" he asked eagerly, his grey-blue eyes regarding her with strange fixity. "I can make a nice one when I want to."

"Thank you!" she said, although in the pocket of her cord breeches reposed her case and matches.

Snatching up his swag of calico sheet and one blanket he unrolled it, folded it, and laid it over a low flat-topped rock. He then led her by the hand to this improvised seat from where she watched his slim fingers carefully roll the finest cigarette he had ever made.

From his hands her gaze rose to the top of his bent head, hatless, revealing to her the two-inch hairless scar of the bullet. "What happened to your head?" she asked, experiencing sudden tenderness despite the lightness of her soul.

When he looked up at her he was grinning in the old way. He proffered the cigarette, and when she took it there appeared with magical quickness a lighted match.

Ned, who had poured water into the billy from a canvas bag, squatted over the fire and carefully fed it with tinder-dry sticks. Smoke was absent. It was very quiet and peaceful up here. The sunlight filtering through the scrub trees tinged the daylight with green.

"Of course, I went to the balancing rock as I said I would do," Tremayne said when he had lighted a cigarette for himself. "There was someone at the foot of the balancing rock. I thought it was you. That someone waved to me in greeting and I stopped Major and waved back. You see, I was so sure it was you that I suspected nothing. I made a fine target for that someone who deliberately shot me."

"Shot you!" she echoed.

He nodded, looking up at her from where he carelessly lounged at her feet. In his eyes there was neither pain nor anger, just plain happiness that she was there. For a moment it was like that; then abruptly his mouth fell into lines of sternness, and into his eyes crept a cold gleam. "Whom did you tell I was to go to the balancing rock on Wednesday at three o'clock?" he demanded.

"Tell! I told no one."

"But you must have told someone. Think!"

"I say I told no one. I'm positive."

For a second or two he regarded her amazed face with pursed lips and half-shut eyes.

"It must have been a sheer coincidence, then, that that murderous beast was there, or perhaps he saw me when a long way off and took position there."

"But I don't understand, Mr Tremayne."

"Well I do, and don't."

"Didn't you see him afterwards? Didn't he go to you to see what he'd done? Are you sure it wasn't an accident?" Frances asked desperately.

"It was no accident," he told her. "I saw the flash of the rifle. He waved to me hoping I would stop and present a motionless target, which was precisely what I did do. I was knocked off my horse, knocked unconscious. I lay there beside an old man saltbush for several hours, and he never came down to ascertain if I were dead or alive for fear of leaving tracks. Later on, your uncle and a stockman named Alec came riding from the south, and, seeing my horse grazing nearby, came over and found me. Your uncle thinks it was a ricochet bullet fired by one of two kangaroo hunters shooting away back from the breakaway edge."

"But you told him about the man who waved to you; the flash of the rifle?"

"No. I didn't tell him that."

"But why not?" she pressed him, astonished.

"Because I didn't want your uncle to know I knew it wasn't a chance ricochet bullet which came to within half an inch of killing me."

"But why not, why not?"

"Listen to what followed," he urged, and proceeded to relate all the happenings of that day and night; the passing revellers, the methods they adopted in the attempt on his life. "Those men came from Breakaway House. They know I'm looking for John. They know I'm a policeman. Are you still sure that you didn't tell anyone?"

CHAPTER XXI

NO DECEIT BETWEEN US

"MR TREMAYNE, I repeat that I told no one about your proposed rendezvous," Frances said in tones which excluded further doubt. "You'll admit that I never did agree to meet you in spite of your persistence. You have no cause to think me cheap."

"Excuse my butting in," he said with a disarming smile, "but let us get things right between us. I never did regard you cheaply, and I want you to believe that my foolery was just foolery. I'm not laundered by gay feminine society and ironed by drawing-room etiquette, and, consequently, I'm not subtle. Because my manhood has been spent in a land where men are few and women are even fewer, I met you rather as man to man than as man to woman. At no time did I think of hurting you; at no time have I held you cheaply."

"Perhaps, I shouldn't have used the word 'cheap'."

"In one respect you were entitled to use it, Miss Tonger. I'm beginning to see that I shouldn't have made the suggestion of meeting you so soon after our first acquaintance, but I sought the meeting for three reasons. First, because I wanted to secure your confidence and your silence regarding my identity; second, because I found pleasure in your society; and third, because with bush people friendship is not dependent on an exchange of visiting cards. Does that clear the ground between us?"

"Yes, it seems to."

His face magically regained its youth. Seated on the ground at her feet, dressed in light khaki drill slacks and open-necked shirt, hatless, and recently shaved, the thought occurred to Frances Tonger that never had she looked into such a frank and open face as that then presented to her. Like every woman since Eve, intuition informed her when in the presence of a wholesome man, and here at her feet lounged the antithesis of her uncle, Morris Tonger.

"In one respect I'm sorry you didn't go to Perth," he said. "I suppose you couldn't manage to take a holiday in Perth right away?"

"No—not even if I wanted to go, which I do not."

What he next said was softened by the good-humoured smile in his eyes.

"I've a good mind to arrest you for being dangerous to the Western Australian Police Force, take you to Perth myself and lock you up in my people's house with my mother for gaoler."

"But why?" she asked, half seriously, half laughingly.

"With you safely at my parents' house, my mind would he relieved concerning you."

He then said to Ned: "Go over to the far side and keep a look-see on Breakaway House. If you see anyone tracking along this way, you run and tell me."

"Orl ri', Mr Tremayne. Tea made," Ned announced, and rose to depart with the silent swiftness of his race, carrying with him a rifle, but leaving behind by the fire a Leonile club, the weapon of his immemorial ancestors.

Tremayne rose, too. He poured tea into half-pint tin pannikins, added sugar, and set one pannikin with a spoon beside the girl.

"What's that?" she asked, pointing to the Leonile.

"The Aborigine's most dreadful weapon," he replied, picking up the club and holding it up for her inspection. It was fashioned like an emu's head and neck, from a mulga root. The head was larger than an orange, while the beak, which was aligned at a right angle to the neck, was tapered to a point and hardened with fire. The long handle, or neck, bore a series of rings which Ned had cut with a flint. "One tap on the head with this makes a second tap quite unnecessary," Tremayne said grimly.

Frances shuddered. "Put it down," she implored. "It's a terrible thing." She sipped her tea, wishing he had milk to offer her.

He was making fresh cigarettes.

"Mr Tremayne, will you take me fully into your confidence?" Frances asked earnestly.

"I would like to. I...I..." For the very first time he faltered, revealed hesitation and doubt, when always he had been so assured, so confident.

"Go on," she requested, leaning a little forward towards him. "What were you going to say?"

"We appear to have arrived at a position of some delicacy," was his prevarication. "Haven't you guessed that I've come to regard your uncle with grave suspicion?"

"Yes, I've guessed that."

"And that the time will come when you'll have to decide whether to stand for him or against him?"

Making no immediate reply to this, she looked pensively at the red-tinged wood coals of the fire. For a little while this mental attitude controlled her.

He waited, watching her immobile features, sensing something of her loneliness, her isolation from youth and happiness, and from life proper to her beauty and her age. If to her he at times looked much older than he was, to him sometimes she appeared aloof, too restrained, as though her youth had been much too brief. When she spoke he knew that her words were the result of no idle observations.

"Mr Tonger is my father's brother," she said slowly. "He has paid for my rearing and my education. I owe him loyalty if little else. It's all so very difficult for me. You see, I owe something, too, to your father and mother who have been kind to me, and to your brother who once proposed marriage to me."

Again she fell silent, and Tremayne made no effort to break in on her train of thought. He was thinking of John, a fearless youngster; could picture his eager face as he poured out his love at the feet of this peerless girl.

She said at long last: "I would like to know all that you know. Then I could the better decide what to do. If I should elect to stand by my uncle I would, nevertheless, not act or think against you. You see, Mr Tremayne, it seems that I must believe you will be fair."

And so it came about that he related the whole story without a shade of doubt that she would respect his confidence. He began with the suspicions of the Myme mine directors, and went on to the killing of Hamilton, John Tremayne's mission and his disappearance, and all the details of his own work; the strange lights in the vicinity of the balancing rock, the tracks of midnight riders and pack-horse strings.

"Now we come to that rock blasting stunt the other night which killed my horse, and would have killed me had I been on his back," Tremayne continued. "The next morning I rode down to the place. I saw that the huge rock slab had been weathered partly from its base, leaving a strip of about three feet wide which held it from falling over the track. I saw, too, about fifty yards further down the track a much bigger slab of rock partly eroded by the weather from its wall base, and there I found two drill holes stopped with wooden plugs to keep the holes clear of earth and dust. The condition of the plugs proves that the drilling was done about a year ago.

"Mr Filson says that his father engineered the road some fifty years ago, and that he, the son, never had any blasting done. We agree in assuming that someone drilled those holes, as well as the holes behind the slab blown out the other night, for the purpose of stopping the Myme mail car should it carry a large consignment of gold to the railway. The mine usually dispatches its gold in a guarded truck by the straight route crossing the breakaways where they peter out up north.

"The holes having been drilled, the motor party, which knew of them, had merely to fill one set of them with gelignite fitted with detonators, and explode the charges with a spare car battery when it was judged that the falling slab would pinch me and my horse. Such a result would have appeared to be an act of nature–an unfortunate accident."

"It's all very horrible," Frances said softly. "But although all those things happened near Breakaway House, there's nothing to connect my uncle with them."

"No…" he said doubtfully. He watched her eyes widen, uncertainty and fear entering them.

"Is there? Is there?" she demanded, sharply.

In reply, he held out his hand towards her, palm upward. On the palm rested a gold-plated matchbox. She recognised it before she took it to gaze at the carved letters on its face–two letters joined, an "A" and an "M" representing Amy and Morris.

"I found that about four feet from where the car was stopped that night. The owner evidently put it down on the offside rear mudguard, for it fell into the wheel track on that side almost immediately after the car was started," she heard him say.

From the box she raised her gaze to meet his, her eyes round and filled with horror, her face pale and her lips parted. "You think he was there?" she whispered.

"How can I think otherwise? For your sake, I wish I could. Listen! After I saw you I resigned from the police force. My father won't accept the resignation, but no matter. I resigned because if your uncle was proved to be mixed up with a gang of criminals and had nothing directly to do with the murder of Hamilton or the possible killing of John, I decided I wasn't going to be the man to bring him to justice. My mission is to find out what has become of my brother. Peace of mind for my father and mother is of greater importance to me than people's criminal activities. The question which I want answered, because it will answer others, is why your uncle has planned twice to kill me. Believe me, I am less concerned by those attempts than with the answer to that question."

"Why don't you ask him? Why don't you have him arrested?" she said sharply.

"Because arresting him on suspicion of having attempted to kill me would be unlikely to reveal John's fate."

"Do you think–do you suspect that he killed John?" she asked, as though stifled.

"I believe that he's mixed up with that gang of criminals. I've an open mind as to whether he himself actually killed John, or even that John is dead. You'll remember that when John reached Breakaway House you were away at the Gatley-Tomkins's. It's quite likely that John stayed at Breakaway House that night. It's probable that he discovered something, and was in turn discovered with knowledge dangerous to your uncle."

When she offered no comment to this, he went on: "A further fact which may, however, have no significance is that the day you were at the Gatley-Tomkins's, the day that John reached Breakaway House, saw the arrival of Colonel Lawton in his aeroplane. Have you ever met him?"

"Twice. I don't like him."

Tremayne's brows rose a fraction of an inch. "I met him once. To me he seemed all right," he said. "What is there about him you don't like?"

"I don't know exactly," Frances replied, flushing. "But he's not nice."

Tremayne noticed the quick drumming of her fingers on her knee, saw the troubled expression in her eyes, and got to his feet.

"What am I to do?" she asked helplessly. "It's all so terrible. What am I to do?"

Bending forward to bring his face on a level with hers, he said: "Do nothing, Miss Frances. I would not ask, I would not want you to do anything for me which might be against your uncle. As you have just said, you owe him loyalty, and until he proves to be unworthy of your loyalty, you must stand squarely by him—not me." Tremayne's voice quickened as he proceeded. "I've told you what I have because I feel that between you and me there can be no deceit; that you had to know just why I'm here. Actually you should regard me as an enemy of the Tongers. But I must find out what's happened to John; find out if he is alive, and, if he's dead, to bring to justice his killer. That's all. Do you think you could get across to Bowgada next Sunday afternoon?"

"Why?"

"I persuaded Mr Filson to invite my lovely Violet and Miss Sayers to spend the afternoon and evening. I want to have a semi-official talk with Miss Winters, and," he added slowly, "I want to give Miss Sayers a chance to impress on Mr Filson what an ass he is to think that a few war disabilities make any difference to a woman's love."

"I'd like to go," she said wistfully. Then she added with a dawning smile: "I thought they were in love."

"Of course they are. Very much so. But Brett Filson thinks Miss Sayers would be making a sacrifice by marrying him. Will you come over on Sunday?"

"Yes."

"Good! I'll fix it." He was smiling at her now, and she was bravely smiling back. There was a hint of wistfulness in his voice too when he said: "I'm afraid you'll have to go now. It's quite unnecessary to ask you not to mention to anyone our little *tête-à-tête*. Tell me—had you not gone to Mount Magnet, would you have met me at the balancing rock?"

Her eyes fell, but her head faintly indicated an affirmative answer.

Tremayne's spirits soared.

CHAPTER XXII

MORRIS TONGER AT HOME

FRANCES did not return directly to Breakaway House. There was too much in her mind to be sorted and classified and studied, too many problems demanding instant solution. On reaching the plain she set her horse at a hand gallop out to "sea", grateful for the cooling air pressing against her face and seeming to pour into her brain, clearing it as Epsom salts clear muddy water.

What was she to do? What could she do? Nothing–as Harry Tremayne had said. And yet she must do something; there must be some action she could take. Supposing that Harry Tremayne and Ned were killed through the instigation of this violent, sensuous uncle of hers? Gold-stealers, thieves and worse were the men who came sometimes to eat with her uncle and herself, and then retire to the office to drink and plan fresh villainy.

Of its own volition her horse eased to a canter, and presently relaxed to a walk. There was no doubt that Uncle Morris was with that party of men who had blasted out rock in an attempt to kill Harry Tremayne. There was now also no doubt that it was her uncle who had planned that shooting, and had sent her to Mount Magnet to be out of the way while it was being done.

When she was finally shaken out of her uneasy reverie by the yells of two riders mustering a small mob of cattle, she realised she was some two miles at "sea" and due east of the balancing rock.

At any other time she would have delighted in joining those riders, but this afternoon she found no joy in living, no room for anything in her world which now seemed governed by vice and wickedness and horror.

What had they done with John Tremayne? Never would she forget his face, his burning hazel eyes, his strong white teeth and clean-cut features when he had told her he loved her as they sat in a single-seater car on a lonely hilly road in the Darling Range. He was as good-looking as his older brother, just as attractive, and yet she could not love John Tremayne. He had bravely accepted his defeat.

And how terrible for poor Mrs Tremayne away down in Perth, waiting, waiting every day and every hour for news of her boy; hoping, always hoping that he lived, continually fighting down the dread that she would never see him again.

Do, what could she do? One thing she would have to do was keep calm. Whatever else, she must not give her uncle reason to suspect where she had been that afternoon and with whom. He must not find out what she knew and suspected.

For a minute or so she contemplated running away to the Gatley-Tomkins's who would welcome her, or to Perth where she could be hidden. And then the mental picture of Harry Tremayne and Ned keeping watch on the island produced a resolve to remain and see it out to the bitter end. For that there would be an end, she felt sure.

No—she could not now leave Breakaway House. It would be too much like cowardice, or desertion. Harry had said: "Do nothing." And for the moment she wouldn't. She would go on as she had been, and wait and watch. She owed it to her uncle to remain loyal if he was innocent of any crime, but did she owe him loyalty if he was responsible for those crimes enumerated by Harry Tremayne? Surely not...surely not!

Before she realised it she found herself approaching the balancing rock, and, with a shudder, looked up at it perched like an egg on the very end of the promontory. Here and now she could so easily visualise Harry Tremayne, hope and joy in his heart at the prospect of seeing her, pulling back his horse to wave his hat in greeting, and then seeing the rifle flash which preceded the sudden darkness of oblivion.

Her heart was behaving strangely, and new and wonderful thoughts were flooding her brain. He loved her! Of course he loved her! Did not his every gesture, his every look proclaim it? It was as though he were with her then, telling her about it, his strong hands gripping hers. She felt the blood surging up her neck into her face. Her face grew hot, and she set boot heels to her horse and galloped him to the breakaway cliff south of the jetty. Only at the foot of a steeply rising cattle pad did she pull him up to make him carry her upwards between walls of granite forming a wide cleft in the lip of the breakaway.

On the open space between the breakaway lip and the line of mulga scrub, she turned her mount round to gaze over the sunlit plain of saltbush towards the Bowgada breakaway.

Well, what was the use of trying to hide it from herself? What use further to deny it? She loved that tall, lithe man who teasingly had asked her how was Perth, who had so coolly intervened when her uncle raged at her. Of course she loved him. Little fool! Else why had she kept that last dance open for him? Why did she thrill and thrill when near him? Why was she thrilling now–if she did not love Harry Tremayne?

Loyalty? Ah! Now she knew where loyalty was due. He loved her and she loved him. She would work for him and against the man who had planned his death, and who would again plan his death immediately he knew that his last attempt had failed.

Death! The thought of Harry Tremayne dead made her gasp. It fashioned her mouth into grimness and forced her rounded chin outward into an expression of the famous Tonger stubbornness. Patting her horse's neck, she whispered into his receptive ears: "Why, I don't feel afraid of Uncle any more."

With a glad cry, she swung him round, made him canter to the bordering scrub and hurried him through the thick grey broad-leafed mulga for several hundred yards before coming out on to an area of surface rock similar to that over which Mug Williams drove duffed cattle from Breakaway House into Bowgada country.

Across this area of granite passed the Breakaway House-Mount Magnet track, and, following the track homeward, Frances presently came to the turn where, at the bottom of a long straight grade, rested the group of buildings she had come to look upon as home.

Later she met Morris Tonger waiting dinner in the dining room. He was standing at the sideboard, whisky glass in hand. Dressed in well-fitting gabardine slacks and tweed coat, the whiteness of his soft linen collar providing startling relief against the dark-red tint of his skin, he appeared at ease in that plainly furnished room. Nodding to her, he refilled his glass from bottle and syphon, drank slowly, and then came to his place at the head of the table.

"Been out for a ride?" he said, in tones which made the question a statement of fact. "Which way did you go?" He spoke with such casual interest that for a moment she forgot the gold matchbox exhibited to her on the browned palm.

"I went down the valley," she replied. "Came home via the balancing rock and the Magnet track."

"See any sheep?"

"No, but I saw two of the men bringing in the killing beasts. Are they killing one tonight?"

"Yes. I'm expecting an important visitor tomorrow or the day after."

She felt rather than saw his gaze fixed upon her and refrained from looking up from her task of serving the vegetables.

For almost a minute they ate in silence, then: "You don't want to know who the visitor will be?" he inquired.

"Frankly, I'm not greatly interested," she replied coolly. "The only visitor I like to welcome is old Mr Wonkford. At least he can talk on subjects other than money, mining, sheep, cattle and the weather."

"Strange old bird," Tonger said, chuckling. "But he's got tons of money, and you could do worse than marry him. What do you think of Colonel Lawton?"

"To be frank again, I don't like him."

"No! Well, he's even richer than old Wonkford. And younger."

"Were I eighty years of age he would be too old for me," Frances said a little hotly. "I...I feel soiled when in his presence."

For a second or two her uncle regarded her with a queer expression on his face, a mixture of pride and determination. "He's the important visitor," he said slowly. "The last time he was here, when you were away, he asked if I would accept him as a nephew-in-law. I told him that I would; I'm telling you that I hope he never will be. If you like, I'll ring up Mrs Gatley-Tomkins and ask if she'll have you over to her place. You could go tomorrow."

"I'm not afraid of Colonel Lawton. If he proposes to me I shall refuse him."

Pride and determination became more pronounced in Morris Tonger's face. "When you get married, Frances, I want to see you married to a good man," he said with strange earnestness. "We Tonger men have been nothing to shout about, but the Tonger women were all good and pure. Even your aunt. She ran away with a shearer, but I drove her away. I don't blame her. I'm a pretty evil sort of beast now, but I'm not that bad that I would like to see you married to Colonel Lawton, or any man like him."

There were occasions when Morris Tonger was much less coarse than usual, and if ever there was an occasion when Frances could have given him affection, this was it. He was a paradox. A stranger paradox of a man she had never met. Violent in temper, yet courteous when not governed by temper. She had seen him embracing one of the maids. She had witnessed him knock a stockman flat to the ground. Outside with the men he swore vilely, but in her presence seldom spoke an ill word. He always drank too much, even for a man of his wonderful physique and outdoor life. He was an animal mastered only by her purity and his family pride was strangely at variance with his own acts.

"Well, you must excuse me," he said at the close of the meal. "I've some work to do in the shearing shed and then I have business letters to write."

Her uncle having gone, she passed into the drawing room and spent an hour softly playing the piano in the half-light afforded by the lamp in the hall. The evening was very quiet. She wished it would blow and rain more often, for these long periods of calm weather became monotonous. A further hour she devoted to her diary, seated at her own *escritoire*, pouring out in ink the meeting with Tremayne and their conversation almost in its exact words. This heavy, brass-locked book was and had been her only friend since coming to Breakaway House. At about ten o'clock she carefully relocked it, and locked it within the *escritoire* and then retired for the night.

She was wearied by her evening of solitude, and her nerves felt tortured by the eternal silence. She suspected that her uncle was drinking himself into a stupor in his office.

When in bed, even before switching off the light, she knew she would not sleep. With the light out, she again clearly saw the gold matchbox held out for her inspection on a brown palm. Vague imaginings consolidated into acute fears for the immediate future of the blue-eyed man who had laughed at her and then come to laugh with her.

Again switching on the light, she saw the time to be a quarter to twelve, and spent five minutes searching for an aspirin bottle before remembering that it was in a vase on the mantelpiece in the drawing room. And so it was that, after slipping into a dressing-gown, she walked along the thick-carpeted corridor to find the drawing-room door ajar and a light on within.

Without a sound she pushed the door open wide. Her uncle was seated at her *escritoire*, the desk-flap was down, and on it lay her diary wide open, the diary she was always so careful to leave locked within the locked *escritoire*. With his back not quite directly presented to her, she was able to observe him intently reading her most secret thoughts.

Of how long she stood there she retained no memory. At first, indignation controlled her, then dismay, then terror. Watching his face in profile, she clearly saw the upward turn of the mouth, the expression of cynical amusement alternating with one of calculating cruelty. And then within her surged a sudden fierce desire to run away and hide, to get away safely from this man who had suddenly become a monster.

Frances closed the door softly. It made no sound. But when she released the handle the lock clicked sharply, and that sound caused her to fly along the corridor to her room, shutting and locking the door behind her. Then her light was out and she was in bed, the clothes pulled up around her face.

So that was how they knew! She buried her face in the pillow. That was how they knew Harry Tremayne was to visit the balancing rock! Into that book she had entered all the little personal items of the dance, even Harry Tremayne's insistence that he would be at the balancing rock at three o'clock the following Wednesday afternoon. That was how they knew he would be there!

Her uncle had been regularly reading her diary. He possessed duplicate keys to her *escritoire* and her diary. So they lay in wait to shoot him like a kangaroo!

And instead of leaving the door open as she had found it, she had stupidly closed it and thereby informed her uncle that he had been observed.

CHAPTER XXIII

THE BUNYIP

THEY knew–they knew about Harry Tremayne! The diary had told them everything about Harry Tremayne!

These sentences ran through Frances Tonger's mind, over and over, again and again. Lying there on her bed in the dark, frozen into immobility by the knowledge that she had, albeit unwittingly, given over to her uncle and his associates Harry Tremayne and the innocent Ned, she lashed herself with the knout of self-condemnation.

So still did she lie, and so quietly, that she heard the handle of her door turn and the door being pushed against the lock. A superhuman effort prevailed to prevent the scream tearing from her throat; for, outside in the passage, was the man who had engineered those two attempts on Harry Tremayne's life, the man who now knew how the last attempt had failed, knew what Tremayne knew and suspected, knew where he had been all that day, and where he might be that night and tomorrow.

"Frances!"

Her name was spoken softly, and she might have made reply had not fear and horror paralysed her tongue. With that paralysis fortune favoured her. Morris Tonger spoke the name again, softly and with cunning, and she then knew why he did not shout it and demand admittance. Had she replied it would have proved to him her wakefulness and her knowledge of him, for he did not utter her name loud enough to waken the lightest sleeper. Not replying indicated to him that she slept; and indicated too, that it was not she who had spied upon him. He had pictured her–if it had been she who had shut the drawing-room door–waiting for him to come, her senses taut, keyed to tautness by the turning door handle and her spoken name.

When finally he went away, Frances knew he would be furiously wondering who it was who had seen him reading the diary, but now that he would be sure it had not been his niece, he would be less perturbed. For that would mean it must have been one of the maids, and a maid would see nothing significant in his action of reading the diary, unless, of course, it was a spy acting for Harry Tremayne.

Frances writhed on the bed, a corner of her pillow stuffed between her teeth, long after Tonger had departed, long after he had crept back to the door to listen for five minutes and again depart. She did not realise the passage of time until it occurred to her that actually a long time must have passed since he uttered her name. Now that her uncle knew of the two men camped on the island, he would at once scheme to get rid of them, understanding their dangerousness; especially Tremayne who knew so much and suspected more, and also held definite proof that he, Tonger, had been in the car when the great slab of rock had been blown out over the truck.

What monstrous thing was it that her uncle directed or was a part of? He now knew all she knew, all that Harry Tremayne had told her, which was all he knew and suspected. If this thing with which her uncle was connected had killed the policeman, Hamilton, and was thought to have killed John Tremayne, then it would now determinedly set out to kill Harry Tremayne who was far more dangerous to it than they had been.

There would, more than likely, be a hunt early the next morning. A man hunt! They would steal up to the island summit, probably before daylight, and shoot Harry and Ned, and hide their bodies in one of the thousand caves along the breakaway. They would get rid of them somehow, for the past had proved that murder was not a rare weapon.

Time! What was the time?

Her illuminated wrist watch told her it was six minutes after two o'clock. It was at the shortest two hours since she had heard her uncle outside the door. Her mind was beginning to function now that the need for action was becoming apparent. It was becoming unclotted by that gritty substance called fear, fear caused more by the shock of new-won knowledge regarding her uncle than by the actual calling of her name through a closed door.

How should she act? How could she act? Pertinent questions, these, which hammered away on the anvil of her mind. She came to see that the only manner in which she could repair the grievous damage she had done through her diary was to warn Harry Tremayne before her uncle gathered some of his men and struck.

Slipping out of bed, she began silently to dress, and got as far as working her skirt down over her shoulders before she gave thought to the style of clothing best suited to the expedition before her. Hastily discarding the skirt, she donned her riding kit and wisely chose thick-soled tennis shoes and putties in preference to the lovely officer's top-boots.

Fortunately she remembered the class of country over which she was to walk, most of it littered with loose stones and here and there surface bars of granite. Rubber-soled feet would negotiate this country much more quietly than heavy leather boots. And more for comfort and companionship, than with any idea of use, she took with her a small-bore plated revolver that her uncle had given her soon after her arrival from the southern city.

Inch by inch she raised the window to its full height, careful not to make the slightest noise. Inch by inch she thrust her body over the sill, and inch by inch she closed the window.

The moon long since having set, the night was dark though starry, and, standing beside the window, she spent a full minute listening. Then crossing the narrow strip of garden, she reached the gate which was open, slipped along the north side of the enclosing fence, rounded the corner and passed soundlessly along its east side until she reached the south-east corner from which she set off due south for the eastward thrusting headland.

Its steep, boulder-littered slope met the level ground about a quarter of a mile distant, but it was level ground gashed with water-gutters, not very deep but liable to give the unwary a nasty jolt. To avoid these, Frances was obliged to move circumspectly until she found herself walking up a gentle rise leading to the long low line of rock rubble skirting the headland. Looking up she saw that from meridian to western horizon, the sky was masked by a cloud bank thrusting eastward. That plus the north wind presaged rain.

Wisely, she walked straight towards the headland looming ever higher, and presently reached the line of rubble beyond which the slope rose steeply. Here, turning to the left, she skirted the rubble bank, her canvas-shod toes jabbing against stones which made her wish she had selected the officer's top-boots after all, although she knew that leather boots would have proved more difficult in the darkness.

It came upon her with the rushing speed of an express train, a horrible wailing shriek, and passed with the sound of mighty wings close above her head, but the shriek rose higher in sobbing notes, the shriek of an evilly tormented woman. Frances fell on her knees, her hands clapped to her ears, her eyes staring wildly about her. Every nerve in her body echoed every note of the awful cry. The pain in the sound of it ran down her limbs from her solidified brain.

Then she saw close to her a tree stump, a stump she had not noticed before the cry froze her blood. Was it a stump? Was it that awful something which had screamed so? She had read of the Bunyip in Aboriginal tales and legends, the formless monster which devoured those rash humans who wandered through the bush at night. Biting her nether lip in a bid to make physical pain banish her mental numbness, she straightened her legs, stood up, took her position, and walked on quickly.

She hoped that she would find Harry Tremayne very soon.

Queer little cold shivers flickered about her shoulder blades quicker than her heart was beating. She felt sure that someone was behind her, but when she turned, which was often, she could see nothing sinister dogging her footsteps, nothing but that dim void on her right, and the blacker void of the featureless headland on her left.

Forward again, with no thought of turning back, Frances at last reached the point of the headland, and from there tried to make out the position of the island. It was a mere five hundred yards away, but its smaller and lower bulk was invisible in the cloud-creating darkness which was now becoming more intense. Then that something was at her back again. She knew it. Every particle of her skin was pricking. Once more she swung round to look fearfully behind her.

Perhaps ten feet, or it might have been fifteen feet, she made out the motionless image of a tree trunk. It stood on the path which she had taken, and she knew she had not passed by a tree trunk during the last several hundred yards of her journey.

For many long seconds she stood frozen with dread, staring at the tree trunk stunted as though broken off by a gale of wind. It was as still and fixed as the bluff point of the headland towering above her. Of course, it was the remains of a once living tree and it was just her imagination, that feeling of something alive behind her, stalking her like the Bunyip; but…but she must make sure; she must be certain that it was a tree trunk before terror overcame her and compelled her to run and run, and probably hurt herself by colliding with a boulder or falling into a water-gutter.

With an impatient movement she drew from her breeches pocket the loaded revolver, resolved to use it were she attacked. Slowly at first, but with quickening steps, she walked resolutely towards the tree trunk, her eyes wide and staring in a terrific effort to pierce the gloom.

She began to imagine its outlines were shaped like those of a human being, yet continued to approach it, praying she might reach it before fear conquered her. Seven feet, now six feet, now five feet separated it from her. It was a man. Surely it was a standing man? Why, that dark putty-coloured blotch was a man's face! And those twin gleams were eyes! And the man said with steely softness: "Put up your hands–quick!"

Frances began to laugh and to sob. She swayed on her feet, extreme weakness mastering her knees. She swayed towards the "tree" and, with a sharp exclamation, Harry Tremayne caught her in his arms. Her arms slipped up round his neck and tightened. Again she began to laugh and to cry.

"Frances, it's all right Frances," he said soothingly. "But what are you doing out here? I saw you and followed you, but I didn't know it was you. I thought it was one of your uncle's scouts. Don't laugh like that, please, please."

With a mighty effort she controlled her hysteria and managed to say: "All right! All right! I'll not again! But hold me—hold me tight! Oh, I was so frightened."

CHAPTER XXIV

THE TREE TRUNK

"TIGHTER, please," Frances pleaded. "I want to laugh. Tighter! Stop me laughing!"

"Laughing! You're not laughing, you're crying," Tremayne said tenderly. Then he exclaimed exultantly, with amazement: "Why, Frances, Frances–you care for me."

"Of course I do," she whispered. "Do you think I would have ventured out here to warn you if I didn't? First Uncle. Then that dreadful scream. Then you standing behind me like a tree trunk. What was it screamed? Did you hear it?"

"It was a curlew, dear. It made me jumpy, too. But your uncle! Come, let's sit down for a little while. You're still trembling. Here's a handy rock. Sit so, close to me, my arm round you and your head against my shoulder."

The words began to fall from her lips like a cascade, traces of strain still in her voice. "It was I who told Uncle about your proposed visit to the balancing rock. I told him through my diary," Frances explained, going on to relate the sequence of events which had so shocked her nerves. When she had finished they sat in silence, she beginning to feel a strange state of peace, he going back over her story and experiencing grim satisfaction that his suspicions concerning Breakaway House were proving to be well grounded.

"Dash it!" he exclaimed, breaking the little silence. "I wish I could smoke. I can't think without smoking. Thank goodness it's going to rain. I felt a drop on my hand just then."

"Why do you want it to rain?" she asked.

"To wipe out your tracks. If, in the morning, your uncle should think to have the ground outside the house examined for tracks, or by chance your tracks are picked up–and that's a good chance, too, because they'll be hunting for my racks–he'll know of this, your early morning stroll, will see that it was taken to warn me, and will know that it was you who saw him reading the diary. Now tell me, if you can remember, when did they finish shearing?"

"I can tell you that because it was the day before I went to the Gatley-Tomkins's."

"That was August tenth. My brother arrived at Breakaway House on

August twelfth. So did Colonel Lawton. Can you remember when your uncle dispatched his wool to Mount Magnet?"

"Let me think."

"Would a kiss help you to think more clearly?"

"It might be worth trying."

For a moment time ceased to exist.

"Well, was it worth trying?"

"Y-yes, I think so," she replied breathlessly. "Um...They trucked some of the wool during the shearing. Then they trucked more after I had returned from the Gatley-Tomkins's. About a week after, I believe. None since then, although a lot of it is still in the shed. Uncle said he was holding it back for the December sales. Why are you asking questions about wool?"

"Early this morning your uncle and his boss stockman, Whitbread I believe his name to be, and Alec were opening the bales of wool in the shed," Tremayne said thoughtfully. "They were pulling out of each bale almost half its contents. I don't understand that."

"It does seem queer, Harry. How did you learn that?"

"I watched them for some time."

"You...you watched them?"

"Yes. At nine o'clock I was snooping round the house. I stayed for nearly half an hour outside the drawing-room window listening to you playing the piano. Ah! It's going to rain right enough. I must take you back."

Frances squeezed his arm. "I don't mind getting wet," she said softly.

"But I mind your getting wet. And I mind your tracks being seen and read tomorrow, which they will be if you make tracks when the ground is soft with water and the following rain is not hard enough to wipe them out."

Already on his feet, he pulled her up and took payment for the courtesy before slipping an arm round her waist. As lovers walk in Lovers' Lane, they set off for the house.

"What about your own tracks?" she asked.

"I don't leave tracks," he replied.

"But you must. You cannot help it."

"Nevertheless, I don't leave tracks. I wear, as you are unable to see, eagle skins over my feet with the feathers on the outside. My feet are then covered and protected with feathers, and my feathered feet leave no marks on the ground, break no twigs, turn no stones. But when the ground is wet, the mud clogs the feathers together into a kind of pug which leaves distinct impressions. Which is why Ned and I must be off

Breakaway House territory before it rains enough to make the ground sloppy. I sent Ned on to the well an hour ago. I was following when I saw you and became a tree trunk."

"The rain's going to set in," Frances said a little later.

"It is. Look, I can see the house, dark as it is. Now, no more talking after this. I'll get Brett Filson to ring up tomorrow, and make arrangements for you to come over on Sunday. We might even invite your uncle as well, although I hope he won't come."

"He won't. He's expecting Colonel Lawton tomorrow."

"Is he?"

For a space Tremayne was silent. Then he said rapidly: "In that case, you might expect me tomorrow. Anyway, we'll see each other on Sunday. I'll work that all right. Now, no more talking. Just a farewell kiss."

They were standing with their faces pressed cheek to cheek when he murmured: "Keep still. Be a tree trunk. Remember that you are a tree trunk. Don't speak."

She felt his body stiffen and become taut. Her heart began to pound. She wanted to ask what was happening, what was going to happen. She could see nothing for the world was shrouded in darkness.

Tremayne heard the soft, padding footsteps six seconds after he heard the low but sharp click of one stone meeting another. And then he saw looming out of the darkness a strange shape which resolved itself into five separate shapes–five men walking in single file.

Then Frances heard them. They were somewhere behind her. It occurred to her then that her lover had been turned into a tree trunk by the Bunyip, so motionless and rigid was he. She strained to control her trembling, fearing that her shaking would betray them.

Then she saw the five figures passing within twenty feet of them, indistinct shapes which glided silently over the ground, four men led by a fifth who walked with the sureness of one heading for a predetermined destination.

Tremayne lifted her off her feet, and slowly he swung her round, pivoting on his feet, so that he might follow those men with his eyes. Together they watched them pass from sight, and for yet another minute he held her before releasing her and chuckling.

"There go the happy huntsmen," he said. "I swear it was your uncle in the lead. They're due for a nice wet march–and so are we, if we don't hurry."

Pressing his arm against her side, she sighed, saying: "I'm so glad I came. They might have surprised you."

"They would not have done so. But you did."

"How?"

"We might have gone for weeks before we found each other had not you mistaken me for a tree trunk."

They walked for a further hundred yards before he spoke again in low tones. "How did you leave the house? By the window, I think you said."

"Yes. I climbed out through the window. I shut it after me."

"Well, go back that way. Go in as quietly as you came out. That may not have been your uncle leading those men, and therefore you mustn't take chances."

"I won't. I wouldn't dare."

"I'll probably see you tomorrow," he whispered. "There's the house. You can't miss it. *Au revoir*, sweetheart! And don't worry about anything. Remember to be sure to write me at once if and when they send you away again."

Embracing, they parted, the girl to hurry to the house fence, the man to stand and watch her figure dim and blur in the darkness until it vanished in the deeper shadow of the house itself. He waited a further five minutes, listening, and then having heard nothing, not even the bark of a dog, he set off on his ten-mile tramp to Bowgada.

WHEN Brett Filson entered his living room for breakfast, he found Tremayne lounging beside the table sipping coffee and smoking a cigarette. The younger man was arrayed in dry clothes. He was shaved and he was smiling, although beneath his eyes were the dark marks of lack of sleep.

"What time did you get back? I didn't hear you," Brett said.

"About an hour ago," Tremayne replied airily. "I've had my brek. I couldn't wait. Say, do you know what firm sells Tonger's wool?"

Filson's eyebrows rose just a fraction. "I understand that Morris Tonger ships his clip to a Bradford buyer direct," he replied slowly. "Why?"

"Sends it to England, does he?"

"Yes. He's done so for years."

Filson regarded his "overseer" sharply before helping himself to porridge but Tremayne offered no comment. He seemed sunk in a reverie. Eventually Brett asked again: "Why are you interested in Tonger's wool?"

Again instead of answering this question, Tremayne asked another. "Did you ring up Miss Sayers about Sunday?"

"I did. Yesterday morning. Miss Winters and she will be glad to come.

They'll be ready to leave about three o'clock."

"Good!"

The squatter found himself regarded by twinkling eyes. "I said, if you remember, ring her up today, Saturday," Tremayne murmured. "Why the hurry?"

Filson's gaze abruptly dropped to his plate in an effort to conceal sudden confusion. Tremayne went on, or rather off, at another tangent.

"I'm not looking for any pats on the back, Brett," he said calmly, "but would you tell me if you like me, or are just indifferent, please."

"Well, whatever next!" Filson exclaimed. "I like you well enough. Why do you ask?"

Tremayne was perfectly serious when he said: "I was thinking of a double wedding, that's all."

"You are, I think, being a little abstruse this morning, Harry. First it's Tonger's wool, now it's a double wedding. 'Please explain', as the nasty taxation people are fond of saying."

Tremayne leaned forward across the table to look straight into the other's hazel eyes. "As a matter of fact," he said distinctly, "Frances and I are going to be married directly I have cleared up this Breakaway House matter, and I thought it would be a good idea if you and Miss Sayers were married with us—making it a double event, so to speak."

With deliberateness, Brett Filson put down his knife and fork, leaned back in his chair, and stared hard ahead of him, a flush mounting into his weather-tanned face.

"You don't offer me congratulations," Tremayne complained. "Are you sorry that I'm to be married?"

"Not a bit," Brett replied bitingly. "I am, however, sorry that you're so damned impertinent."

For the next five minutes neither spoke. Filson declined to look at his companion.

Then with unusual earnestness Tremayne said: "Just between pals, Brett, what's against that double wedding? I know it's no cursed business of mine, but what is against it?"

Filson turned his eyes to glare at this young man who would not take a snub. Abruptly he stood up to pass round the table and stand squarely before Tremayne. Bending his head downward he placed an index finger against his almost white hair. "This," he said. "I'm not yet forty." Pulling up the left trouser leg, he revealed an artificial leg. "And this," he said softly. Rapidly he removed his coat and waistcoat. Tremayne saw the padded harness which supported his body. "And this," Filson said, with almost a sob in his voice.

"Doesn't she know?" Tremayne asked quietly.

The young-old squatter nodded and began to replace waistcoat and coat.

"Did she know before the ball?" Tremayne pressed.

"She did," Filson replied shortly. "Don't let's talk about it any more."

"Then you can take my word for it that the harness and the leg and the colour of your hair do not make the slightest difference to Ann Sayers. That's no excuse for the double wedding not to take place. Tell me–do you love Ann Sayers?"

"You seem to have guessed it," Filson said bitterly.

When Tremayne spoke again it was very cheerfully. "That being so, Brett, old man, it's about time I made you understand that denying yourself you are denying Ann Sayers, my very good friend. Hurting yourself, you are hurting my very dear friend too. And it hurts me confoundedly to see you both unhappy. Whether you like it or not, there's going to be a double wedding, and be damned to you."

CHAPTER XXV

COLONEL LAWTON ARRIVES

AS usual on Saturday mornings, Frances entered the dining room at half past nine, having been summoned by the gong struck in the hall. The sun was shining from a clear sky, and the mild rain-freshened air entering through the French windows was laden with bush scents. The maid who brought the breakfast foods on a tray was the girl who had conveyed her mistress's note to Tremayne.

"Good morning, May! Mr Tonger not yet up?"

"Good morning, Miss Frances! Yes. Mr Tonger went out very early this morning and he hasn't returned," answered the girl, whose complexion was dusky and features pleasant.

"Oh! Do you know where he went?"

"Not exactly, but Cook says she heard from one of the men that Mr Tonger, Mr Whitbread and Alec went off to track some cattle duffers."

"Cattle duffers?"

"Yes, Miss Frances. Mr Tonger was heard to say that if they caught them, and they would not surrender, he was going to shoot them."

Frances strolled to the window, her brows drawn together by a frown. She drew back the billowing curtains, experiencing a slight sense of relief engendered by the knowledge that she had found one "cattle duffer", or he had found her, and that he knew his danger. Thank God he was well away from Breakaway House! That he had left her to go back to Bowgada. Carelessly she peeped outside before turning back to the maid standing by the table. The girl noted her mistress's peculiarly direct gaze.

"Close the door, please," Frances instructed. "With both the windows and the door open, the draught is a little too strong."

Having obeyed, the girl found her mistress still regarding her steadily.

"Come here, May," Frances said quietly.

Her expression one of puzzlement, the girl came to stand squarely before Frances, who said: "How much did it rain last night?"

"They say there are eleven points in the glass. No one has taken it out because Mr Tonger does that when he enters the amount on the weather chart. Why do you look at me like that, Miss Frances?"

"I'm wondering, May, if I can trust you," Frances said softly.

"Why, of course! Have you not always been kind to me?"

The vivacious round face indicated earnestness; the dark eyes, bordered by long silken black eyelashes, were wide. Altogether a frank face revealing a thinking mind. Her mother lived with her tribe in the vicinity of Meekatharra; her father was a prospector who admitted and had fulfilled his obligations. After her rearing in a mission, May had gone to live with him in his shack outside Mount Magnet before coming to work at Breakaway House.

When Frances put her next question, she flushed a little. "Are you going with any of the men here?"

"No, miss. I'm a good girl. I only stay here because you are mistress. I have a sweetheart. He works on Kyle station," the maid said with pride.

On impulse, Frances took both May's hands in hers. "I'm glad to hear you say that, May," she said. "I've always liked you, and I've always thought you to be a good girl. Would you like to be my friend? You see, I have no one here with whom I can be friends."

"Oh, miss! I would like that. I would do anything for you," the young woman cried in a trembling voice.

"Very well. You shall be my friend. That will be one secret between us. Can you keep secrets?"

"Yes. Try me."

"I will. I'll tell you another secret. You remember the gentleman who called the other day when I was away at Mount Magnet–Mr Tremayne? He and I are going to be married some day. That's our secret number two. Now listen. Mr Tonger hates Mr Tremayne and I want you to come and tell me if you hear at any time plans being made to hurt him. Will you do that for me?"

The girl's eyes gleamed. Between her red lips pearly teeth flashed. Nodding, she said: "You can depend on me, miss. I'll learn things."

"Very well, May. You can go now. Remember our two secrets. We are both lonely here, but we won't be lonely any more, will we?"

"No. I shall be happy here now. There have been times when I was sad. The others are cold to me, and all the men want to flirt. I tell them that if they annoy me my father will come and shoot them all. He would too. He said he would. He said he wasn't going to have his daughter taken cheaply."

"May that never happen," Frances said fervently. "Why, that's the telephone! I must answer it. Get me the office key please."

With an unusually buoyant heart, Frances left the house and crossed the open space to the office. The homestead was very quiet that morning, wearing its unmistakable Saturday aspect which, even here in the heart of the bush, was not to be denied. Beside the men's quarters, two stockmen were washing clothes. The huge fat cook was seated on the doorstep of his kitchen reading a newspaper, his breakfast work accomplished and his dinner prepared.

The office occupied one end of a long weather-boarded building devoted to store-room, and paint and saddlery shops. The office room was spacious and furnished with several easy chairs, an American roll-top desk, a writing table, shelves of books, a safe, and many pictures of racehorses and stud sheep on the walls. At the head of a stretcher bed set against one wall was a lowboy in which Frances rightly guessed her uncle kept his narcotics, for set out on top were a glass jug and several glasses.

Lifting off the telephone receiver and giving her name, she heard Brett Filson's voice. "How are you this morning, Miss Frances?"

"Quite well, thank you, Mr Filson. How are you?"

"Very chirpy. That was a nice rain we had last night. It'll freshen up the herbage and wipe out old stock tracks, making the men's work easier. Is your uncle at home?"

"No. He's away. He went out early."

"Did you hear where he went?"

"I'm not certain, but I understand he thought some cattle duffers were at work, and he's gone out to try and track them."

"That sounds serious," Brett said, laughing.

"Yes, doesn't it?"

"I rang up for two reasons," Brett stated. "Firstly, to congratulate you."

"Thank you!"

"I wish you every joy, Miss Frances. You picked a good man. My second reason was to ask if you could come over tomorrow afternoon early and stay the evening. Miss Sayers and Miss Winters are coming out for the day, and we want to make it a jolly party. Could you manage it?"

"Yes, I think so. I don't think Uncle would raise any objection."

"You might ask him to come with you."

"He's expecting Colonel Lawton. I don't think he would be able to come."

"Be sure to ask him, nevertheless. Our mutual friend is fast asleep, so you'll have to excuse him. Goodbye then, until tomorrow. If you can't borrow your uncle's car, ring me up and I'll come and get you myself."

"Until tomorrow then. Goodbye, and thank you!" Still smiling, tempted to sing, and her heart light with happiness, Frances locked the office and sauntered back to the house and her much-delayed breakfast. Even with Mr Filson, the coming of Harry Tremayne had made a world of difference. Before the ball she had hardly known the Bowgada squatter, he had seemed so coldly aloof, so resigned.

She was still at table when her uncle came in to go at once to the sideboard and silently mix himself a whisky and soda. He did not speak, even when he sat down opposite her.

"Good morning, Uncle," she said brightly, declining to be subdued by his black mood.

"Morning," he replied boorishly, then snapped at May when she placed a cover before him: "What this? I hope the confounded food is hot. I hate cold grease."

Frances thought it strange that she no longer felt afraid of him; strange because now she knew him for what he was. Bowgada seemed much nearer than it had before; it had become a haven into which she could slip for safety.

"Mr Filson just rang up," she said, ignoring Tonger's ugly mood. "He's invited me to spend tomorrow afternoon and evening at Bowgada. They're having a party. Miss Sayers and Miss Winters are coming out from Myme."

Tonger's face cleared with astonishing rapidity. He sat more upright in his chair and the dull angry look in his dark eyes vanished.

"That's kind of Filson," he said. "I hope you accepted his invitation. It'll be a change for you; you don't get out much. You can drive yourself over in the car because I'll not want it."

"Thank you, Uncle. Mr Filson thought you might like to go, too. His invitation is extended to you."

"I'm afraid I couldn't. Lawton will be here this afternoon, and he's sure to stay two or three days. But you go by all means and have a good time. Perhaps Filson will ask you and his friends to stay over till Monday. If he does, accept. The less Lawton sees of you the better. In fact I wish you were away from now until he's gone. He's all right as a friend, but I don't want to see any Tonger woman married to him."

"Don't worry, Uncle," she said cheerfully. "I'll not fall in love with the man. And remember, I can manage him."

He gave her one of his rare smiles.

"Well, you can manage me, and that's something of which to be proud," he told her. "It's time we went on a long holiday. I haven't had a real holiday for seven years. What do you say to we two clearing off to Europe rather than just New Zealand when I've got the last of the wool away? We've been living well within our income, and I've made money in spite of the depression. I feel like splashing some of it."

"It would be lovely," she agreed, successfully infusing enthusiasm into her voice.

"That's what we'll do then, directly I've got the wool away. Is the spare room ready for the Colonel?"

"I think so. I've not made a final inspection. Will he be here for lunch?"

"No, not before two o'clock, and it might not be until six."

They fell to discussing the menu for dinner that evening and when Morris Tonger rose to leave, saying he had to make sure that the wind kites were working properly to assist the Colonel in landing, his mood continued to be cheerful.

He was full of the projected holiday trip to Europe when they met at lunch, and again expressed pleasure that she had accepted Filson's invitation. Casually he suggested that she should make no mention of the tentatively planned holiday to Colonel Lawton.

She was softly playing on the piano and singing an old Italian love song when the note of an aeroplane engine sent her quickly out to the veranda, where almost instantly she saw the twin-engine bi-plane speeding down from the north, its silver-painted wings and fuselage shimmering in the upper light.

From three thousand feet it dived steeply for the homestead and with a whistling scream arrived over the shearing shed, its engines breaking into a full-throated roar. Then the machine flashed by overhead, but she saw the arm thrust over the side and the waving handkerchief held in the gloved fist.

Up and up it zoomed, circling westward and northward before returning to alight beneath its master's hands on the open ground east of the homestead. Like a waddling cockatoo it taxied right to the shearing shed wall where Tonger and his men were waiting.

From behind the window curtain, Frances saw the bulky figure of the airman clamber out of the machine, shake hands with her uncle, and give orders to Whitbread whilst he removed his kit. Together, he and the Breakaway House squatter walked across to the office talking earnestly.

An hour later as she was trying hard to concentrate on a book, the afternoon tea set out on an occasional table, the door was thrown open, and she rose to meet Colonel Lawton whose exploits had rung round the world in 1918. Her uncle followed the airman.

"Hallo, Miss Frances!" he said in greeting, his voice strangely soft and weak for so big a man. "I declare you grow more beautiful every time I see you. You remind me of a flower shut down in a coal-cellar."

"I'm a thirsty flower, Colonel. I've been waiting to give you afternoon tea. Has your trip been good?"

CHAPTER XXVI

THE TEA PARTY

IT was with a decided feeling of relief that Frances drove away from Breakaway House across the wide expanse of saltbush flats on her way to Bowgada. Never a place of light and happiness, the coming of Colonel Lawton seemed to cast an even deeper shadow over the homestead.

To be sure, he was a charming man in some respects. He talked well and had the knack of drawing vivid word pictures taken at random from a vast album of personal experiences. She would never forget the story of fighting a typhoon over the raging Timor Sea, a story in which the machine was the hero, not the puny man who controlled it. Seldom was the masculine "Great I am" so skilfully submerged.

It was the expression on the Colonel's scarred and battered face–the result of several crashes–which repulsed her; not the broken nose and the red wrinkled skin bridging his left temple which drew the adjacent eyelid upward to make that eye look markedly oriental. Physically, the man was a perfect specimen, almost as big as her uncle but harder, cleaner of flesh and clearer of eye. He did not smoke, and he drank nothing but water.

Perhaps it was the extraordinary control he exercised over his facial muscles and his command over his emotions which disturbed her. When he smiled, which was seldom, she knew that it was mechanical and that there was no laughter in his heart.

"Well, goodbye," he had said lightly but unsmilingly as he stood beside the car. "You're fortunate to be able to enjoy a game of bridge. Cards bore me frightfully. If you're not home by midnight, I shall come after you on one of the station trucks."

It was then that his mouth expressed humour, but in his eyes she sensed stern determination to do what he had said. He had not uttered a word which even remotely referred to his proposal of marriage made to her the evening before. A proposal to which she had of course said no, but he gave her the impression that her rejection of him would be merely temporary; that to fail in his suit simply did not occur to him.

And strangest of all was the peculiar fading into the background of her uncle. Immediately Colonel Lawton arrived, the personality of Morris Tonger waned, became as colourless and as uninfluential as that of one of his stockmen. He seemed to take on the characteristics of one who was merely a deputy to a far more important person than himself.

It was a strange day; one of those days when a high-level haze neutralises the sunshine; but with distance rapidly lengthening between herself and Breakaway House, her mood continued to lighten until by the time she reached the boundary gate she was singing. She had opened the gate and was driving the machine slowly through, intending to close it after her, when Fred Ellis's shout caught her attention.

"Don't trouble about the gate, miss. I'll close it. Look at them smoke signals, they're at it again," he yelled from the doorway of his hut.

Slowly she drove the car forward and finally stopped it in front of the stockman's abode.

Ellis hurried to the car and leant nonchalantly against the front door. "Gonna rain, Miss Tonger," he said casually and yet not familiarly, his blue eyes beaming and draggled moustache quivering.

"I hope it doesn't until tomorrow. You're Fred Ellis, aren't you? Have you got over that nasty blow you received the night of the ball?"

"Too right, miss. It was Matthews who downed me. I'll be waiting, calm like, for him to come this way again–silly fools, 'im and Buck Ross, to think Mr Tremayne would be getting away with a black woman. Look at them signals, they've been going strong all day."

"What do they mean, do you know?"

"No, they beats me. Them blacks are cunning chaps. Ask them anythink and they only laughs for an answer."

It was the first time Frances had spoken to Fred Ellis, although she had seen him on several occasions. Simple and open, she found that she liked him, and remained talking to him for several minutes. She noted how five large cats rubbed themselves against his legs and purred.

"Do you read much?" she asked presently.

"Yes miss, anythink I can get 'old of. Reading a book now by a bloke called Charles Lamb. Sooner read somethink with blood in it. That there Nora pinched all me books when Ned and 'er went south."

"I'll send you over some books one day. Now I must be going along. Anything you want brought back from Bowgada tonight?"

"No miss, thank you. If I hear you coming I'll slip along and open the gate for you."

"Thank you. Goodbye."

Her last impression of him was of a tall figure crouched to gather into his arms several of the cats which might have got beneath the wheels.

As she was driving up the steep grade to the summit of the eastern breakaway, she thought of the recent attempt made there to kill Harry Tremayne. She slowly passed and noted the place from which the rock slab had been blown out over the track. The newly exposed rock bed was easily discernible, and she shuddered when she saw how the horse had been knocked off the roadway to drop thirty feet to the steep slope below. She was still thinking of that, her heart smouldering with rage, when she brought the car to a stop outside the Bowgada homestead. Brett Filson hurried out to meet her and, standing in the door-frame, she could see a large matronly woman.

"It's very good of you to drive over, Miss Tonger. Especially when you have a guest," Brett said, smiling cheerfully. "Miss Sayers and Miss Winters should be here at any moment."

"It was kind of you to ask me, Mr Filson," she told him, her face flushed and her eyes sparkling. "I do get bored at Breakaway House, and Colonel Lawton seems to have such a lot to say to Uncle. They are very old friends, you know."

"So I understand. Well, come on in. Here's Millie waiting to receive you. She's my housekeeper, and what I should do without her I don't know."

Side by side they walked the short pathway to the house, she exclaiming over Jackson's vegetables which in those parts are far more important than flowers, and he lifted out of himself by this unusual excitement of receiving guests at Bowgada. Before the coming of Harry Tremayne he had seldom had visitors.

The smiling Millie, neatly dressed and a fitting mate for the honest boss stockman, took charge of her so completely that she experienced an unknown type of happiness, unknown because there was no one to welcome her to Breakaway House like this. The Bowgada homestead itself welcomed her. It was so solid-looking, so peaceful and clean and light. The room to which Millie conducted her was evidently a guest room, and yet there were bush flowers arranged tastefully in vases.

She found Brett Filson waiting for her in the living room, a room which breathed masculinity. The writing desk, the pictures of horses and sheep, the rack of pipes, and the tin of tobacco and rice papers on the high mantel over the great open fireplace all portrayed this man's character.

"I do like your house, Mr Filson," she told him with charming directness.

"Do you? It's not quite so ship-shape as it was when my mother was alive. Still, it's kept comfortable and clean by Millie. Would you like tea now, or shall we wait for the others?"

"Oh, we'll wait if you don't mind. They shouldn't be long. Mr Tremayne will not linger on the road."

"Not like he did when he drove you back to Breakaway House the night of the ball?" Brett queried teasingly.

"Did he…did he tell you that he didn't go over five miles an hour?"

Looking down into the bright eyes and observing the flushed face, Brett replied in the affirmative. "I warned him that people who began by being antagonistic towards each other end by falling in love," he told her lightly. "I'm glad you two have fallen in love. I like Harry Tremayne. Life here has been much brighter since he came. And through him I'm getting to know and to like you."

"You're very kind, Mr Filson. You cannot imagine how nice all this is. It seems such a different world to me. Listen, I can hear a car coming."

"That will be English with the Myme ladies. Shall we go out to meet them?"

"By all means. But…but didn't Harry go in for them?"

Brett's face gained a degree of gravity. "No," he replied. "English went. Harry's not yet back."

"Not back! Where did he go?"

"That I don't know. He went away early last evening, and said he would be back this afternoon. He should be here at any minute." Again Brett smiled when he added: "He knew you would be coming over."

Feeling just a little perturbed, Frances accompanied her host to the front door and along the garden path to the gate before which the Bowgada car came to a stop. Brett welcomed the passengers and assisted them to alight, and Frances observed how Ann Sayers' eyes shone when she looked at the squatter. Then she was regarding the ample figure of Violet Winters enshrouded in sea-green chiffon. When her gaze returned to Ann Sayers she was pleased to note that her impression gained in the artificial light of the ballroom was well sustained in brilliant sunshine. She was rather nice, this girl from Myme, and of course madly in love with Mr Filson. And equally, it would appear, he with her.

All talking together, the ladies were taken away by Millie to the guest room, and later they found Brett Filson waiting in the living room beside the table on which Soddy Jackson was setting out afternoon tea.

"How did you get that confectionery from Perth, Mr Filson?" Frances asked.

"It didn't come from Perth. It came from the Bowgada kitchen," Brett explained. "Jackson here does all that."

"Did you make those cream puffs? And those lamingtons, Mr Jackson?"

"Yes, miss," the cook assented, his face reddening with pleasure, taken off his guard and forgetting that he was being addressed by one of the hated capitalists. "Old Mrs Filson showed me how to turn out do-dahs for afternoon tea. She was a cook, if you like."

"I shall come again," Violet Winters announced decisively. "That is if you ask me, Mr Filson. Those lamingtons make me want to be greedy."

"There's plenty more," Jackson said with slight disapproval in his voice, then withdrawing to bring in the teapot.

When he finally closed the door, Violet said: "I'd like to marry a man like that. I could put up with his undertaker's face as long as he made me lamingtons like those. Lamingtons I never can resist."

"Good! Will you pour out the tea?"

"I'd like Miss Sayers to. I'd like to be waited on for once."

"So you shall be. Miss Sayers, please serve us with tea."

Having voted Ann Sayers to the position of tea-pourer, the afternoon tea party proceeded with much gaiety, although Violet Winters, who wanted to know when Harry Tremayne was expected, appeared slightly put out by his absence.

Jackson again entered, this time to remove the tea things, and still Harry Tremayne had not come.

Ann and Frances gravitated to the gramophone, leaving Violet talking with Brett who was lounging on the window seat. The windows were open, and the thickening haze had at long last blotted out the sun.

Presently Violet abruptly broke off relating local scandal to ask pertinently: "Where did Mr Tremayne go?"

"I don't really know," replied Brett.

"When did he go?"

Her red face became suddenly stern and into her small eyes crept a hard glint.

"When did he go?" she repeated.

"Last evening. He said he would return at noon today."

For a space she glared at her host as though he had offended her.

"I've found out things about him," she said grimly. "He's a policeman. He's after those gold-stealers whom my brother was mixed up with. It was policemen shot Tom dead, but..." The sternness faded from the rugged face. Her features relaxed and appeared to fall into a different shape. "I hate policemen, but I can't hate Mr Tremayne. He's so different from other men. He's just a rampageous boy. He says to me with his eyes all bright and his mouth widened into a grin, he says: 'If I give you a nice cold bottle of beer, will you give me a nice hot cup of tea?' What could I say, Mr Filson? I don't care if he is a policeman. I can't hate him, I can't. But he's got to look out. They'll get him..." Beyond the windows came drifting the sound of quick drumming hoofs. "That'll be him, likely enough," she said with evident relief.

The horseman was riding from the direction of the Bowgada outstation situated due east of the homestead, and not along the north-east Myme track. They saw him emerge from the mulga beyond the sheep yards and watched the dust rise from the pounding hoofs, a pregnant silence having fallen between them. Brett wondered just how much this big woman knew of the gold-stealers, and remembered what Tremayne had said about her based on the information gained from Mug Williams.

A few seconds later, Violet Winters exclaimed: "Why that's not him! That's Mug Williams!"

CHAPTER XXVII

HURRIED ARRIVALS

THE gramophone music stopped. In the ensuing silence those in the Bowgada living room heard the pounding hoofs rise in crescendo, reaching finality in rapid tattoo when the animal was pulled sharply back at the stockyards.

"Is that Mr Tremayne?" asked Frances quickly.

"No, Miss Tonger," replied Brett without looking at her.

She and Ann Sayers came to stand behind him, and they watched Mug Williams leap from his saddle, shut the horse in the yard, and come hurrying to the house. In the room no one spoke, for this haste on the part of Williams appeared to be pregnant with possibilities.

From the door of their hut Ned and Nora called a greeting to the little butcher, but he neither slackened his gait nor answered them.

"If you'll excuse me!" Brett said, rising.

"If he's come about Mr Tremayne, you will let us know?" said Violet a little sharply.

The squatter nodded: "Yes," he assented. "Yes, I will let you know at once. I have an idea that you may be of assistance to Harry Tremayne, and, in a way, to me."

He met Mug Williams at the kitchen door, observing the little man's dust-laden clothes, his unshaven chin, and his grey eyes lit by the current of excitement. Their sudden meeting relaxed the strain so clearly depicted on his weathered face.

"Glad I found you at home, Mr Filson. I want to see Mr Tremayne at once."

"Mr Tremayne isn't in, Williams."

"Not in! Then where is he? I must talk to him at once."

"Out on the run somewhere," Brett informed him. "I'm expecting him back at any moment."

"Oh!" Clearly Mug Williams was nonplussed. Then he said desperately: "Well, I must talk to you. In private—in your office room."

"I have visitors. We'll go over to the stockyards."

Together they reached the well-built yards where Brett turned to the little man to ask quietly: "Well, what's the matter?"

"They're after me—that crowd who put Hamilton away, and, likely enough, a young feller named Robbins. That wasn't his name. He's Mr

150

Tremayne's brother. Do you know about that, Mr Filson?"

Brett nodded. "I believe I know just as much as Mr Tremayne knows. Why are 'they' after you? Who are 'they'? Better explain everything. You seem to be upset."

"Betcher life I'm upset. They must have learned what I told Mr Tremayne—and he swore he'd never say a word. It's them gold-stealers. They're after me. You see, it was like this: My brother, he's a good and bad bloke by turns. For weeks he sings hymns and goes to church; then suddenly he breaks out on a bender. He's been on a bender since last Thursday, and last night he camps on the doorstep of the pub waiting for old Sayers to open up this morning. About two o'clock two men meets at the kerb right opposite where he's lying, and one of 'em is Buck Ross and the other is a feller called Jake Matthews. It's so dark they don't see him lying down in the doorway, but even though they talks quiet like, my brother hears what they said, and what they said sobered him up quicker than a week in the jug.

"One says: 'We got to fix Mug Williams. He knows a little and guesses more, and talks more than that.' That was Buck Ross. Then he said: 'We got to catch Mug in the bush when he's out on his next night ride. He's to be taken to the plant and kept there to work with the other bloke. It's you and me for that job, Jake.'

"'Wot about that Tremayne feller?' asks Jake Matthews.

"'I'm not worrying about him for the present,' says Buck. 'It's Mug who's our meat. We've got to put him in the safe; we've got to keep an eye on him from first thing in the morning. You come along to my place early and we'll map out a plan of action.'"

When Williams paused in his recital, Brett asked: "Where's the plant they spoke about?"

"I don't rightly know."

"You'd better come clean if you want me to help you," warned Brett.

"I tell you I don't know," reiterated Williams seriously. "I reckon it's somewhere about that balancing rock over on Tonger's breakaway, but I ain't sure."

"All right. Go on. What did you do—or rather, why are you here?"

"Well, when they two cleared off, my brother gave up the idea of waiting on the doorstep until the pub opened, and he comes out to our slaughter yards where I was camped. And me—knowing what kind of push Buck Ross leads—I sees that I'd best clear out of Myme. If I don't go on a night ride, they'll think up some way of getting me in Myme.

"So I wraps the moke's hoofs in bags, and rode north and then east round Myme till I reached the Pinnacles, which, as you know, are humps along a five-mile bar of granite. I hid up among 'em until close on two o'clock today, and then, when I felt a bit sure I hadn't been tracked there, I come on here via Tilcha. I got away all right, but I must lay up somewheres till I can think out a plan on me own. You see I never did nothink to them but now they're going to put the hoots into me. I wants to join Mr Tremayne. I've got to join 'im, or fight 'em on me own, 'cos if I don't they'll get me, and there'll be no peace for me to carry on me legitimate business of butchering."

"And cattle duffing."

"Oh, that's only a side line."

"It would be a most important line if you were ever caught, Williams. So you would join Mr Tremayne in hunting down these people?"

"There ain't nothink else for me to do, Mr Filson. I'm not gonna run away from the district–sacrifice my business."

"Hum! It's possible that you're over-estimating your danger," Brett said slowly. "On the other hand, you may be underestimating it. You'd better stay here until Mr Tremayne returns. It will be for him to decide. Look! Here comes someone else in a hurry. You loose your horse, and go along to Jackson for a feed. Do you know that Aborigine?"

Mug Williams was too agitated to be anything but careless in his reply. "No," he said. "Stranger to me."

"I think it's Ned's brother, Wombera," was Brett's opinion. "Not on a casual visit, either. Well, you go in for a cup of tea."

Leaving Williams to hasten to the kitchen, Brett Filson hobbled across to the hut where the Aborigine was eagerly talking to Ned and Nora. The visitor had rushed straight over to Ned and Nora without waiting for an invitation to approach, and that was unusual.

"What's the trouble, Ned?" the squatter asked, seeing that trouble certainly lay behind the visit.

"N'gobi come back, Mr Filson. N'gobi coming here for Nora."

"I'm not going with N'gobi," Nora exclaimed fiercely. "N'gobi's no good. He beat me. He kill people. He's bringing his relations with him to take me and beat Ned; perhaps point the bone at him."

"I'll not have any fighting on Bowgada, do you understand?" Seeing the varnish of fear painted on the features of Ned and Nora, Brett's severity waned. "Where's N'gobi now? Are you Wombera?"

The stranger nodded. "N'gobi, he get here tonight. He say he kill Ned, he take Nora. Nora belonga him. She right to go back with him. Much trouble if Nora not go alonga him."

Wombera spoke with less facility than Ned and much less than Nora. He was dressed in tattered dungaree trousers and a brown shirt, and he was without hat and boots. He was emphatically in favour of Nora going back to her rightful husband so as to avert a quarrel between the two tribes, a quarrel which would otherwise be certain to result from this domestic irregularity.

Brett considered ringing the police station at Myme; for, after all, N'gobi was a gaol breaker and should be arrested and returned to gaol. In fact he had been asked to report any information concerning N'gobi's whereabouts. Brett wished with increased fervour that Tremayne was home or that he would quickly put in an appearance, for he was unsure what Tremayne would want him to do.

"Ned, you and Nora will stay here," he commanded. "I'll decide what to do with Nora later on. I might arrange for her and Millie to sleep inside the homestead, and for you, Ned, to camp with English. If you believe in the pointing bone you're a fool. You just stay quiet and do what I tell you. Get some tucker from Soddy for Wombera."

"I'll not go away with N'gobi," Nora burst out passionately. "He beat me. He's a bad man. I'll not go. Ned's my man."

Brett smiled into her stricken eyes, and his smile appeared to allay her terror. Frances was calling to him from the open window, and he crossed to see what she wanted.

"It's the telephone," she explained when he reached the French windows. "I hardly liked to answer it."

She saw the cloudiness in his eyes when she stepped back to admit him.

"I'm glad you didn't answer it," he said. "Please put on the gramophone again."

The bell rang once more, insistently. The Merry Widow waltz broke into its lilting melody. Brett lifted off the receiver. "Filson speaking," he said loudly.

"Oh, day, Filson," he heard Tonger say. "Frances arrive all right?"

"Yes. She's here now. Did you want to speak to her?"

"Not particularly. Just wanted to know if she got over. Think it's going to rain?"

"Yes, I do rather. Wind in the right quarter. We could do with an inch."

"We could that. Hope it keeps off for another twenty-four hours, though. Colonel Lawton is here as doubtless Frances has told you. Wants to return north tomorrow. An inch would make the take-off ground a bit boggy. Well, goodbye Filson. Pack Frances back if it should rain, and rain or no rain, set her off before midnight. That is, if she's not staying over until tomorrow."

"Very well. Just heard that N'gobi is on his way here to claim Nora. I'll have to ring the police, I suppose, and have him arrested."

"Shoot the swine, Filson. Save trouble. Oh! By the way, I'd like to have a word with Tremayne if he's there."

Now smiling grimly, Filson turned to the company who were watching him with not a little intentness. He held the receiver about a foot from his head and said loudly: "Harry, Mr Tonger wants a word or two with you."

The women regarded him with astonishment. The waltz played on. After a distinct pause, Brett again placed the receiver against ear and lips to say in a remarkable imitation of Tremayne's voice: "Hello, Mr Tonger! Tremayne speaking."

"Ah, that you, Tremayne?" said the Breakaway House squatter. "What about those stitches I put into your scalp? Better come over tomorrow or the next day and have them pulled out."

"Righto, thanks, I will," assented the overseer's voice. "All right. Bye-bye!"

Replacing the receiver, Brett turned thoughtfully to his guests.

Violet Winters cut off the gramophone. "Who was that?" she asked.

"Mr Tonger."

"What did he want?" It did not occur to him that she was rude, so evident was her anxiety.

"Mr Tonger first wished to know if Miss Frances had arrived," he said slowly. "Then he wanted to speak to Harry Tremayne."

"In that case Mr Tremayne can't be at Breakaway House, and that's something to be thankful for." Violet Winters was standing squarely on her feet, hands on hips, her attitude that of a fighting Amazon.

Ann and Frances remained silent, waiting for her leadership.

"Why did you answer in Mr Tremayne's voice?" was her next question.

"Because he wanted me to do so should Mr Tonger ring up and ask for him," Brett replied. "He made me practise mimicking his voice. He said that it would be important for Mr Tonger to believe he was here and that..."

"So he is at Breakaway House," Violet cut in swiftly. "He was expecting them to do something, before which they would make certain he wasn't there to see them do it. He's over there all right." Abruptly she swung round to face Frances, to stare at her with such concentration that Frances flushed.

"Why do you look at me like that?" Frances asked with sudden coldness.

The big woman's voice was equally cold when she said: "I'm wondering how far you're to be trusted."

"In so far as Mr Tremayne is concerned, I think I'm to be totally trusted," Frances said, coldness replaced by heat. "You see, we're going to be married some day."

"Be married!" echoed Violet. With surprising swiftness Violet reached the girl's side and stared hard at her. "Is he in love with you?"

Frances nodded. Into her eyes had leapt the truth.

Silently Violet turned away and walked heavily to the window.

CHAPTER XXVIII

COLONEL LAWTON EXPLAINS

THE interior of the great corrugated iron shed was commanded by quietness akin to that reigning in a church. Within, peace; without, the mundane noises of life; in this instance the bellow of a far-distant steer and the regular chug-chug-chug of a petrol engine.

Anyone standing just inside the closed double doors would face several rows of sagging wool bales; sagging because half the contents of each were piled on tarpaulins laid before each row. On the far side of this part of the building a stack of wool bales rose in tiers halfway to the roof. Should the observer turn half right, he would look along a shuttered wall surmounted by the shearing machinery. The wall abutted a straight aisle of wool-polished flooring skirted by heavily built wooden pens which in turn were skirted by larger pens or yards constructed with lighter material. It was possible to keep under one roof twelve hundred sheep to await barbering the next day.

This particular Sunday afternoon the shed interior was less brilliantly illuminated than usual by the daylight filtering through the far open end, for the sky was overcast by a thickening haze which had slowly blotted out the sun.

Above the beat of the petrol engine rose the murmur of men's voices, and a moment later the side door opened to admit Morris Tonger, Colonel Lawton, Whitbread the boss stockman, and three hands.

"Ah…everything ready, I see," remarked the Colonel in peculiarly silken tones. It was a voice general to youths and sounded incongruous with his stature. His left eye was drawn up into its habitual half-closed position, presenting a further incongruity beside the right eye which remained fixedly open. He was dressed in immaculate flannels.

"I prepared the bales directly I knew you were coming," Tonger said quickly. "We'll have a clear run, and I'll be damned glad when this consignment's shipped."

"I shall be pleased, too, but it's a pity it will have to be the last consignment for some considerable time," Lawton said coldly. "There would have been no necessity for it to be so had you not mixed with that other organisation. Why you should have desired to pick up pennies when you were picking up pounds with greater security is very difficult for me to understand."

To this Morris Tonger offered no further explanation, if he had made any former explanation. Flushing slightly with impatience, he asked: "Shall we get on with the work?"

"Of course, have the stuff brought from the plane."

Languidly, Colonel Lawton stooped to pick up a sample of the Breakaway House wool and closely examined the snowy fibres. The squatter gave orders to Whitbread and the boss stockman, a powerful, swarthy man growing a jet black moustache, motioned the hands to follow him. They began to bring into the shed small boxes made of heavy iron, each box about a foot square and some six inches in depth. After making several trips forty of these boxes were piled on the floor between two wool presses.

Lawton made no attempt to assist in the operations. He sat on a filled wool bale, one of those forming the bottom tier of the stack and idly fingered the wisp of wool, gazing abstractedly at it, as if he were trying to work out a solution to a vexing problem.

Whitbread and his assistants worked the two wool presses, dragging the half emptied bales to them. When the open ends of the bales were fixed to the top of the presses, Tonger placed an iron box inside each one. The wool formerly removed from the bales was then rammed down on top, the plunger of the press forcing it compactly into each bale, and the bales were then clipped shut. As they were brought out of the presses, Morris Tonger stencilled letters and numerals on the outside which to the uninitiated would be puzzling, but which to wool brokers and shipping agents were quite plain in meaning.

Thus were the iron boxes, brought by Colonel Lawton in his plane, disposed of. Whitbread was then ordered to bring in another lot of boxes, and then he and his assistants departed in a truck which roared up the grade rising westward from the house.

"There are sixty to come from the store, aren't there?" inquired the Colonel.

Tonger nodded but did not look up from his task of branding the refilled bales. The Colonel carelessly slipped off his seat and began casually to pat and punch those bales which were stacked. Just why they interested him was not clear. He then climbed up to the first tier, and sauntered along it a little distance before climbing up to the next tier. When he reached the fourth and topmost tier, his expression was one of slight interest, and without haste he produced an automatic pistol. Still maintaining his habitual softness of voice, he said: "Should you emerge head first, I'll riddle it with a point forty-five bore nickel-plated, soft-nose bullet. Come up with your hands held high above your head. I want to see your hands first."

Tonger, who was regarding the Colonel with amazement, called up from the floor of the wool room: "What the devil are you about?"

"Patience, my dear Morris, patience," Lawton urged. "We have here, I feel sure, someone who should not be here. Now, Mr Spy, like Lazarus, come forth, but hands if..."

The astonished Morris Tonger heard from the depths of the stacked wool a dry chuckle. That was followed by faint scratchings, and a moment later he saw two human hands rise above the topmost tier, between it and the shed wall.

Following the hands rose the grinning countenance of Harry Tremayne. "Good afternoon, Colonel. Is it going to rain?" he inquired blandly.

"It appears to be quite probable," replied Lawton.

"Tremayne!" Tonger burst out. "By heck! Shoot him and end his cursed business."

Lawton's right brow rose level with the permanently raised left brow.

"So you are Police Constable Harry Tremayne," he said wonderingly. "Ah! Now I recognise you. You once called on me with census papers, or a summons or something."

"Those golden days are gone never to return, I'm afraid," Harry said mockingly.

"I'm compelled to agree with you," murmured the Colonel.

"There are moments when I regret having resigned from the police force. How long do you require me to stand like this?"

"Pardon. Just a moment longer. Morris, come on up and...er ...fan Mr Tremayne."

"Hurry, Tonger! My arms begin to tire," Tremayne cheerfully urged. "By the way, Colonel, how did you discover me?"

"It was your cheap watch that betrayed you. It ticks a little louder than a good one does. We quite thought you to be at Bowgada, or rather, Mr Tonger did."

"I could have sworn it was he who spoke over the telephone," the squatter said vehemently, clambering up to them. "I'll get even with Filson for that trick."

Lawton was now smiling with his lips.

Tonger reached them and was coolly informed by Tremayne that he would find a pistol in his right-hand pocket. Tonger was smiling too, a wolfish, triumphant smile. His red blotched face was thrust close to the overseer and his hand was groping for the pistol when Tremayne's left fist smote him against the jaw.

It sent the big man staggering sideways and he slipped over the edge of the wool tier to fall down the stacks like a piece of jetsam sliding down a waterfall. At the bottom, on the floor, he lay still for an instant and groaned, but long before that, Tremayne had swung round upon the Colonel with panther-like agility.

"Of course—if you really wish to die," Lawton said, and Tremayne knew that he would die if he sprang. Destruction was looking at him out of hard, ice-blue eyes. The quiet voice said gently: "You can go for your gun if you think you have a chance."

"I don't think I have a ghost of a chance," was Tremayne's opinion.

The smile on Lawton's mouth became pronounced. His mouth was the only feature, the only part of him which moved. His eyelids were frozen, and the muzzle of the squat pistol and the hand which held it remained as steady as though carved in bronze.

"You may produce your pistol and lay it down on the bale at your side," suggested the Colonel. "Let me entreat you not to hurry. Haste on your part would give me a wrong impression of your intentions."

"Had much practice with a pistol?" Tremayne asked conversationally whilst transferring his pistol from pocket to bale.

"Well, yes, I must admit I've had a good deal of practice one way and another," Lawton admitted. "I was in South America for four years, in those parts where pistols, knives and poison are considered necessary adjuncts to life. Now if you will kindly step backward six paces—good. If you wish, you may smoke, but remember my request not to hasten when your hands are in your pockets. You see, I'm not quite sure that you don't have a second weapon."

Morris Tonger came clambering up the wool bales. "What are we going to do with him," he demanded, twisting a crowbar in his hands. "He knows too much. He's got to be put out. We can't..."

"Try to be calm, Morris. Believe me, I feel for you. A smack against the jaw, I know, upsets one, but nevertheless, try to be calm."

"Shall I make you a cigarette, Tonger?" Tremayne inquired, having lit the one he just rolled. He spoke casually enough, but inwardly he was angry at being thus trapped. He was stung by the ease of Lawton's victory, and before he had even found out what those iron boxes contained! Gold. Surely not! The amount of gold that could be contained in those boxes would not be enough to tempt a man of Colonel Lawton's calibre.

When he spoke his voice was impersonal. "I'm wondering just what is inside those boxes you packed away amidst the wool," he drawled. "Do you mind enlightening me?"

"Not at all, Mr Tremayne. Only too pleased," came the soft voice. "Kindly refrain from interrupting, Morris. Each of those boxes contains seven pounds weight of cocaine–pure cocaine. We are about to consign to England seven hundred pounds weight of the finest grade cocaine."

"Quite a nice little parcel," Tremayne said admiringly. "Dispatched like that the Customs people wouldn't worry too much."

"Exactly, Mr Tremayne," Lawton agreed calmly. "As you doubtless know, Java produces quite a lot of cocaine which isn't controlled by the League of Nations, the shrub having in the first instant been imported from Peru and Bolivia, to which countries it's indigenous.

"Just after the war, when the demand for cocaine was at its peak, a lot of people were concerned in supplying the demand. One man I knew used to receive one hundred pounds a trip for taking a few ounces into England, thereby earning a comfortable income. In a general way, everyone was earning a comfortable income, bar we fools who thought we were putting an end to war forever.

"That, of course, is a digression for which I ask pardon." The Colonel shrugged. "I will not weary you with an explanation of the whys and wherefores I went into the drug trade. My reasons were personal. I've never been concerned with the morals of others, or interested in human weaknesses, save to exploit them. I'm convinced that men and women have a free right to do with their bodies what they will. If they wish to destroy themselves, what is it to me if they use cocaine in preference to strychnine, excepting, of course, the monetary angle. Weak people should always be assisted to leave this world they so encumber.

"You see, my dear Mr Tremayne, the save-my-brother philosophy is not for me. When I returned to look after my station which borders the Ninety Mile Beach on the northwest coast of this State, I saw the possibility of importing cocaine from Java and re-exporting it to England. The official mind, which invariably runs in a groove, always looks for drugs entering from the Continent or from Asiatic ports. I saw that hidden within such a commodity as wool, and coming from Australia, cocaine could be got into England with comparative ease. A ship..."

"Say no more!" interrupted Tonger, his face livid. "Tremayne knows too much as it is."

"Please be quiet, Morris," he was blandly reproved, and to the interested Harry, the Colonel continued: "A fast ship brings the contraband to a point off the Ninety Mile Beach, and my own fishing launch brings it ashore. It's very simple; just routine, for as you well know, the Ninety Mile Beach isn't devoted to tourist resorts and it isn't patrolled by coastguards. Even the Navy never steams near it. I believe that a foreign nation could occupy the country for a fortnight before anyone knew about it. The contraband is transferred from the launch to motor trucks which bring it to my homestead, and, because I own cattle stations which do not produce fabrics exportable in bales, I bring the contraband to Breakaway House per aeroplane."

"Have you taken leave of your senses?" Tonger broke in.

"You'll presently observe the method in my madness, Morris," Lawton said carelessly. "Having brought the cocaine to Breakaway House we pack it, as you have observed, into the middle of each wool bale. Stout iron boxes are necessary to withstand the tremendous strain exerted on them by the dumping presses at the wool stores, each bale being compressed into less than half its length to permit more of them occupying a ship's available space. Our wool is consigned direct to a Bradford firm which takes over the business over there."

The Colonel permitted himself to smile. Then he added: "Being unaware of just how much you know, my dear Mr Tremayne, I have followed my practice over many years of telling you everything in order that you may be so dangerous to us that to kill you will be an absolute necessity."

CHAPTER XXIX

AN OUTRAGED HUSBAND

BRETT FILSON'S party at Bowgada that Sunday was not a success, a state of affairs owing entirely to the absence of Harry Tremayne.

Violet Winters became strangely silent after Frances's avowal that Tremayne loved her and was to marry her. And as each long minute passed, the Breakaway House girl became more and more uneasy when Tremayne still failed to appear. It seemed so odd that having convened the party, and having promised to be present, he did not return. Surely he would have sent a reason for his absence, had he been able. Brett decided that if he did not turn up before dinner was cleared away, he would himself enter this dangerous game. Matters had gone far enough.

Talk was desultory during the meal, despite the host's valiant efforts to keep the conversation running smoothly, and despite his able backing by Ann Sayers who shrewdly guessed his worry. When the cloth had been removed by Millie she was asked to send in her husband and Jackson.

When they had arrived Brett said: "No doubt you'll both remember N'gobi who was imprisoned for killing an Aborigine. And of course you know that he's escaped from prison and is almost certainly making for Bowgada. According to Ned's brother, Wombera, he'll reach here sometime tonight, and he'll be bringing with him some of his friends to take it out of Ned.

"Nora swears she will not go back to N'gobi, and I've sworn that I'll protect her and Ned. So, Charlie, I want your wife and Nora to occupy a room in the house tonight, and I want you to look after Ned and bring him into the house when N'gobi gets here. You understand, I don't want any fighting. You and I, Jackson, will effect the arrest of N'gobi, and we'll keep him here until the Myme policeman takes him over tomorrow morning."

"Why not get the policeman here now and let him do the arresting?" asked Jackson.

"Yes, why not, Mr Filson?" echoed Ann, regarding the squatter with troubled eyes.

"That's a question which I shall not answer," Brett said grimly, presenting to Ann a facet of his character she had not even suspected. "Now where's Mug Williams?"

"Across at the men's hut," English answered.

"Send him back to the kitchen and tell him to wait there until I call for him. You have a rifle, Jackson?"

"Too right! And a Mauser pistol. And a shotgun–double-barrel."

"Have them where you can get at them quickly. Should you hear a car approaching, or see a horseman coming, tell me at once. That will be all now."

"Wot about Mr Tremayne? Shall I keep his dinner hot? He said he would be here for dinner for certain," demanded the cook.

"Evidently he has been delayed by something, Jackson," Brett pointed out quietly. "Keep his dinner warm, by all means."

When the cook and the boss stockman had withdrawn, Brett turned to his interested guests and came straight to the point without preamble. "I think that we're all interested in Harry Tremayne and that we all like him," he said. "His non-appearance this afternoon is perturbing in view of his mission to the Murchison, and, too, in view of certain happenings. I'm going to take you into my confidence for several reasons, one of which is that I want to learn what Harry hoped to learn this afternoon. It was he who suggested this party, and, frankly, one of his reasons for doing so was to seek certain information from you, Miss Winters. Might I assume that had he been here you would have given him the information he sought?"

Violet was sitting bolt upright on the extreme edge of her chair. Her rugged face was red despite the powder, her small nose shone defiantly, and her eyes were mere pin points of dark brown. Her mouth was set in a long, thin, straight line.

"You can assume that, Mr Filson," she said grimly. "I'd made up my mind to tell him certain things when I learned what he was and what he's doing here." Her eyes closed for a moment and her face softened.

When she went on her voice was less hard, and certainly not bitter. "I'm getting old and I forgot that. I've had silly thoughts for a woman of my age but they'll be memories now. Yes, I'm in love with Mr Tremayne, even though I've wakened up; and even though he's a policeman."

Brett noticed how Frances's eyes shone and then became clouded as she continued to listen to Violet. They all felt for Violet, all sensed what she was going through. Little real affection had swayed her rough life before she met "the boy" who took her to a dance.

Brett's voice then filled the ensuing silence, every one of his listeners magnetised. He told of Harry Tremayne's mission to the Murchison, all that Tremayne had learned, all that he suspected, and of the determined attacks on his life. He concluded by asking Violet another direct question.

"Miss Winters, will you tell us what you know of those gold-stealers?"

"Yes," she assented without hesitation. "I know for a start that Morris Tonger is not in with them unless he joined them this year."

"Oh...I am glad!" Frances exclaimed.

"I don't mean to say that Morris Tonger may not be mixed up with something much worse," Violet said swiftly, her show of feminine tenderness replaced by the habitual hardness she turned to the world. "What that is I don't know, but it must be something bad, else why should young Tremayne disappear near his house? Why should he twice plan to kill Mr Tremayne? It seems certain that, like his brother, Mr Tremayne has stumbled on something that bad that Tonger would commit murder to keep it hidden.

"You see, when I first went to Myme, I kept house for my brother. Buck Ross was there two or three nights a week, and there were times when some of his pals came with him. I got to know their business and Tom's, and, because on the goldfields stealing is not reckoned much of a crime among the miners, I didn't try hard to persuade Tom to give it up.

"When he was killed, Ross and his friends sort of made me hate policemen. They were afraid I might talk, knowing so much, and Ross wanted to marry me to make even more sure of keeping me silent. I refused, and he threatened to kill me if I said things. That was in the Myme kitchen." Violet's eyes suddenly blazed. "He had to go to the doctor when I'd finished with him!"

"Tonger never associated with your brother and Ross?" questioned the squatter.

"Never."

"Where is Ross's secret treatment plant?"

"About seventeen miles north of Breakaway House, up near Telfer Range."

"Oh! Not near the balancing rock about three miles south of the homestead?"

Violet shook her head.

"You don't think you are, or could be, mistaken?"

"I do not," she replied emphatically. "I know just where it is because I once went there."

"How do you account–forgive me for cross-examining you–how do you account for Buck Ross being associated with Morris Tonger?"

"I can't. I don't understand that. The only reason I can think of is that Tonger joined Ross and his gang some time this year. They weren't associated last year, that I know."

"Well, they are associated now, Miss Winters. It appears probable that, as Ross is joined to Tonger, Ross's gang are joined too."

The door to the kitchen was opened and round its edge peered Mug Williams. "Car coming from Myme," he said meaningfully, absent from his face the usual smile.

Brett looked at the clock to see that it was twenty-seven minutes after seven. "Tell Jackson to show you to his bedroom," he said sharply. "And tell Jackson I want him."

The round face vanished, and, just as they heard the sound of the car, Jackson came in.

"If this car stops, don't go beyond the kitchen door," Brett ordered. "And no matter who it is, if one of these ladies or I is asked for, tell me who it is before you admit them here."

Jackson nodded.

"And," Brett said further, "be in a vile temper and stress your undying hatred of capitalists."

Again Jackson nodded, into his eyes leaping a gleam of dry humour as he returned to the kitchen.

With complaining brakes the car pulled up at the side of the house. The horn was sounded peremptorily and the murmur of men's voices reached them.

Then a man called out: "You there, Jackson?"

When Jackson made no answer the lowered voices again drifted through the open windows.

Then there was a short silence, followed by a man's voice at the kitchen door. "Pity you can't come out when you're wanted."

"If you think I'm gonna run round money-grabbing capitalists, you're mistaken," Jackson snarled. "I only got one taskmaster, and don't you forget it. Slavin' 'ere orl day, Sunday, too. What do you take me for? The day ain't far off…"

"Cut it out. Where's Miss Winters?"

"How do I know?" again snarled the cook. "Am I looking at 'er? She was in the dining room ten minutes ago with the blinded boss, but I wouldn't bet a razoo she's there now."

"Well, you just tell her I want to speak to her. And keep that gun off me. I don't like even empty guns pointing at my stomach."

"I'll do wot I like with me guns in me own kitchen," roared Jackson. "You don't come 'ere giving me orders on me own parade ground." Then the living-room door was pushed open and Jackson entered back first in order not to remove his gaze from the man at the kitchen door. "Stay where you are," he ordered. "I don't aim for you to pinch me new frypan." Over his shoulder, he added with heavy sarcasm: "Mr Buck Ross wants to speak private like with Miss Violet Winters."

Violet took a step towards the door, but Brett restrained her. "Show Mr Ross in here," he said.

"Come in here," Soddy snarled.

"Can't stop. I'm in a hurry," Ross said from the doorway. "Ask her to come out here."

Brett pushed Jackson out into the kitchen before him. The cook sat down at the table and continued to clean and oil the double-barrelled shotgun.

When in the centre of the kitchen, Brett said: "You here again, Ross!"

"Yes, Mr Filson. I just stopped, wanting a word with Miss Winters."

Brett, indicating the room at his back, invited the big man to enter.

"I haven't got…"

"Come in," Brett repeated, ice now in his voice.

"I tell you I haven't got time," Ross said angrily. "I want a word or two with Miss Winters in private."

"I think you'd better get on your way, Ross," said Brett in a low voice. "Leave your most private interview till tomorrow. Later this evening I shall be taking Miss Sayers and Miss Winters back to Myme, and it might interest you to know that I've insured my guests and myself against accident with the police."

"Wot do you mean by that?"

"I will leave you to guess my meaning, Ross. Now, will you come in, or shall we say 'good night'?"

"I can't stop, I tell you. I'll be gettin' on."

"Very well. If you're not off Bowgada in half an hour…"

"I'm on a public road," Ross objected heatedly.

"Half an hour, Ross. No more than half an hour."

The man's fury whitened his face.

As an accompaniment to the dialogue between him and Brett, Jackson hummed tunelessly. Seated at the kitchen table facing the caller, he handled the oiled shotgun carelessly, whilst within reach of either hand lay the Mauser pistol.

From behind the curtains in Brett's bedroom he and his guests watched the car pass along the road to Breakaway House. They saw that Ross was at the wheel and that the two passengers were careful to keep their faces turned away from them.

"I think, after all, that you and Miss Winters had better stay tonight, Miss Sayers," the squatter said thoughtfully. "We can ring up your people and allay their anxiety. If you'll excuse me, I'll go out on to the breakaway where I can observe Ross and his friends."

166

"We'll all go, if we may," suggested Ann, her face a trifle pale.

"Yes, please, Mr Filson," Frances seconded.

"By all means. Come along."

At the garden gate Brett asked for silence to listen. The roar of the departing car could still be heard, and Brett judged that it was then down on the valley speeding towards Acacia Well.

A man shouted from the back of the house. He shouted again from within the house. Then Ned appeared at the front door, and ran to them. Nora followed, and behind her was English.

"They're coming!" Nora panted. "N'gobi and all his relations are coming! Give me a gun, Mr Filson. Soddy won't give me one of his. Give me a gun. I shoot–I shoot that N'gobi!"

CHAPTER XXX

THE BATTLE

FOLLOWING Nora's demand for a gun, the little party at the Bowgada front gate were stilled as if it were a tragedy accomplished rather than a tragedy impending. Everyone appeared to wait on Brett Filson's leadership, and he, sensing their attitude, accepted leadership less by right than by silent election.

"Millie, take Nora and Ned to your room," was his first instruction. To his guests, he said: "You would render me great assistance by remaining in the house."

"Why not ring the police, Mr Filson?" urged Ann Sayers.

He smiled, thrilled by the concern for him he saw in her wide eyes. For the first time since the war he forgot his disabilities and permitted himself to look Ann straight in the eye, physically sure of himself. "I was hoping that Harry Tremayne would come," he said slowly. "Now it would be too late anyway so you may ring the police station at Myme, and tell the constable that N'gobi's here and that we'll detain him."

"Who do you mean by 'we'?" she asked anxiously.

"Why, English, Williams, Jackson and myself. There's no reason to be uneasy about N'gobi. We won't hurt him."

Laughing gently at her and forgetting the others, Brett was glad of this chance providence offered. With all his heart he wanted to make her forget, if only for a little while, his crippled condition, and when he led the way into the house he barely used his stick.

When they were back in the living room, Ann at once crossed to the telephone to ring the Myme exchange. Brett went to his writing desk, took out a nickel-plated Smith and Wesson revolver and rapidly loaded it from a box of cartridges. Violet Winters sat down and eyed the heavy poker lying in the fender. Frances was watching Ann, now frantically ringing Myme.

"I expect Ross and his friends have cut the Myme wire," Brett said, actually chuckling. "Now you three remain here. I'll be back in a minute or two."

He was at the door when Ann Sayers reached him, her face working with anguish. Her dark-blue eyes were wide, and she seemed to hold her breath; and, because he forgot his infirmities, he also forgot his resolutions concerning celibacy. Before the others he placed his hands on her shoulders, drew her to him, and kissed her. "Don't worry, dear," he said, holding her back to smile at her. "I'll be quite all right."

"Don't go! Don't go!" Ann pleaded. "Let Nora go back to N'gobi. Let Ned fight for her if he wants her. What does all this matter to us?"

The last pronoun was breathed rather than spoken; as though the word had become sanctified at long last; as though they two, to which it referred, were set apart.

When he shook his head she knew his resolve. "I've given my word, Ann. Nora wishes to remain with Ned. They belong to Bowgada. Now, I shan't be long."

When he had left, Frances went over to Ann and gently restrained her from following.

In the kitchen, Jackson, Williams and English stood bunched in front of the door waiting for Filson.

The light was failing, for the sun was setting and black clouds were sliding eastwards beneath the grey haze. The outbuildings were brought out in sharp contrast to the dark green background of mulga in this strange twilight. Near the stockyards was a group of Aborigines in excited conversation with Ned's brother, Wombera.

"English!" The three men at the door swung round at Brett's approach.

"I want you and Williams to guard the house and at the same time cover Jackson and me. You take the rifle, English, and you, Williams, the shotgun. Cover us from the windows and don't fire unless you know we're in danger or the blacks rush the house. Don't let them see you until they start something. You, Jackson, come with me."

"Yes sir! But can't you get the police? They got more right to be killed than we have."

"No. I think Ross must have cut the telephone wire to Bowgada. We have to arrest N'gobi before the daylight goes. Once we've got him under lock and key those others will go away and camp quietly. They're not that wild that they don't appreciate what will follow if they start something, but there's no knowing what they might do if we permit N'gobi to stir them up. Remember, you are not to produce that pistol you love so well until I say so."

"Righto! Quite like old times, ain't it? Wot about that night me and you went on that walkabout east of Corbie?" For the first time for many years, Soddy Jackson was smiling.

Together, ex-officer and ex-digger left the house to walk unhurriedly across the open space to the party at the stockyards. There were, Brett counted, fourteen Aborigines besides Wombera. The majority was dressed only in trousers and shirt, but two wore better clothes with boots and hat, proclaiming the fact that they were in employment as stockmen.

Towering above his companions was a huge man whose sole garment was a pair of tattered dungaree trousers. His hair and beard were greying, and, at Brett's approach, he swung round to glare at him with wild bloodshot eyes. He was clearly mad with rage. "What for you takeum Nora in homestead, eh?" he shouted. "Nora belonga me. You sendum Nora out quick, or by cripes we put fire-stick into place and smoke her out."

"No, you won't, N'gobi. And you others won't help N'gobi, either," Brett told them sternly. "You others will get tucker off the cook and go back to your camps. Now, N'gobi, you come with me. You have to go back to gaol. The white man's law says so."

"White man's law no good, boss. Blackfellas' law say Nora belonga N'gobi, go back with N'gobi," shouted one of the flashily dressed men. "Blackfellas' law make Ned fight us for taking Nora from N'gobi."

"N'gobi hasn't any right to Nora. N'gobi was in gaol and will have to go back to gaol. Someone had to look after Nora while he was in gaol, and Nora chose Ned. If you break the white man's law you will all go to the white man's gaol."

There was a sudden movement from the small crowd, and, soon after that, the crisis. N'gobi shouted strange curses, taking two paces towards Brett and his companion. Neither saw who threw the spear which pierced Brett's right shoulder. The force of the heavy missile spun him right round and on to the ground. He heard N'gobi's savage yell; then was deafened by the crack of Jackson's pistol. Following the explosion came a sudden silence broken by the sound of a heavy body crashing to earth.

Brett was on his knees holding the heavy spear in his two hands, trying to lift it to stop its leverage bending him forward. He had to get up to prevent that fool of a Jackson from shooting all the others. Didn't he know that Jackson when once his blood was fired? Yet somehow, strive as he would, he could not rise to his feet. The spear was too heavy, holding him to the ground as though it were fastened there. He could see Ned running from the house, the dreadful Leonile club swinging round his black head. As he twisted his agonised body he saw N'gobi's relations break and run towards the scrub.

N'gobi was lying still, the dim light glistening on a round blob slowly issuing from the exact centre of his forehead.

Soddy Jackson began firing into the air and yelling terrific oaths. From the house the shotgun roared twice and the rifle began to bang at intervals. Yells from the departing blacks drifted back to join with the shrill cries of women.

The daylight faded at last, but it was not the darkness of night which swept over Brett Filson.

"Take it out! Take it out! Why don't you take it out?" The woman's voice was low, shot through and through with anguish. She was kneeling beside Brett Filson, gazing at the heavy spear as though she would never see anything else.

She heard Williams say in staccato tones: "It don't look like one of them barbed ones."

"Take it out! Why don't you take it out?" reiterated Ann Sayers.

Although Jackson merely whispered, she heard him say with a shudder: "Fetch a good saw, Charlie. We'll have to saw off the shaft and see if we can get out the point after we've got him on his bed. He'll bleed a lot and we'll want swabs. Where's Millie?"

Ann felt herself lifted up, and she struggled because she did not want to leave the man she loved. After all the waiting time, to have found him, and now to lose him!

"Miss Sayers," she heard Violet say. "Me and you have got to get busy. Come on! You hunt up clean linen for bandages and I'll see to the hot water. The men will bring him in."

Ann experienced exquisite weariness but when they neared the kitchen door strength suddenly returned, and it was she who urged Violet into the house.

As they entered Millie came running towards them. "She's gone! She would go! I tried to stop her, but she would go!" she cried vexedly.

"Who do you mean?" Violet demanded.

"Why, Nora! She said she wouldn't stay to be taken by N'gobi. The shooting! Are they coming to the house?"

"No," said Violet quietly, "N'gobi is shot dead and the others have cleared out. They speared Mr Filson. The men are bringing him in now. Now get to the stove, and heat up water," she added more loudly. Violet then became positively dynamic. "Come on! Lights! Get the light going! Where's Miss Tonger?"

Frances had remained with Brett. She was calm, was wondering at her calmness as she supported Brett's head while Jackson cut through the spear about six inches from Brett's shoulder, with English steadying the wood for all his worth.

"Now we'll take him inside, Charlie. You lift his legs. No—I'll take his legs. You're stronger than me. You take his head. Lift him steady. Steady, now. Here, Ned! Pass your hand under him. Take Ned's hand, Miss Tonger. Easy, now! Remember his harness. Cripes! He's heavier than he was when I carried him back after that stunt, or maybe I'm getting weaker. Easy does it."

Soddy Jackson's face was transfigured. Gone was the perpetual melancholy, the habitual grouch at all the world. Even his voice was altered. It was deeper, resonant, revealing a sense of power.

When they arrived at Brett's room and Brett was lying on his bed, Jackson glanced round at the others crowding near the open door. English and Mug Williams looked on with strained faces, Ned's eyes were rolling, Millie was crying, Ann Sayers appeared to be a statue and Frances was steady but very pale. Only Violet Winters seemed unchanged save for the glare in her small round eyes.

"All you get out and be ready to bring them things," Jackson snapped, waving his long-fingered hand to everyone but Violet. "Miss Winters, you're for it and no faintin' allowed. You got to be the nurse. Now then, towels, linen, potash. A basin of water and a can of water, quick. Keep that range stoked, Millie."

It was fortunate that the spear was plain pointed, not barbed. The point was drawn out easily but much blood was lost before the deep wound was washed out and plugged.

"Wonder if it touched his lung?" Jackson whispered. "Might have done," whispered Violet. "Mighty close if it didn't. We'll have to get the Mount Magnet doctor as quick as he can get here. Old Jonton at Myme will be too drunk, like as not, even if we could reach him on the telephone."

"That's so. We don't want no medical drunks round here. Put that harness out of sight. He wouldn't like Miss Sayers to see that. Bit gone on 'er, he is."

"So's she on him. Let's lift him so we can put a clean sheet under him. That blood…"

"We'll have to ring the police, too. Boss didn't want 'em here tonight, but we'll have to ring 'em now."

"Who threw the spear? N'gobi?"

"Dunno. No, it wasn't N'gobi. N'gobi jumped when the boss was hit. I didn't wait no longer. He got wot he was looking for. Them Mausers hit hard."

"Where did you get him?" was Violet's morbid question.

"Head. Dead centre," replied Jackson, as though shooting people in the head, dead centre, were a natural thing to do.

When everything these inexpert hands could do for Brett had been done, Ann and Frances were called in. Ann was "ordered" to watch the patient and report any change. Frances remained with her, and she could hear the telephone in action.

Violet Winters rang up Breakaway House from where Bowgada could be switched through to Mount Magnet. Morris Tonger, who happened to be engaged with Colonel Lawton in his office, replied to her call.

"This is Miss Winters, speaking from Bowgada. Put me through to Mount Magnet, quick."

"You appear to be in a great hurry, Miss Winters," Tonger said with assumed cheerfulness.

"I am. Look! Your friend and accomplice seems to have cut the wire to Myme, so I can't ring up old Jonton. I want the Mount Magnet doctor quick. So don't you start arguing and waste time. No, No! Mr Filson has been speared by N'gobi or one of his cobbers. Of course, N'gobi's dead. Didn't expect him to be alive, did you? My friends here shoot straight, and you can tell that to Buck Ross. And tell him, too, that next time I meet him I'll put him in hospital for six months, and in the home for blind men for the rest of his life, or until the hangman gets him. Don't you start, now. You put me through to Magnet. I'll talk to you after I've spoken to the doctor and the police. The police–remember?"

CHAPTER XXXI

THE COLONEL'S PLANS

BECAUSE he was sure he would be shot if he offered resistance, because he was so sure, Harry Tremayne permitted himself to be tied in such a fashion that to escape was out of the question. Vigilantly menaced by Lawton's pistol, he was compelled to sit on the floor with his back against one of the wooden pillars supporting the roof. Tonger then tied his hands behind the pillar, lashed his body to the pillar, too, and gagged him. Effective concealment was provided by a number of bales of wool-packs walling him about like the walls of a small room.

There was only one policy to adopt–obedience, with the knowledge in mind that dead men can no longer even hope.

"It's unnecessary for Whitbread and his helpers, who will be shortly returning with more of the iron boxes, to know of your presence here," explained the Colonel. "Even though you're gagged you're capable of making gurgling noises which would attract their attention. As it is not my wish that you should attract their attention. I shall strike you with this iron bar if you do so; and, because I'm not practised, it is possible that I might strike too hard and kill you. Being a thug is not my usual role, I assure you, and therefore I fear that my inexperience could produce results fatal to you."

Harry Tremayne forced mocking amusement into his eyes, since the gag prevented his registering amusement in his face. Actually he considered his position to be extremely grave; for, seated opposite him, a long bar of iron across his knees, was one of those rare mortals not shackled by fear, emotion and selflessness, a man who could kill with much less feeling than the average man swats a march fly.

The first time they had met Lawton had effectively kept hidden the cold, passionless, ruthless facet of his nature; but now there was no necessity to retain such a veneer, which after all was a boring task. This was the truth forced on Tremayne. Seated opposite him was the natural man; on the former occasion, Colonel Lawton had been cramped and cabined like a small boy dressed in his Sunday clothes.

He had never before met a man like Lawton. His sergeant had once described to him a man he had taken for murder who perhaps belonged to Lawton's type; the type of human being who kills without experiencing emotion, without feeling the lust to kill, who kills merely to remove an obstruction or a danger as the ordinary man might cut down a tree which blocks a splendid view.

The policeman found it difficult to understand why a man of Lawton's calibre should traffic in cocaine. He was reputedly rich long before he engaged in it. He seemed to be a man without the human weaknesses which demand satiation by the power of money; the one possible reason behind his activities lay in the danger of the life, the excitement, such as had dominated his activities during the war. With the coming of peace tens of thousands had yawned their heads off with boredom.

Whitbread and his assistants returned on the truck and they could be heard re-baling the wool. The presses whirred and thumped for an hour or more, and the day was waning when at last Tonger ordered them to their quarters on the completion of their labours.

"How does the weather look?" he was asked when he entered the small space about the prisoner.

"Much like rain," replied the squatter, glowering at Tremayne. "What are we going to do with him?"

"Nothing drastic, Morris, until it becomes certain when I can leave," Lawton said, his brows knit in a frown of perplexity. Quite abruptly his face resumed its habitual expressionless placidity, and to the bound man he said: "You see, my dear fellow, you know so much it's absolutely essential that you die in the near future. Dead, you'll not feel the loss of a few years of life. Actually, the loss is imaginary, for the loss will be of the future. We cannot really lose what we've never had. If I'm a little hazy on the point, please forgive me.

"The last time I was here, a swagman calling himself Robbins proved to be an inconvenience. It appeared that he knew a little about a gold-stealing gang with which Mr Tonger is associated, and because he learned a little of my organisation, it was necessary to remove him.

"I left orders that Robbins—I've recently learned that he's your brother—was to be put to sleep, but I find that he's been employed by the gold thieves at their treatment plant. That's a small matter for settlement between Buck Ross and me.

"My intention is to incapacitate you both—being brothers you will have no cause for jealousy—with expertly given injections of cocaine, and transport you in the charge of Buck Ross to my north-west station, tomorrow if the weather permits. You'll then be taken to sea in my launch, still in the care of Buck Ross, and when a school of sharks has been attracted by the killing of a goat you'll be passed overboard to them.

"A peculiar thing about sharks in Australian waters is that they'll seldom take a dead man. As fish abound off the north-west coast they are rarely hungry. I've found that to effectually dispose of a man it's necessary that he be given to them alive for his struggles in the water arouse the sharks. However I can assure you that a school of aroused sharks cause death much more quickly than drowning. It may be of some consolation to you to know that after Buck Ross has fed you to the sharks I'll send him after you. I've no objection to you telling him that. In fact it will interest me to watch how he reacts for, although he won't believe you, the idea will persist and make him cautious of me. He'll use what little brain he has and it will amuse me to watch him use it. You see, I'm a strict disciplinarian."

So John was alive! That was indeed good news. And he, Harry Tremayne, was not dead yet either. If it rained, Lawton's departure would be delayed, and every moment added to his span of life would increase his chances of longevity. "Lucky Tremayne" it had been up in the Kimberleys. To date, "Lucky Tremayne" it had been on the Murchison. The news that John still lived was splendid. If only he could send off a telegram to his anxious mother!

Lawton was looking at him with calm but terrible eyes as he discoursed on the failings of men and women who killed without plan or foresight, and of the extraordinary efforts of some to destroy their victims' bodies when there were to hand such simple methods.

No wonder they had tried to shoot him from the balancing rock, Harry Tremayne thought. Unaware of what Violet Winters had told Brett, Tremayne still thought that the treatment plant must be in the vicinity of that rock, and thus his brother must be there too, instead of it being seventeen miles north. In fact the midnight lights indicated the position of Lawton's cocaine store.

So Buck Ross was due for a gruesome end. If the worst came he would not inform Ross of Lawton's little plan. Tonger had gone to the office to telephone to Ross to come at once just before Whitbread came back with the truck, and Ross should be arriving at any moment. Frances, Ann, Violet and Brett would all be over at Bowgada, wondering why he did not turn up. It was a shame that they had to worry, but he could not have left the Breakaway House shearing shed until he learned why all these wool bales had been half emptied.

Of course, the wool had to be baled during the shearing. In the first place, nothing else could be done with it, and even were it possible to defer the baling–an unheard-of procedure–far too much suspicion would have been aroused among the shearers and shed hands. And the cocaine could not have been buried in the bales during the shearing operations.

Clever–damned clever–to get cocaine into England via Australian imported wool. What Customs officer would think of that channel?

Left alone the prisoner's optimism evaporated. It began to dawn on him just how desperate his position was, and the assertion that he and his brother were to be kept in a state of paralysis with cocaine injections was an even more horrible fate to contemplate than the awful death promised. Once his body was paralysed, even the hope of escape would be taken from him. He wished that he was not so confoundedly uncomfortable.

He heard the oncoming car long before it stopped–as far as he could judge–outside the office. Two minutes later it went on, humming up the long grade towards Mount Magnet, and, he supposed, the area of surface rock directly behind the promontory on which stood the balancing rock. Without doubt, that area of surface rock was used to turn a car or truck so as to leave no tracks to arouse curiosity. Now the silence was broken only by the petrol engine working the electric light dynamo. Tremayne waited patiently for the next development.

And it came from a quarter which astonished him. Round one of the walls of wool-packs slipped a well-built girl whom Tremayne recognised as the one who had given him the note from Frances. Her features were fixed by the temperature of fear, frozen despite the warmth of determination. With the fingers of one hand laid against her red mouth and a butcher's knife held firmly in her right hand, she advanced upon him, and in a few seconds cut him free from gag and lashings.

"Don't speak! Rub! Hurry!" she whispered swiftly gathering the rope and the gag into a heap.

She revealed intelligence above the ordinary when she said on her return from a short absence: "I've hidden all that. It'll make them wonder if you were really tied to that particular pillar and it might give us a little time when wanted. Come with me. I know where we can hide. Go on, rub. I'll watch at the door."

She flitted beyond his range of vision, a winsome, graceful figure, and he fell to massaging his cramped legs and arms, fighting the exquisite pain of returning circulation, his wonder at her mingling with plans for the immediate future.

There was one thing of which he was certain. If discovered by Lawton, Tonger, or Ross, he would be shot down like a dingo. They would have to do it out of self-preservation, and the thought made Tremayne understand that devilish cunning and foresight of the Colonel. Make an enemy so dangerous that his death is inevitable and lesser men become ruthless. What a man! One to whom fear, repugnance and human frailties were unknown; a tyrant who played on fear, repugnance and frailties in others.

The pain in his arms and legs, and about his neck, was quickly easing beneath his fingers. Cocaine from Java! Of course! Along that two thousand miles of unguarded coast they could land anything. As the Colonel had said an army could invade unobserved. No wonder there had been agitation to have modern seaplanes stationed at Port Darwin.

He now managed to walk with little difficulty from his prison to the side wool-room door before which the girl was crouched. "Where do we hide?" he asked.

"We can both squeeze into the fire box of the steam engine which runs the machinery, or we can take a chance and get out of the building from the back and make for the breakaways," she replied, glancing down at the Colonel's bar of iron which Tremayne carried.

"How long have you been in the shed?"

"About two hours. I crept in from the back when they were taking those boxes from the flying machine. I wanted to know what they were doing so that I could tell Miss Frances." Suddenly she smiled. "Miss Frances and me are friends," she informed him proudly. "Miss Frances said so."

Again she stooped to look through the crack between the door and the jamb below the heavy lock. Then she was up again—quick as a clock spring.

"Buck Ross is coming here from the house," she breathed, her voice a soft hiss.

"Alone?"

When she nodded, he grinned and drew her away from the door. "Hide," he commanded. "When I've fixed Ross you hunt around for rope and a piece of cloth. He shall take my place at the pillar." When she hesitated, he added sternly: "Hide, do you hear? I want his gun."

Running from him, she disappeared among the wool bales like a rabbit dashing down a burrow. Tremayne moved quietly back to the walls of wool-packs, his eyes flaming and his brain like ice.

They heard the door being opened and closed. Then came Buck's dry chuckle. "So, my flash gentleman! I'm to nurse you for quite a time," he said, before his hand left the door, eagerness in his voice and an underlying vindictiveness striking a dreadful note of triumph. "Gonna squirt cocaine into you presently, but before that a match or two held against your fingernails for old times' sake."

That threat brought him to the wool-packs, a great, strong-boned, evil brute of a man. He was again chuckling when he rounded an angle and so came to see the wooden pillar to which Tremayne had been tied. There he stopped short, triumph replaced by perplexity, and then a realisation that he must have come to the wrong place within the shed. Possibly it was intuition which made him look up to see Tremayne's grinning face and the bar of iron then descending. It struck him across the forehead, and he collapsed as though shot. Tremayne jumped down from the position he had taken between two bales.

The interior of the shed was once again ruled by silence. The light was dim. The man lashed to the wooden pillar did not move. Anyway, his movement was restricted and his eyes were closed. He might have been dead, for the skin across his forehead was split open in a red-raw gash. Blood assisted the gag to mask his face.

Abruptly footsteps sounded beyond the side door. When the door was opened, yellow light silhouetted the tops of the wool bales against the roof. Men's boots tramped across the wooden floor.

"You there, Ross?" Tonger called sharply. "Come on, dinner's ready."

He and Lawton came into the cleared space about the pillar and the bound man. They looked round for the figure of Ross, not yet having realised that it was he who sat motionless and made the gurgling sounds. Then swiftly Tonger stooped and thrust the lamp he carried close to Buck's face.

"There's Ross," he said with remarkable calmness. "I told you to fix Tremayne when we had him. I objected to you telling him everything. Now if we don't get him quick we'll be done."

When Ross was released, he grinned like an ape. "I don't want no dinner," he snarled. "I want a drink. Can't you see that Tremayne downed me with a bar of iron. He's got my gun for sure."

"What a great pity it is that he didn't kill you—you fool!" remarked the Colonel.

CHAPTER XXXII

FALLING DARKNESS

"I don't like it!" murmured Colonel Lawton, although neither dislike nor perturbation showed on his smooth round face or in his ice blue eyes.

"I still can't get over your stupidity in telling Tremayne everything," Tonger snapped.

"Why harp on one matter like a woman wanting to have her throat cut?" exploded the Colonel with such shattering violence that both Tonger and Ross blanched.

The three of them were seated in the Breakaway House dining room eating rapidly, although without appreciation, the well-cooked food the cook had taken such care to preserve long after the scheduled hour was passed. Despite his assertion on being released, Ross ate heartily, the blue kerchief round his head giving him the appearance of a pirate.

"No–I don't like it," reiterated the Colonel with regained composure. "Ross, step out to Whitbread and tell him to have two men on guard over the plane. How many road miles are we from Mount Magnet, Morris?"

"Eighty-one."

"Time? Ah! Ten minutes to nine. Bowgada rang Mount Magnet at seven-fifty-five. We may assume that the doctor and the policeman–there will, I think, be only one policeman–probably left Mount Magnet by eight-fifteen. As it hasn't rained sufficiently to impede progress, they should arrive before eleven-thirty. It's essential that they're not held up by Tremayne. Who, do you think, cut him loose, if he did not free himself?"

"A maid named May. She cannot be found. I never liked her. It was Frances who insisted upon retaining her. Her disappearance just now points to the obvious."

"You never made love to her?"

"No," replied Tonger abruptly.

"She and Tremayne will have to be located."

The Colonel fell into reverie and Tonger continued eating, his face glowering. The squatter was visualising a prison, for a sense of inevitability was mastering him.

"Let's reason," said Lawton presently. "Tremayne doesn't know what's happened at Bowgada, and, therefore, doesn't know that a doctor and policeman are coming from Mount Magnet. Further, he doesn't know that that fool cut the telephone wire beyond Bowgada. Depend on it, he'll make for Bowgada, or send the girl to Bowgada with instructions, although I don't think he'll do that. It's a dark night. Whichever one of them does go, or if they both go, they'll keep to the road. We have to decide, being limited in number, whether to concentrate on capturing Tremayne, or on getting the stuff out of those bales and put in a safe hiding place so that we can deny all knowledge of it. Which shall it be?"

"We should concentrate on Tremayne. The last consignment is still at sea and won't reach Jefferson in Bradford until next Thursday. If Tremayne gets clear the police will cable to have that consignment held up and examined anyway."

"Of course! Yes, we must pick up Tremayne and that girl before they can do any damage. Ross's crowd ought to be back soon with the brother. We'll return him."

Buck Ross returned, and before he could resume his dinner he was ordered to bring the dry batteries from the telephone box in the office. When he grumbled the Colonel's eyes emitted blue gleams.

"We should have dismantled that telephone before this," Lawton pointed out when Ross had departed. "You're not very helpful tonight, Morris. Order all your reliable hands to come here immediately. Can you count on any of those at the camp?"

"Yes–nearly all the adults and many of the women. In fact I could rely on the whole damn lot."

"Leave the women. Send for the men. Get them all here as quickly as possible. A large scale map of the district would be helpful. Bring one."

When the eleven hands entered the dining room, they regarded the big man seated at the table studying a map he had spread over the cloth and the remaining table appointments with curiosity. They murmured among themselves and the Colonel looked up, sharply commanding them to be silent. The truck which had sped away returned in a few minutes, and fifteen more came in, along with Tonger and Ross. Lawton spoke for some time to Tonger in low tones before Tonger addressed the gathering.

"For many years I've been your father and your mother," he said earnestly. "All of you know me, and I know every one of you. I've fed you and allowed you to make your camping grounds on Breakaway House. Now there's a man come to Bowgada as the overseer who wants to harm me. May, the daughter of old Johnson, is helping him. They're either hanging about here, or they're making for Bowgada. If they reach Bowgada, I'll have to leave Breakaway House, and then you'll lose your father and your mother, and your happy days will be gone. Will you let that be?"

"No!" they chorused fiercely.

"Well, we've got to get Tremayne and that girl. We've got to find them. They must be brought here and kept quiet. Whitbread, you take four men on one of the trucks to Bowgada. When you reach the top of the breakaway, park the truck and walk on to the homestead and lie in wait. Should you capture them, bring them back at once. Ross, you take the second truck and fifteen men as far as the boundary gate. Park the truck off the road. Never mind about Ellis at Acacia Well. Then spread out your men either side of the track and beat back. If you meet a car on its way to Bowgada, stop it and see if Tremayne or the girl is in it. If either or both are passengers, let me know as quickly as you possibly can. You others—hunt round the homestead, look into every place, hunt like you were dingoes after rabbits.

"You each know your work and you all know what will happen to Breakaway House and you if Tremayne and that girl get away. For this night's work you'll be paid five pounds each, and whoever gets them will be paid fifty pounds. Go to it! Remember, you've got to capture them. That's all."

The crowd drifted out silently, fierce eyes glinting in the light. A few minutes later two trucks roared away eastward, and among the homestead buildings flitted almost invisible shadows.

"If Ross does find them in the doctor's car we'll have to get the boxes out of the bales in mighty quick time," decreed the Colonel. "To shoot up the doctor and the policeman as well as them would make matters worse. Ah, that cat coming now—it must be Ross's crowd with young Tremayne for it's too early for the Mount Magnet people. That Mount Magnet car will be the weakest part of our line. I don't like it."

Matthews came in to report that they had brought John Tremayne from their secret treatment plant. "He's out in the car," he said, an evil leer about his mouth. "Trussed up like a fowl."

"See that he's locked up in a secure place, and lock a guard in with him," Lawton directed Tonger. "We might want the car as your trucks and car are away."

Morris Tonger went out with Matthews. He came running back half a minute later to gasp out, his face purple: "John Tremayne's gone! He's escaped! Someone must have cut him loose."

Lawton gave one of his rare smiles. He stood up, shaking himself like a dog. "Good!" he ejaculated. "We now know that Tremayne's still in the vicinity of Breakaway House."

IT was now ten minutes to midnight and there had still been no results of the efforts of some twenty-five men to locate and capture Harry Tremayne and his brother, and the girl, May. Colonel Lawton and Morris Tonger sat on stiff-backed chairs in the deep shadow of the house veranda. It was not so much raining as trying to rain. A soft warm wind came from the west. The night was so dark they could not distinguish the adjacent buildings save that usually occupied by the men, from which poured a solitary light.

"I don't think it'll rain now," Tonger said irritably, his nerves strung taut. "The wind is veering to the south, and it's too late to bring rain. What are we going to do if they don't find the Tremaynes by daybreak?"

"I have a secret retreat," replied the Colonel smoothly. "In fact, I've several lines to which to retreat, prepared for such an emergency as this might prove to be. Assuming that we don't locate the enemy by sunrise, we'll fly away–you, your niece, and I. You needn't worry unduly, my dear Morris, about us. What does concern me is that consignment at sea. It'll be necessary to have a cable sent to the Bradford people warning them. Shouldn't Frances have returned from Bowgada by now?"

"I told her she needn't leave till midnight if she was having a good time."

"Oh! Well, I can't think that Bowgada would be providing her with a good time. Do you think she might remain to nurse Brett Filson?"

"Perhaps," Tonger agreed doubtfully. "If it comes to a getaway, we'll leave her behind. She'd be all right. She could take over Breakaway House."

"You forget that she's to marry me."

"I thought she'd declined your offer of marriage?" Tonger said, stiffening.

"So she did, but women always alter their decisions. She will go with us, Morris. She will be the price you'll have to pay for your freedom–if we have to retire temporarily."

"That's a price I shan't permit her to pay," Tonger announced angrily. "You don't intend to marry her. You'll leave her alone."

"Even if you go to gaol?" Lawton asked smoothly.

"Even if that. I know you, and you know me. You will not get your hands on a Tonger woman. I've sunk pretty low, but I can sink a hell of a long way further, and I am not going to."

"Well, well! We won't quarrel over it. I can hear a car coming from the south-west."

"I can't!" Tonger countered surlily.

The Colonel persisted. "I can," he said. "My hearing is infinitely better than yours."

Morris Tonger was listening for the car when from out of the darkness towards Bowgada a man shouted. Those on the veranda waited tensely. A rifle shot electrified them, although the Colonel moved not a muscle. A woman screamed. They heard padding feet, and presently, into the shaft of light streaming from the house door, the figure of a woman appeared at the gate. Then she was running along the short path to the veranda step. Tonger lurched to his feet with an oath which expressed neither pleasure nor anger. The woman was Miss Nora Hazit.

"Why have you come, Nora?" the squatter demanded sharply before shouting to an approaching figure: "It's all right, Moses."

Nora halted at the veranda step, the hall light partially blinding her. Then she made out the squatter's bulk within the shadow and with a little rush was beside him, clinging frantically to his arms.

"N'gobi come," she panted. "He came to Bowgada, he and his relations. He came for me, and to kill Ned for taking me. Mr Filson, he say me and Ned to go with Millie into one of the homestead rooms and wait."

Nora paused, fighting to regain normal breath, Tonger's left arm supporting her. Further in the shadow, Colonel Lawton sat listening and watching. Had he thought of it, Morris Tonger then would have been able to hear the throbbing hum of the approaching car.

"There was shooting," Nora went on. "I heard Miss Sayers cry out that Mr Filson was killed with a spear. The men were firing from the kitchen windows, and I knew N'gobi would come and take me. I ran out through the front, and came straight down the breakaway and so here.

"I saw N'gobi behind me just this side of the boundary. He was running fast, but I ran faster. Near here I see other men–N'gobi's relations, I think. They're all after me; they were all round me. They're all round here, Morrie." Her voice rose, broken by breath-catching sobs. "One of them shouted at me to stop, and when I didn't, he shot at me. I heard the bullet. I cried out. I was frightened. I not go back with N'gobi. Morrie! Morrie! Let me stay here! Let me stay here! Send Miss Frances away and let me stay here with you always."

"Silly! That wasn't N'gobi after you. It was some of my boys. N'gobi's dead. Jackson shot him when Mr Filson was speared. Miss Winters told me so."

"N'gobi dead! You sure, Morrie?"

"Yes. Miss Winters telephoned for the Magnet doctor. Look, here's his car coming now. Presently I'll see what we can do."

"I wait! You'll come soon?"

Colonel Lawton pondered on the weaknesses of men, their primitiveness despite education, training and tradition; the way they could be easily mastered by emotion. The corners of his mouth twitched when Morris Tonger picked up the woman in his arms, and strode with her into the house, an arm round his neck, a wavy-haired head cuddled against his shoulder.

"And I'm not to look at a Tonger woman!" the Colonel murmured to himself.

The car came humming down the long grade from the western high land, its headlights illuminating a strip of ground beyond the house fence. Tonger reappeared at the door, the courteous, welcoming host. But without reducing speed the machine swept on towards Bowgada, presenting those on the veranda with a brief glimpse of a man's set face.

"I wonder, now, why didn't they stop?" Lawton said.

CHAPTER XXXIII

VENGEANCE

"WISH I'd known that car was coming," Harry Tremayne murmured thoughtfully. "I could have sent word to Brett to keep Frances over there until tomorrow."

"Not being me, I'm glad she's chosen you," the man at his side whispered in a rasping hiss. "It could never be me now. It'll be years before I'm a man again."

"Rot, John! You'll be all right. Wonder what the time is. Must be after midnight."

"Haven't you a watch?"

"No," replied Harry grimly. "I threw it away. It ticked too loudly."

They were laying full length on the cart-shed roof which was thatched with cane grass. They had been there since Harry freed John from the police manacles fettering his feet using the key of his regulation policeman's handcuffs; severed the rope which bound his arms; and then carried the numbed figure to the cart-shed roof. Together they had observed the human bloodhounds beginning the hunt about the homestead buildings. They had heard several efficiently searching the shed below them, and now they spoke in low whispers.

Before the moon rose it had been one of the darkest nights the elder brother remembered; now, with the cloud-masked moon above Bowgada, the blackness was replaced by a dull opaqueness permitting them to make out the other buildings and the outline of the aeroplane between them and the giant shed.

"That woman who ran to the house veranda—it wasn't Frances, I suppose?"

"No. I think she was an Aboriginal woman named Nora. Tonger has been making love to her," Harry replied, still wondering at his brother's changed voice. It had been pleasantly modulated when he had last seen him years ago. Now it sounded coarse, harsh.

"You had a pretty rotten time?" he asked.

"Foul. I've been treated worse than an animal. Their plant's in a series of caverns. I was kept with manacles on my feet, and chained up when not worked. A Russian who lived at the place was my master. He made a sort of cat-o'-nine-tails out of a stockwhip. He'd flog me without any reason; just for the lust of inflicting pain. I'm going to get him. I'm going to choke him to death. I've got to…"

"Hey…! steady, old man. Speak softly."

"If you knew!" John's voice held a sob. "I tell you I've got to kill that Russian, and Buck Ross, and a fellow called Jake, if I'm ever to get back my self-respect. I ought to be mad; I can't understand why I'm not mad. How many guns have you?"

"One."

"Give it me."

"I'll keep it, John. Go easy," Harry urged, his own blood at boiling point.

"All right, but let's do something. Let's get going. I can't stop here like this much longer. Let's clean up the crowd here so that we can tackle those who are away when they return. We must stop Lawton getting clear in the plane."

"I've an idea it's guarded. Go carefully."

Without noise they gained the ground, and there John Tremayne gripped his brother's arms with such power that Harry stiffened.

"You give me that gun. I want it," the younger man breathed fiercely. "Hand it over."

"I'm keeping it," affirmed Harry steadily, nauseated by the odour of his brother's clothes.

"Hand it over, I say."

"Don't be a fool. You'll get your chance. Remember that you're still in the force."

"No I'm not. I'm not a policeman. I'm not a man. You haven't seen me yet in the light. Wait until you do. I'm only a beast, and I'll always be a beast until I can clean myself with blood."

"Steady! Steady! It'll come out all right. You'll get a bath and change of clothes presently and you'll be a new man."

Round the corner of the shed stepped a tall figure which halted as its peering eyes found the two brothers. The figure raised a heavy waddy but was not quick enough. The man died slowly, iron fingers closed round his throat, a sickening smell in his gaping nostrils.

"One–the first one," snarled the semi-human being which rose from the body. "I don't want the waddy nor your gun. I want to feel 'em die in my hands."

If John Tremayne was not mad, he appeared to be verging on it. And with the passing of every moment Harry Tremayne was becoming more and more uneasy. A minute later he lost sight of his brother. Filled with foreboding, he decided to make for the house.

"I can hear another car coming–from the east," murmured Colonel

Lawton. Morris Tonger and he were still lounging on the dark veranda, although the time was after one o'clock.

"It'll be Frances," was Tonger's opinion. He spoke with a note of regret in his voice which the Colonel did not fail to pick up.

"I hope so," came the soft voice. "We three will get away in the plane at daybreak if your hunters fail to obtain a bag. Why fidget so? My retreat will be safe, and our money's safe in foreign banks. We can start afresh with nothing to fear." Presently he said: "Here's someone with news."

Out of the darkness sprang the figure of a running man. He wrenched back the gate and raced up the shaft of light streaming through the open doorway. It was Alec. He halted on the veranda breathing heavily, unable to make out the two figures until Tonger sharply asked him what was going on.

His reply was hysterical: "Jimmy–he's dead. So's Jacky Sparrow. So's Billy. Billy and Jacky are under the plane. They're both dead, boss."

The squatter uttered an oath.

The Colonel got to his feet.

"You sure?" demanded Tonger.

"Yes. Too right, I'm sure."

"You heard nothing? Where have you been?"

"Sneaking about. I heard nothing, not a sound."

"Morris, you stay here," ordered Lawton curtly. "I'll get my torch and this man can come with me. It's about time I took a hand in this hunting game in the dark. Send Miss Frances to bed when she arrives. Keep her quiet, anyway."

Slipping along to his bedroom, Lawton entered and then emerged with a torch through the French windows. With Alec, he walked swiftly from the house.

Tonger, knowing that the cook was asleep in her room, had left Nora in the kitchen; but knowing, too, that Frances would want coffee after her drive, and would go to the kitchen to make it, he entered the house to take Nora to another place.

Her coming at this time was damned inconvenient. Showed him up, too, to Lawton. What a mess they were in, to be sure! All through Lawton being so cocksure of himself. Telling Tremayne everything to make him more dangerous! Pshaw! Devilish clever, but there were times when Buck Ross's crude methods were preferable to finesse.

Nora cried out when he came into the kitchen and ran to cling to him.

Tonger scowled, but then relented and smiled. He kissed her passionate mouth, and soothed her with promises. His embrace lasted but a moment, for the squatter did not forget that this was hardly a time for love and kisses.

Beyond the house came the sound of the approaching car. With his arm round Miss Hazit, her head laid back firmly against his shoulder, they walked the long passage to the hall off which opened his bedroom. And in the hall Morris Tonger died without ever knowing what killed him.

LAWTON was flashing his torch on the bodies of two men lying beside the shadowy aeroplane, experience revealing to him the manner of their death, when a scream rang out from the house, a high-pitched dreadful scream. It came a second time but was cut short, as though shut off by the closing of a sound-proof door.

The car from Bowgada was quite close, and for an uncertain instant Colonel Lawton contemplated climbing into the cockpit of the plane and attempting to take off in the dark and with cold engines. It was, however, merely an impulse. In the approaching car was Frances Tonger. Once she was with him, that fool Tonger and his stupid gold-stealing could go hang.

"Wot's up, Colonel? Who's that yelling?" demanded Matthews, running up with a hurricane lamp.

"I don't know. Those Tremaynes are evidently keen sportsmen. They've strangled the guards here. Seen anything of them?"

"Nope."

"Have you a gun?"

"Too right."

"Where's your companion?"

"Dunno," replied Matthews. "I bin lookin' for 'im. Perhaps he's bin corpsed, too!"

"You stay here. Keep your eyes open. I must see who's coming in that car. Damn! That Alec's disappeared. Wind up, I suppose."

"Bout time we all got away, I'm thinkin'."

"Fool! The game's only just started. You'll stay here to guard the plane. Shoot on sight. Do you understand that?" Lawton asked with silken politeness.

"All right," Matthews said surlily. "Only don't be long, or send me a mate. I ain't as young as I was, and them stiffs..."

The Colonel strode off to the house, his giant figure illuminated by the headlights of the approaching car. The car had almost stopped when he reached the gate and he turned to welcome Frances Tonger. The dash light revealed the faces of the woman in the car and the tight-lipped man who drove it. The woman was not Frances.

"Good night!" she said grimly. "Mr Tonger about?"

"I believe he's inside the house," the Colonel replied casually. "Will you come in?"

"No. I'm stopping here. Tell him to come out. Tell him a lady's wantin' to speak to him."

"Very well. If you'll excuse me."

Lawton bowed and set off for the house, his mind working furiously at the problem this rude woman presented. Why the devil didn't Tonger come out?

He stood motionless in the doorway for three seconds, then turned and came slowly down the path to the gate.

"I regret," he said softly, "I regret to say that Mr Tonger has been murdered."

"I'm not surprised to hear that," announced Violet Winters. "It's a wonder he wasn't murdered years ago. I think I will come in. Mug—if there's any funny business, shoot first and ask questions later. It'll be safer."

SMALL brown eyes screwed into pin points regarded the steady figure of Colonel Lawton. Pale-blue eyes examined the Amazonian proportions of Violet Winters. They stood either side of the dead squatter. Lawton's hands thrust lightly into the pockets of his jacket, Violet's hands concealed by the light rug hung over one arm.

"Did you kill him?" she demanded, like a woman asking a small boy if he had stolen an apple.

The Colonel experienced admiration, a rare emotion in him, for this square-cut woman who appeared to possess none of the weaknesses of her sex.

"No, I didn't kill him. He was killed while I was over by my plane near the shearing shed."

"Well, it's a pity he couldn't have got himself murdered outside the house. He's spoiling the carpet."

"It's not our carpet," the Colonel reminded her, unable to forbear giving her a wintry smile. What a woman! Indeed, what a woman!

"It's nothing to laugh about," she said severely. "Who are you?"

"My name is Lawton. I'm the dead man's guest."

"Oh! Have you seen Mr Tremayne, Mr Filson's overseer?"

"Mr Tremayne! I don't think I know him."

"I don't think you're telling the truth. Take your hands out of your pockets when you're in the presence of a lady. Bring 'em out slow like."

No man cares to be addressed like a child, and no man likes to be reminded of his manners. The Colonel's face paled and his eyes narrowed. He could not but note that Violet's hands remained concealed within the folds of the rug, and he could not divest his mind of the idea that concealed, too, was a pistol unwaveringly pointed at him. His own right hand was wound round the butt of an automatic, and he had no doubt of his being able to fire first.

There were so many men dead at Breakaway House that his "retirement" to his second line, or retreat, no longer was a matter for speculation. A few more dead people would make no difference–but he wanted Frances. He drew his hands out of his pockets, slowly. They were empty.

"You've not yet told me who you are," he said politely.

"I'm Miss Winters. I've come over from Breakaway House to find Mr Tremayne, as the policeman from Magnet who came with the doctor has gone to try and contact the Myme policeman. To stop you wastin' time asking questions, I'm telling you that I think you know very well where he is."

"Really, I don't know your Mr Tremayne. I haven't..."

"Where's the telephone here?" Violet rudely broke in. "If you're so innocent as you make out, why don't you telephone the Magnet police about this murder?"

"The telephone's over in the office. Please permit me to point out that you've hardly given me the opportunity to leave and telephone. All this business is going to be..."

"Very serious for you, I agree. Where's Buck Ross and Matthews?"

"You appear to think..." the Colonel was saying as they turned towards the doorway. He broke off. Beyond the car at the gate–that used by Matthews to transport John Tremayne from the treatment plant, and behind which Mug Williams had halted Tonger's car–a brilliant white flame was leaping skywards higher than the shearing-shed roof. The Colonel gave no indication, even then, of any emotion, but he was placed in the tightest corner of his adventurous life. Somebody had set fire to his aeroplane.

CHAPTER XXXIV

AGAIN SUNSHINE

WITHOUT undue haste and with a low murmur of apology, Colonel Lawton stepped to the doorway and passed through it to the veranda. Suddenly a voice ordered him to raise his hands above his head. Turning to his left, he saw clearly revealed by the burning plane the rock-like figure of Harry Tremayne.

"Back–into the house, Colonel," came the sharp command.

With his hands held on high, his face as passive as always, Lawton obeyed, stepping backwards into the hall.

At the sound of Tremayne's voice, Violet Winters, who was still behind the Colonel, experienced both astonishment and happiness. "To my unfortunate brother is due the deaths of three of Tonger's men and Jake Matthews, and the burning of your aeroplane, Colonel. He has suffered badly at the hands of that gold-stealing gang, and it will require time to heal his poor mind. Your game is finished, and you'd better be resigned to that fact," Tremayne explained. "Miss Winters–if you don't mind–kindly relieve the Colonel of the pistol in his right-hand pocket."

Lawton remained immobile, the vacuity of expression making his face terrible.

"Do not pass in front of the Colonel, Miss Winters. Take the pistol from behind him. I'll shoot to kill if you move, Lawton."

"I thought he looked a scoundrel from the first," Violet said calmly.

She was drawing close to the airman when the engine of one of the cars standing at the gate broke into a roar and was driven away with terrific acceleration. Tremayne dared not remove his gaze from the Colonel. Violet now was directly behind the Colonel, and, too late, Tremayne saw that he dared not shoot if Lawton went for his pistol for fear his bullet would pass through the man and wound her. Lawton's hand streaked for his weapon directly he felt her behind him, and he attempted at the same time to spring at the overseer.

But he had not reckoned with Miss Violet Winters, a woman of the mining camps of Western Australia. Her mighty arm went round him, her left arm, and sent him staggering to the right, and even as he was staggering, trying to pull out his pistol, the machine wrench she had hidden beneath the rug, and which he had thought to be a pistol, crashed down on his head and sent him to the floor like an expertly pole-axed bullock.

"Oh, boy! What a night!" she exclaimed, and sat down on one of the hall chairs. "And it isn't over yet. Buck's due to come. He's around here for sure. And the shearin' shed is alight, caught afire by the plane. What a night! Tie him up quick, and hunt out a drink. I'm dying."

When Tremayne stood up from his task of handcuffing Lawton's hands behind his back and tying his ankles together with window-blind cord, she smiled at him in a way that was different from her usual grim humour. Softly, almost crooningly, she said: "What a night, what a night to remember."

"What are you and Mug Williams doing here? Have you brought Frances?" he asked.

"She's over at Bowgada helping Ann Sayers to nurse Mr Filson," Violet explained, going on further to tell him all that had occurred there. Then, a little defiantly: "Mr Filson was thought to be dying, so I told the Magnet policeman who came with the doctor all about you, and all about what you had been through and what you thought. Mr Filson told me, you see. And I knew a lot more. And you never came home when you promised. I knew you were up against something over here and I was afraid. You don't mind, do you?"

"Not a bit, old thing. The job's a little bigger than I can manage with John in such a bad way from the treatment he's had."

"I'm glad you're not angry. The Magnet policeman and English took Mr Filson's portable telephone with them on a truck to try and locate the break in the telephone wire and get in touch with the Myme policeman. They'll be coming across as soon as they can get here. Where's Mug now?"

"He's outside keeping an eye on things. How's your nerves?"

"A bottle of beer would soothe 'em. What killed Morris Tonger?"

After Tremayne had examined the dead squatter and covered the body with the dining-room table cloth, he said gravely: "Clubbed. Were Ned and Nora at Bowgada when you came away?"

"No. Nora cleared off when Mr Filson was speared. We reckon Ned went after her. Say...do you think she came over here, and that Ned followed her and did...that?"

"Confidentially, I do think so. What's more, I think Morris Tonger has been looking for what he got for a long time."

"Perhaps Tonger was killed with that thing half hidden under that chair. Looks like the handle of something."

She pointed at a lounge chair set in a corner of the hall, and from beneath it, where possibly it had skidded after being thrown down, Harry Tremayne drew out the Leonile club he had seen in Ned's possession.

"So it was Ned," he said steadily. "Ned came here through the line of men sent out to net me, and he's departed with Nora to get through them again."

"Burn it," Violet suggested. His brows rose.

"Burn it," she repeated. "They've got feelings like the rest of us. Forget you're a policeman."

"I'm not a policeman," Tremayne assured her with a grin. "I resigned some time ago."

"Why?"

"Because...oh, because I wanted a free hand. I think I will burn it. By the way, did you stop at Acacia Well on your way over?"

"No. Why?"

"I sent a young girl across to Fred Ellis with a note asking him to take great care of her. She had more than an hour's start on Tonger's men. Her name's May. She rescued me just as I was thinking what a damn fool I was."

"I see. Looks as though the Colonel's coming round."

IT transpired that Alec had not actually deserted Breakaway House until he had learned in some way of the death of Morris Tonger. The killing of the squatter had proved to be the breaking point on the strain produced by the earlier three deaths and the others had deserted with him, so when Buck Ross and his party reached the homestead, having made all haste on account of the burning shed, the Myme bully suddenly found himself to be alone.

That somewhat damaged his nerve, and the sight of the plane burning beside the shed further affected his courage. Within the confines of the homestead, which he approached with cunning caution, the conflagration revealed no human being, not even the men's cook who was not an active member of the gang. But at one corner of the office building he met the man whom he had pleasured to torture.

John Tremayne was smiling when he later entered the hall of the house but his face was a dreadful grey colour and his awful clothes hung in shreds from his scarred and work-toughened body. Violet Winters, refreshing herself with beer, the wrench lying handy to her hand on her lap, cried out at the sight of him.

"I feel better, now," he told Harry with a beaming smile which made his face even more tragic. "I got Buck Ross. There's only that Russian. He'll keep. I'll get him in the morning." Pointing to the visible form of Colonel Lawton, he asked: "Is he dead, too? Is that a dead man under the cloth?"

"They're all right, John. They're our prisoners. Mustn't kill prisoners, you know. What about a bath and clean clothes? Afterwards you'll feel as right as rain."

"You come with me," urged Violet. "I'll fix you up."

She smiled sadly at the gaunt figure, and slipped an arm round the filthy rags. John Tremayne smiled down at her like a child joining its nurse in a new game.

JUST as the sun was about to rise into a sky streaked with blue, the two policemen arrived. They brought with them Whitbread and the two men they had found hanging about Bowgada. Before they left with their prisoners for Mount Magnet on Filson's truck, they used the portable telephone to send reports to their district headquarters, since no one could find the batteries Ross had taken from the office telephone.

The shed was a smouldering ruin, and, other than the engines, little remained of Colonel Lawton's plane. Until the police reinforcements arrived, Harry Tremayne consented to remain in charge of Breakaway House, while Violet Winters volunteered to look after John Tremayne who required her strong will to master him. There appeared to be no reason why he should not completely recover, given time and attention.

Having dictated a telegram to be dispatched to his mother by the policemen, Harry mooned about the smouldering mass of wool, from which he raked a number of iron boxes, until Violet suggested that since Mug Williams was staying, there was no reason why he should not slip across to Bowgada for an hour. There was nothing of great importance for him to do, and at the earliest the first draft of police and detectives would not reach Breakaway House until the evening. When she pointed out that May would be still at Acacia Well, and an embarrassment to Fred Ellis, Tremayne consented to leave Williams in charge.

Of course, he should have stayed to write reports and gather evidence, but instead he drove off in Tonger's car with a heart full of anxiety, wanting to reach Bowgada and see his wounded friend. On reaching, Acacia Well he was welcomed by the stockman and the still wild-eyed girl who wanted to sob her relief at the news he brought. She was quite willing to go on to Bowgada and assist Millie English. Tremayne then sauntered across to the clump of acacia trees where Ned and Nora had made a temporary camp.

He carried a sack containing a heavy object and was watched by two pairs of keen eyes set in two strained and frightened faces. In front of the roughly and hastily constructed bough shelter the couple had built a fire, and, when standing beside this fire, Tremayne silently withdrew the Leonile club from the bag.

"All right, boss. I go with you," Ned said.

Sternly, Harry Tremayne looked at him, and Ned's eyes never wavered from his.

"Take me, too, Mr Tremayne. It was my fault. It's always been my fault. Old Mrs Filson said I was a bad girl, and she spoke true," whimpered Nora.

They watched with increasing amazement as he buried the club in the heart of the fire and then waited in silence as the weapon was slowly consumed by the flames.

Finally Tremayne spoke: "What are you two talking about?" he asked them, still without a smile.

"You know, boss," replied Ned wonderingly.

"I know this much, Ned. If I have any more trouble with either you or Nora, I'll take a stockwhip to you."

"You can beat me now if you want to," wailed Nora.

"I've a good mind to. Now you pack up, get some tucker from Fred, and clear out on walkabout. You make camp in some cave and have a long shut-eye. You get me? And keep your mouths shut."

These two had become used to obeying the white man's laws and never receiving justice from them. Now Harry Tremayne gave them a justice they understood.

Ned seized his hands. His eyes were shining when he cried: "You good fella, Mr Tremayne. I tell Nora next time she behave like that I bump 'er off."

"If you bump anyone off, Ned, the police will bump you off, remember. So long, Ned! So long, Nora!"

And Nora this time did not attempt to "make eyes" at him.

Half an hour later he reached Bowgada with May beside him, and having explained her presence to Millie, he devoted five minutes to Frances. Then he passed into Filson's room, where he found the doctor seated on one side of the bed drinking the patient's whisky, and Ann Sayers seated on the other holding the patient's hand.

Brett was conscious but looked pale and was very still beneath the bedclothes. The doctor was smiling, which was not wholly due to the whisky, and Ann looked wistfully happy, which indicated that Brett's chances of recovery were excellent.

When Tremayne grinned at the patient, he looked not older than twenty-one. "Just dropped in, Brett, old man, to tell you that the double wedding will take place on Christmas Eve," he said. "I've a lot of work to do cleaning up the mess, but I'll be free on that day. Have you proposed to Ann, or must I do it for you?"

"I wish you would take the doctor outside for a little while," Brett said quietly. "I want to talk to Ann."

"No talking," ordered the doctor. "I won't have you talking. You can say what you want to say with your eyes as well as I said it to my wife eighteen years ago."

"You can come and talk to me that way, too," commanded Frances from the doorway. "Not you, doctor dear—Harry."